I0725359

Hidden RESOLUTION

STONEBROOKE SERIES

T.M. CROMER

BOOKS BY T.M. CROMER

Get your printable list here:

https://www.tmcromer.com/printable-booklist

CONTEMPORARY & ROMANTIC SUSPENSE

The Stonebrooke Series:

BURNING RESOLUTION

HIDDEN RESOLUTION

The Fiore Vineyard Series:

PICTURE THIS

RETURN HOME

ONE WISH

The Holt Family Series:

GOODBYE TO YOU

THIS TIME YOU

INCLUDING YOU

A LIFE WITH YOU

PARANORMAL ROMANCE

The Sentinels of Magic Series:

THE AETHER

THE DEATH DEALER

THE SEER

THE TRAVELER

To Deb:
You'll see I kept your favorite line.
You're welcome.

CHAPTER

ONE

Mason Sharp slung his carry-on into the overhead bin and collapsed into his first-class seat with a contented sigh. In a few hours, he'd be soaking up the sun and diving into the Caribbean's crystal-clear waters.

Christ, he needed it.

Ten glorious days. Zero responsibilities. No work, no drama, no bullshit.

All he required was a peaceful flight without Chatty Kathy next to him. A scotch and a long nap would work nicely, helping the resort-level relaxation kick in.

His phone buzzed, and he debated whether to ignore it. After a glance at the screen, he grinned and changed his mind. Seemed his brother Zack, who was also his business partner and best friend, was excited about their newest client.

You wouldn't believe who signed up for a membership today! ERICA SUTTON! Remember her from high school?

Mason stared at the name, gears turning. Erica Sutton didn't

1

ring any be—ah! He vaguely remembered a shy, soft-spoken girl who'd spent more time staring at her shoes than making eye contact.

> The mousy chick with the glasses who tutored you?

> Yep. Not mousy anymore.

Mason smirked.

> See? Told you New Year's Day was prime for sign-ups.

> Seriously? I drop a nostalgia bomb, and you go full business mode? I thought you were on vacation.

> Exactly. Turning off my phone now. Buy her a smoothie and stop bothering me.

> Whatever. Enjoy your overpriced drinks, asshat.

> Yeah, up yours, dickhead. And thanks, I will.

Mason was powering down his phone when a sultry voice interrupted him. "Excuse me. I think that's my seat."

Honest to God, he tried to look up, but his gaze stalled, captivated by a pair of high-octane, centerfold-worthy breasts that were one sneeze away from liberating themselves from her deep V-neck. Full, round, and absolutely mesmerizing.

"Up here, buddy," the woman said, her sultry voice dry with humor.

Mason tore his gaze away and swept over her face. Sweet hell, her visage was just as breathtaking. Moss-green eyes, framed by thick, dark lashes, twinkled with amusement. The kind that suggested she was used to turning heads.

"Pardon?" he asked, more rattled than he'd ever admit. He met beautiful women all the time. Hell, he co-owned three gyms, for crying out loud. So why was this one throwing him off his game?

"Lady, you're holding up the line," groused an impatient jackass behind her.

She half turned, fixing him with a glare so lethal it should've come with a warning label. Mason grinned, delighted, as the dickhead blanched, muttered an apology, and scrambled to lift her carry-on into the overhead like an obedient schoolboy.

Dismissing him, she returned her attention to Mason. "Do you mind letting me by? I'm in 3D. Says so right here," she said, flashing her boarding pass.

Feeling like a dumbass, he stood and promptly smacked his head on the overhead bin.

"Goddammit!"

Seriously, could manufacturers make airplanes any less friendly to the vertically gifted? At six-four, even first class was a cramped shoebox. He rubbed his head, then cut her a sharp glance when she tsked.

"Sorry."

She didn't look the least bit sorry. In fact, she appeared downright gleeful and on the verge of laughter. If he hadn't been the one suffering, he'd have thought her reaction almost cute.

Shifting into the aisle, Mason had little choice but to brush against her as he maneuvered out of their row.

She sucked in a breath, and their gazes collided. 3D wasn't as cool and collected as she pretended.

After she was situated, he took his seat and waited for the rest of the passengers to trickle through first class to their economy accommodations. It wasn't long before the boarding was complete and the flight attendant asked for their drink requests.

"Scotch. Neat," he said.

"White wine," his seatmate requested.

After their beverages were delivered, Mason took a large, appreciative swallow. How long had it been since he took time for himself or indulged?

Too long.

He debated the merits of conversing with the beddable bombshell next to him. Most days, he was up for mild flirtation, but it had been a helluva week, and he wanted to relax without any distractions.

"I'm Shonda."

The decision was taken away from him, and he could either be rude or introduce himself. Although he leaned toward the first option, his upbringing required the second.

"Mason."

"Where are you heading?"

"St. Thomas. You?"

"St. Thomas," she replied with a breathy laugh.

Her voice was the kind of sexy that curled around a man's dick and settled in low. Phone-sex operators only wished they were as gifted. Speaking of sex... If he didn't get his mind out of the gutter, he'd suffer the consequences. But the forever-horny bastard inside refused to listen and took his thoughts straight to Fantasyland. He was deeply entrenched and almost missed her following words.

"So, are you part of the Mile-High Club?" She gave him an expectant smile.

Caught mid-sip, he choked, spraying the seat back in front of him.

"Excuse me?" he croaked when his throat and lungs stopped burning enough to respond.

She tilted her head. "The Mile-High Club. I'd assume you'd be a member if you fly often. Isn't that what it's called when you're a frequent flyer?"

Oh, sweet, innocent Shonda!

Her curiosity appeared guileless, if a little misguided. After an internal debate about letting it go, Mason decided the question deserved honesty.

"Yes, I am a member," he replied. "And no, it's not for frequent flyers."

He desperately wanted to go a step further and offer to initiate her, but the plane was taking off, and they were a long way from the Islands. Sleep beckoned.

She blinked, and her flash of uncertainty caused him to lean forward and whisper against the shell of her ear, "To be a member means you've had sex during a flight."

Then he sat back and waited.

As soon as his comment registered, her skin flushed.

The sight made him grin.

"Oh my God!"

Shonda was mortified.

Too late.

She *had* heard the term before.

Her only excuse was fatigue and how bootylicious Mason was. With his midnight-colored hair, dark slashing brows, and light-blue eyes, he'd scrambled her brains more thoroughly than a granny's farm-fresh eggs in a cast-iron skillet.

Taking a sip of her wine, Shonda frantically sought another topic, but came up empty. Giving up all hope of a normal conversation, she reached for the Sky Mall magazine in the seat pocket and flipped through. Odds were he viewed her as a complete ditz.

Pretending interest wasn't difficult. As a marketing director, she liked perusing fliers, magazines, and advertisements to discover new trends. And the doorknob security bar for only $24.99 was a steal.

She whipped out her phone and captured a snapshot of the ad. When she reached her destination, she intended to order one for her apartment.

"You live in a bad section of town?" asked Mason.

She looked his way to find his eyes closed and his head tilted back. How had he known what she was looking at? Easing up her hand, she waved it in front of his face, careful not to create a breeze. When he didn't react, she shook her head.

"No," she replied, returning to thumbing through the magazine. "But a girl can't ever be too careful."

"Think that's going to stop someone who truly wants in?"

When she glanced back, he was watching her intently.

"Aren't you supposed to be sleeping or something?" She gave him a pointed stare.

The lines beside those incredible sky-blue eyes deepened with his amusement. "I'm just saying if you think that little piece of junk will keep anyone out..." He trailed off with a dismissive shrug.

The disparagement of her soon-to-be-added security measure was irritating. If the stick could buy time for the homeowner—or, in her case, apartment dweller—to call the police, then it did the job.

"My friend will help me test it when I get home."

"Save your money. Get an alarm," he advised, closing his eyes again as if his word was final.

"I have an alarm." She didn't, but he didn't need to know. "I happen to think this is a brilliant product."

He snorted.

"You know, I don't believe anyone asked your opinion," she said, annoyance causing her to scowl.

One eyelid lifted to study her and dropped shut again. When no comment was forthcoming, Shonda's temper spiked.

Who did this arrogant jerk think he was?

"Asshole," she muttered.

He came alert and glared at her. "What did you say?"

"I called you an asshole. A-S-S-H-O-L-E. Asshole," she said as if speaking to the dullest tool in the shed.

If looks could kill, she'd be dead and buried at twice the required depth. But Shonda had taken crap from people all her life and, for whatever reason, decided it stopped there and then. Her bestie, Erica, would be proud. Empowerment in action.

Telling this overbearing, self-entitled, gorgeous—*whoa!*

Damn, her mind went sideways. It had to be all those manly man pheromones he was emitting.

She leaned in and inhaled.

Mason stared as if she'd spontaneously sprouted a second head. "Did you just sniff me?" he asked incredulously.

Shonda froze mid lean, eyes wide and shocked.

Ohdeargod!

Had she? She had! Her body had responded to his delicious scent, acting purely on animal instinct.

"No!" But she was a bald-faced liar, and they both knew it. Heat flared in her face, betraying her, so she decided coming clean was the best course of action. "Okay, *yes*. But can I help it if you smell like bottled temptation?"

His obnoxious bark of laughter turned heads.

Face within five seconds of spontaneously combusting, Shonda ducked lower in her seat. An eyeball peeped through the seat crack, and she resisted the urge to poke it, thereby blinding her nosy neighbor and teaching them to mind their own fucking business.

Mr. Egotistical concluded it would be fun to tease her.

"Soooo," He drawled as if they had all day, and damned if it didn't sound provocative in his Southern baritone. "You like the way I smell."

The smirk was uncalled for, though.

She glared. "Yeah, well, I like how cupcakes smell, but it doesn't mean I indulge."

"Pity."

"That I don't eat cupcakes?"

"That you don't… indulge."

"I didn't say I don't *indulge*, indulge."

"'*Indulge*, indulge'? Code for sex?" he taunted.

"What else would it be code for?" she snapped. "As if you didn't start it with your sexy bedroom eyes and that voice and your suggestive—"

Jesus, Mary, and Joseph, she'd done it again! What the hell was this man doing to her brain? Melting it, that's what. "Stop talking to me now. Please."

His deep chuckle hit her right between the eyes, dumbfounding her.

"If you change your mind about *indulging*, I'll gladly initiate you to the club," he said with an elevated self-confidence no person should possess.

She shouldn't have wished for their plane to go down in a fiery crash, but the embarrassment of their stupid conversation was killing her way too slowly. Shonda opened her mouth to retort, with no real idea what she'd say, when a crackling announcement drowned her out.

The passengers were asked to return to their seats and fasten their safety belts. Flight attendants raced to collect cups and other items they'd passed out, urging everyone to put their tray tables upright as they hurried past.

Mason touched the woman's arm to get her attention. "What's happening?"

"Just turbulence." Her pseudo-calm reassurance gave way to a yelp as the plane dipped.

A second announcement directed the crew to find their seats and buckle up. The plane rocked and righted itself, sending a symphony of gasps throughout the first-class cabin.

Shonda gripped Mason's hand.

When the captain spoke next, it was to inform them of engine failure and the need for an emergency landing.

"Okay," Shonda blurted.

"Okay, what?" Mason asked her, clearly confused.

"Okay, let's do the Mile-High thing. If we're going to die, we might as well go out with a bang."

For the longest minute, he stared at her.

Unspeaking.

Unmoving.

An instant later, he shoved the divider out of his way and captured her lips with unerring accuracy.

Shonda moaned. If this was to be her last moment on earth—or in the air, as the case may be—she would die happy. And damn! The things Mason could do with his mouth had to be illegal in forty of the fifty US states, but if that were the case, she was subscribing to the criminal life.

CHAPTER

TWO

Mason had never tasted anything sweeter than Shonda.

Her soft moan and the breathy mewl against his mouth went straight to his groin. He was rock-hard and two seconds from forgetting they were on a packed plane. They hit another turbulent patch, snapping the moment in half and waking him from his fantasy. She muffled a cry of fright, and he automatically tightened his grip on her hand.

"It's okay, love." He winked, hoping to ease her nerves. "Let's readdress the club membership when we're not plummeting into air pockets."

She managed a trembling smile. "You're incorrigible."

"So I've been told."

Mason brushed his thumb over her knuckles, noting how her pupils dilated at the contact. A subtle shifting of her legs suggested she was into him. Perhaps they could share a few days of island-style R&R. No strings. No drama. Pure fun. Of course, he'd be upfront and make the rules clear. Having been cured of his romantic delusions long ago, he didn't do complicated.

Another jolt rocked the aircraft, earning a squeak from Shonda and a chorus of screams from the back. His stomach slow rolled in sync with the dip. If they survived this flight, someone was receiving a strongly worded email.

Pain pulsed behind his eyes in relentless waves, and his ears were ringing from the banshee wail of the woman seated behind them. With each passing second, his mood soured.

Her final scream broke his control.

"Shut the hell up, or I'll open the damned door and toss your sorry ass out!" he snapped. Yeah, less-than-kind and likely to bar him from future flights, but for the love of all things holy, he was moments from murder.

The screamer clamped her mouth closed, sending him a stunned stare. In fact, all those close to them were gaping in astonishment.

Except for Shonda.

He was almost positive hero worship lit in her eyes.

By the time they were herded off the plane, all amorous thoughts fled.

Mason picked a couple of chairs in the next terminal, beating out a hundred or so disgruntled travelers waiting for a replacement plane and crew.

The delay had him out of sorts and craving caffeine. He was halfway to the nearest kiosk when he stopped and retraced his steps.

"You want coffee?" he asked Shonda.

Her tight, tired smile made him glad he'd bothered.

"Two creams, no sugar." She gestured to his carry-on. "I'll keep an eye on it."

As he stood in line, he recalled her pale, brave face during the worst of the trip. She'd handled it better than most, especially the guy reciting Psalm 23 on repeat. Once would've sufficed. If the man truly feared no evil, why the endless loop?

When Mason returned, Shonda was in deep conversation with

the same jackass who'd hassled her while boarding. Apparently, the guy thought surviving a near-death experience gave him a shot. But body language never lied, and she leaned so far away she was practically in another zip code.

Mason put his towering frame to good use and dropped his voice an octave. "You're in my seat."

The guy hesitated, eyes darting between them.

After handing Shonda her coffee, Mason leveled the horndog with a flat stare. Wannabe Romeo took the hint.

"Thanks," she breathed, appearing genuinely relieved.

"My pleasure. I assumed he was bothering you, but if you're into sweaty, balding creeps, please don't let me stand in your way." He shrugged, indicating it was no big deal either way.

She shuddered. "Yeah, no."

Biting back a grin, Mason reclaimed his seat and stretched out his legs. She sipped her coffee and let out a moan of appreciation that made every hair on his body stand at attention.

Jesus, that sound! He nearly groaned in response. It was impossible to recall ever wanting a woman this badly, this fast. Usually, he let them come to him. Let them flirt a little, throw out a signal, and take the lead. But this one? She had him on a hair trigger after one kiss.

He took a chug of his brew and tried to analyze why. Gorgeous? Check. But he'd dated stunning women before. The appeal was more than looks. Perhaps it had to do with her dry humor and whatever spark he'd felt when they kissed. Whatever it was, it made him want to dig deeper, stay longer.

His last thought scared the fuck out of him, but he'd let it play out to see where it led.

"Are you meeting anyone on vacation? A group of girlfriends? A boyfriend?"

Christ. Did he seriously just ask about her relationship status?

"Um, no." Her eyes widened, honest and unguarded.

And because chivalry wasn't dead, he leaned in, careful to keep his voice low. "Do me a favor. Don't advertise traveling alone. If you have to, lie. Say your boyfriend or husband is joining you." At her startled look, he added, "A woman by herself could attract the wrong kind of attention."

She blinked, and a half-formed "oh" rounded her lovely, pink lips.

"Just be cautious. I'd hate for you to be one more statistic." Inside, he cringed at sounding like an overprotective dad.

"Thanks."

Smooth, buddy. Real fucking smooth. Way to kill the vibe and taint her vacation with worst-case scenarios. He could almost hear Zack braying like an ass. But statistics and probabilities drove everything he did. Apparently, he'd morphed into the kind of guy who warned women not to talk to strangers.

They fell into a slightly awkward silence. Not Mason's usual MO. And the damnedest part was he hadn't felt this off-balance in years.

Her hand landed on his thigh, and he nearly shot out of the chair, spilling coffee on his shirt.

"Fuck!" He drew the material away from his skin, intent on preventing a burn.

"I'm so sorry." Shonda's face turned crimson. "You looked so lost in thought, and I wasn't sure you heard me."

With a pointed glance at the hand still on his knee, he arched a brow.

"Ohmygod! Sorry!" She jerked back faster than if she'd touched a hot stove.

"No harm, no foul. It was barely warm." Mason couldn't help but smile when she frowned at his chest.

"Do you want me to get ice or something to cool the burn?" Shonda offered.

Her concern spoke well of her, and he felt terrible for his over-reaction.

"I'm good," he said. "Swear."

She seemed unconvinced.

He sighed. "What were you going to ask me?"

"I… It's just that, well, I was wondering if maybe you'd keep pretending we're together? Just while we're at the resort."

"You want me to play your pretend-boyfriend?" he clarified.

"No. Yes. I mean—" She blew out a breath and laughed. "I'm such a hot mess, and here I've made you one. Let me get something to clean your shirt."

Her about-face rattled him, and he watched her go with a shake of his head. That walk of hers was straight fire. Confident, sexy, and effortless. Hot as fuck.

His jeans were growing tight as his thoughts detoured to places they shouldn't, and he shifted in his seat. What the hell had gotten into him? But it wasn't just him. Every guy in the terminal was observing her, too. Perhaps even a few women.

Knowing how she affected others made him uneasy. She was going to get hit on, propositioned, and maybe worse. Leaning on his mother's do-the-right-thing teachings, Mason couldn't just leave Shonda to deal with the hassle alone.

A minute later, she returned with a soapy paper towel and an apologetic smile.

"It was all they had," she said.

"Yes."

She blinked. "Excuse me?"

"Yes," he repeated. "I'll be your pretend-boyfriend shield in St. Thomas."

They discussed resort details and discovered they were staying in the same hotel.

Convenient.

Maybe too convenient.

. . .

As Mason scrubbed the stain from his shirt, Shonda questioned Fate's wicked sense of humor. Self-sufficient by nature, it had never occurred to her exactly how vulnerable a woman could be while traveling solo. Hell, she flew back and forth to Miami for business all the time.

Instinct told her Mason was safe. At least physically. Emotionally? Yeah, that was another story. If she indulged in a fling—and let's face it, all signs pointed to go—she'd have to guard her heart. Her track record of falling too fast and later regretting it was Olympic-level gold. Most men she'd dated weren't worth the time investment. Deep down, she'd always known it, but listening to her inner voice meant a life of loneliness.

Mason felt different.

And not just in appearance, though God knew those movie-star good looks didn't hurt. She'd recognized him the instant he picked up his duffel bag. What girl from Stonebrooke didn't know the Sharps? Their sex appeal was genetically encoded in their DNA, and their reputations as lovers were the stuff of legend.

Mason clearly didn't recall her. But she certainly remembered him. His swagger demanded attention. Older by a couple of years, he'd been one of the few genuinely nice football players. And if memory served, he'd been utterly devoted to his high-school sweetheart.

She'd envied their kind of love. The hand-holding. The stolen kisses. The way he looked at the girl as if she were his whole world. Though his girlfriend had been on the same cheer squad, her face escaped Shonda. Funny how she recalled him so clearly, but not the person he'd been so crazy about.

Her breath caught.

Crap! She'd made an assumption he was single, based on his

solo travel and his easy agreement to play boyfriend. But maybe he was simply being chivalrous. Maybe he had a girlfriend, or worse, a wife, waiting for him.

"You… uh, do you have…?" Her brain stalled the moment his blue eyes found hers. She gave herself a mental facepalm. Where did her college-level vocabulary go around this man? At the moment, she sounded like she had never passed the fifth grade.

Those eyes crinkled with amusement. "No. I'm single."

Relief gushed out of her like steam from a pressure valve.

"Okay. Good." She winced at how eager she sounded.

Get it together, Shonda. You're a grown woman, not a lovesick teenager.

"Time to board." Mason's deep voice cut through her mental scolding.

Startled, she glanced around. Lost in thought, she'd managed to miss the announcement. Lord, help her! This man was turning her brain to pudding.

BY THE TIME they arrived on the island, Shonda was running on fumes and ready for a twenty-four-hour coma. But wasting valuable vacation time wasn't an option.

A restorative shower washed off the worst of her travel grime, helping to cool her after the wild fantasies starring a certain sexy companion. And okay, she'd turned the water a few degrees colder than comfortable after visions of Mason under a waterfall began to feel too vivid.

When she stepped out onto her suite's veranda, there he was.

Mason Sharp.

Who, from their high-school days, would have believed it?

Leaning casually against a railing across the courtyard, he looked out at the horizon like he owned it.

Relaxed.

Confident.

Utterly delicious.

Then he turned and met her gaze across the distance.

A slow smile curled his mouth before transforming into an all-out, knee-weakening, wicked grin. Startled, Shonda immediately glanced down to make sure she hadn't forgotten an essential article of clothing and exhaled a relieved sigh. Everything was accounted for. When she looked up, Mason was striding in the opposite direction.

"So much for holding him enthralled, you silly woman," she muttered.

With a shake of her head at her foolishness, she pushed away from the railing. Her stomach gave a not-so-subtle grumble, reminding her to get food fast. The tropical breeze kicked up, suggesting a walk on the beach after dinner would be a perfect way to end the evening. Followed, of course, by another cold shower to cool her overactive hormones.

Her debate was between room service and the resort's main dining room. It boiled down to the question, did she want solitude or a little pampering after the long-ass day?

Prickling started along her skin, creeping up her spine. Her body's early warning system.

Someone was watching her.

With a seemingly casual eye and a slight smile, Shonda surveyed her surroundings, pretending to appreciate the view. Nothing appeared out of the ordinary, and she mentally shrugged off her unease. She slipped inside and locked the glass slider, an old habit after a scary experience she'd never forget.

The sharp rap on her door surprised her, making her muffle a scream. Crikey, she was getting jumpy. And as she debated answering, another knock sounded, more impatient this time. She was approaching the peephole when Mason's voice called out. Her relief felt over the top, and she put it down to fatigue.

"You looked lonely," he said as she swung the door wide.

Warmth curled low in her belly. Three little words. How the hell did he manage to make her a puddle at his feet with so simple a sentence? She inhaled to steady her nerves and smiled wryly. No way was she letting him know he affected her this much.

With a tilt of her head and a raised brow, she aimed for casual. "Did I?"

Studying her, he didn't answer straight away. And it was like he could see through her faux expression and read every thought in her head. All of them still revolved around her shower fantasies.

Wordlessly, and with a boldness only seen in movies, he stepped closer and slid an arm around her waist. With his free hand, he unclipped her updo, sending waves tumbling over her shoulders and down her back. He raked his finger through her hair as if memorizing its texture, fascinated by the play of gold.

When his eyes met hers, the intensity stole the air from her lungs.

"Yes, you absolutely fucking did."

Then he kissed her. Their second one of the day. It was hotter, deeper, and a helluva lot more dangerous than anything she'd ever experienced.

Dear God, she was a goner!

CHAPTER

THREE

One kiss, and Mason was toast. What the hell was that about?

Shonda's soft, supple mouth so willing to open to him. Her slender waist, seemingly made for his hands. The subtle, fruity scent clinging to her silky skin. Sure, all of it was a turn-on, but another sensation, more tangible, tugged at him. The pull wasn't anything he could explain. It was primal and possessive, leaving him feeling as if his soul wanted to stake a claim on hers.

What the fuck was wrong with him?

The dangerous urge cooled his reactor real quick.

He set her away, but his eyes refused to obey and lingered on her mesmerizing face. Flushed, dazed, her lips swollen and glistening, she was a vision.

Her lashes fluttered open, as if waking from a dream. "Um, wow," she muttered, voice all husky and sex-kitten soft.

Apparently, a purr came out when she was turned on.

Great. Just great.

Lust was going to wreck him. She had him by the short hairs, and she didn't even know it.

"Dinner," he bit out. It was sharper than intended, and she blinked her surprise. Trying to soften the blow, he said, "Let's head down, get a bite."

Bite her, more like, his inner devil urged.

He clamped down on his wayward thought. Later. Maybe. For now, he needed to rein that shit in.

Her stomach grumbled, and his roared back louder, making them laugh.

"Let me grab my purse."

Mason took her hand on the way to the elevator and again when they entered the restaurant. A show, he reminded himself, for appearances only, to warn the vultures off. It had absolutely nothing to do with how naturally her fingers laced with his or how good it felt when he kissed her inner wrist while seating her.

Her glowing smile disconcerted him, causing him to freeze mid-motion. An unintentional frown drew his brows together before he could stop it, and hesitation flashed across her features. When her apprehension filtered into his sluggish brain, he shook off his momentary lapse and took a seat across the small, intimate table.

"Sorry." It was his only concession to hovering and unintentionally intimidating her with his commanding height. He hated when other men dominated with their size, and he felt like a complete ass.

She nodded, gracious as ever, and perused a menu.

Once the orders were placed and drinks arrived, small talk picked up.

"So, what do you do?" she asked.

"I co-own Workout World with my brothers, Zack and Dane. Three locations as of this year: Stonebrooke, Wisteria Heights, and Sagefield. I handle the marketing." He tilted his chin toward her. "You?"

"Marketing director for WTKO news. I oversee all the stations statewide. Periodically, I get drawn in for national stuff, since our parent company is in Miami."

He accepted a salad plate from their server with a smile and "thank you" before returning to their conversational thread. "That must keep you busy," he said.

"Ten-hour days minimum, half-days on Saturdays. I love it, but it's exhausting." Her shy, self-effacing smile told him she was downplaying how much work she put in.

"WTKO? We have an account with them for our local commercials."

"Yes. I've run across it. Amber Harrington is your rep, I believe."

"Yes." He sipped his wine. "I know Amber."

The slight hesitancy in his voice must have tipped her off.

"Ah." Her brows arched as she forked another bite of salad, and her gaze skimmed past him.

Did he detect censure? He would be disappointed if it were. As a grown-ass adult, he didn't need to justify a handful of forgettable dates, damn it. Especially not to a woman he'd met today.

But she pivoted the conversation before he could get defensive.

"How long are you in St. Thomas?" she asked brightly.

"Ten days, and I'm really looking forward to it." He smiled in the face of her unspoken curiosity. "This is my first real vacation since we opened four years ago. I've taken some weekend trips here or there, but nothing for any extended length of time. It's overdue."

"Same. I was supposed to come with my best friend, Erica, but she got hit with an unexpected deadline. She's an author, and it happens, but a girls' trip would have been fun."

"Erica?" The coincidence was too great. "Not Erica Sutton?"

"You know Erica? Don't tell me you read romance, because I won't believe you."

He snorted. "Not hardly. My brother sent me a text to say she'd just joined our gym. He knew her as a kid."

"Erica? Joining a gym? We can't be talking about the same woman here. She *hates* exercise."

Mason chuckled at her emphatic use of the word hate, suspecting she'd said it for entertainment value. "The average person doesn't like to work out. They do it to stay healthy."

"You don't understand. Erica lives on donuts and coffee. She wouldn't set foot in a gym if her life depended on it. Even then, it would be to escape out the back door." Shonda lifted her wine for a quick sip. "I'm pretty sure she breaks out in hives at the mention of a treadmill."

She launched into additional stories about her friend, animated, funny, and utterly unaware that Mason couldn't take his eyes off her. Her husky laugh and the way she lit up with each tale were magnetic.

The plates were eventually cleared, and yet they lingered, trading stories and laughter like old friends. It struck him how much he enjoyed her lively state. She was luminescent, and her sparkling wit enhanced her beauty.

And that was the problem. It wasn't just attraction anymore.

Shonda wasn't acknowledging any of his flirtation cues, and it was pretty damn clear she wasn't a casual-fling kind of woman. Which meant if he wanted to protect both of them from complications, he needed to pull back. Fast.

Damn it.

It was too bad, really. Tonight was the most fun he'd had in years. But it was the dangerous kind, hinting at his deep-down loneliness, tempting him with the possibility of true companionship, and reminding him he was sick to death of meaningless hookups and one-note conversations.

Perilous thinking for a man who intended to avoid forever.

Sure, he'd hoped for a few nights of mutual pleasure, but the truth was spelled out in neon. He needed to distance himself, no matter how much his dry spell protested. Emotional entanglements were too difficult.

Abruptly, he stood, startling a wide-eyed gasp from Shonda.

"Time to call it a night. It's been a long day."

"Oh. Yes. Sure," she replied, a bit off-balance.

By the time they reached her room, he almost caved and asked if she was up for a walk on the beach. The expectation on her face suggested she was hopeful, but he merely kissed her cheek, promising to check in the next day so they could coordinate their schedules.

Then he walked away before he changed his mind and did something truly stupid.

SHONDA STOOD FROZEN in her suite, replaying the night and wondering what went wrong. She wasn't crazy. Their chemistry had been off the charts. And his pre-dinner kiss wasn't at all polite. Nope, it was pure, bone-melting fire. So what the hell happened?

Maybe in dragging Mason into her hare-brained fake-boyfriend scheme, she'd killed the mood. The chaste kiss to her cheek and polite, *"I'll check in tomorrow so we can sync schedules,"* wasn't exactly the behavior of a man dying to get her into bed. Clearly, he wasn't interested in more, and there was little point in forcing things. After all, there were plenty of solo travelers at dinner. Surely she could survive a week on her own without inventing a relationship?

With a sigh, she changed into shorts and a tank, then wandered out to the balcony. The ocean breeze whispered sweet nothings, brushing across her skin and tempting her to dip her toes in the gently lapping waves.

And there he was.

Mason.

Backlit, he stood at the railing of his balcony, drink in hand, and stared out at the sea as if it held all the answers. His silhouette was carved from moonlight and shadow. Broad shoulders. Bare arms. He didn't fidget; he simply leaned there, stoic, remote, and devastating.

Her lungs tightened.

His presence was electrifying in ways she could never describe. God help her fanciful imagination, but he belonged to the night. If vampires existed, he'd be the one to have women lining up and volunteering to be bitten.

Mason had presence. Gravity.

She couldn't figure out why he, of all people, had her tangled up in knots. Plenty of men were more handsome than Mason Arrogance-is-my-middle-name Sharp. She'd dated the polished, pretty, and charming. None of them had ever left her weak-kneed or lit her up like he did with a single look. The memory of his kiss made her cheeks burn, and the evening breeze did nothing to cool the heat simmering beneath her skin or the hum in her blood.

Right as she shifted away, she caught it. A flicker of stark loneliness on his face. But it was gone in a flash, masked by a sip of his drink.

Her pulse sped up as her mind was inundated with questions. The primary one: Why would someone so charismatic choose solitude?

Shonda ran through everything she'd heard about the Sharp family. Aside from their father leaving when the boys were young, there hadn't been any whispered tragedies. At least none she could recall.

Mason straightened, raised his glass in a silent salute to the stars, and turned.

"Good night, Shonda," he said, his voice low and clear across the courtyard.

She wasn't surprised he'd known she was watching the whole time. Hell, she should be embarrassed, but she wasn't.

"Good night, Mason," she replied, but he was already gone.

The magic of the night vanished with him, leaving her chilly and flat.

She was being ridiculously fanciful. If she wasn't careful, she'd start spinning fantasies around a man who didn't want her. A man who'd made it very clear, intentionally or not, that she was better off keeping her distance.

She needed to sleep this fascination off.

And if that didn't work, well, her battery-operated backup never failed.

CHAPTER

FOUR

The morning dawned bright and beautiful. Sunlight and sea air streamed in past the billowing curtains. Shonda stretched as she enjoyed the smell of the ocean.

A jolt shot through her, like being hit with a live wire, and she shot up in bed, heart hammering with the force of a resonating steel drum. She was positive she'd locked the bedroom windows last night. She distinctly remembered setting the AC to seventy-two and the fan on low. The curtains had most certainly been drawn. No way would she feel comfortable in a strange place with potential onlookers close by.

Yeah, that left window shouldn't be open at all.

Without leaving the bed, she scanned the room. Everything appeared to be untouched. She eased from under the covers, careful not to produce a sound. After padding barefoot to the bedroom door and peeking into the living area, her pulse spiked.

The slider was open!

Only a few inches, but enough to indicate a visitor.

Panic clawed at her rib cage, leaving her short of breath, and she bolted for the door. Whipping it open, she charged out and *straight into a brick wall.*

Nope, make that a man's chest!

Steel bands came around her to break her fall, supporting her as her knees gave way.

"Dear God, I think I broke my nose," she moaned.

"Let me see." Gentle hands tilted her chin.

Mason. His identity was evident by the way her body betrayed her, warmth intensifying and heartbeat quickening. All thanks to his deep, sinful voice.

He examined her nose as tears leaked from the corners of her eyes.

"I don't think it's broken," he said. "Want to tell me why you ran out of your room like hellhounds were chasing you?"

"Oh!" The reason slammed back into focus, and she gripped his wrists. "Someone was in my room. I don't know if they're still there."

"Stay here. Let me check it out."

"No! You're not going in there by yourself. What if they have a weapon?"

He snorted his disbelief. "Chances are they've already escaped out the back with all the commotion you caused here in the hall."

Annoyingly, he made sense.

Shonda folded her arms. "Then I guess there's no reason I shouldn't go in with you." Sarcasm slipped out, but she didn't feel bad. His alpha act was starting to grate.

"Are you always so difficult?" Mason asked, exasperation riding every syllable. "The longer we argue, the more time the perp has to escape."

She fumed in silence while he checked every corner of her suite. Of all the high-handed attitudes! Right now, she was finding it difficult to remember what had made him so attractive to her in the first place.

"All clear," he announced, stopping in front of her. "Let's call the front desk and report it. Also…" His finger traced the thin strap of her tank top. "You may want to put on something less revealing, love."

The spark in his eyes was the polar opposite of last night's cheek kiss. She'd never given thought to her sleepwear being particularly revealing before, but Mason's interest made her reconsider.

And now she was covered in goosebumps.

Damn the man and all his sexy energy.

While they waited for management and local police to conduct their investigation, she wrapped herself in silence. Mason said little, standing like a sentinel at her side.

Nothing appeared to be missing, and the officers were less than impressed with her story. Their polite disbelief was infuriating.

"There's no sign of forced entry. You probably forgot to lock up," one said with a tight smile.

She bristled and tamped down the desire to punch his smug face.

"I *did* lock up," she replied through clenched teeth. "I'm a responsible adult who knows how to secure a fucking door."

"We'll make a note of the incident," another offered, kinder but just as dismissive as his partner. "If anything happens again, please call."

"Yeah, sure," she snapped, stalking forward to see them out. "I'd absolutely love it if you came back and condescended some more."

Shonda slammed the door behind them with more force than strictly necessary. It helped. A little. Smashing things would've made her happier. She shifted on her heel and froze.

Mason was leaning against the wall, arms crossed. His face was unreadable.

"You think I made this up, too?" She stormed closer, working up the nerve to tell him to go to hell.

"No," he said evenly. "Not in the least."

Under his watchful gaze, her rage cooled.

"Why should you believe me when they didn't?" she asked curiously.

"I couldn't sleep last night. When I stepped outside, I glanced over to see if your lights were still on. From what I could see, everything was shut up tight."

"Then why didn't you say anything to the police?" she demanded, circling back to pissed off.

"It wouldn't have done any good," he said matter-of-factly. "They weren't interested once they'd discovered nothing valuable was taken."

Shonda dropped into a chair, deflating. "So that's it? Some fucker breaks in, and no one gives a shit?"

He pushed off the wall to stand directly in front of her chair. His intensity lit her nerve endings.

"Want to tell me why someone would break into your suite, leave everything untouched, and vanish, Shonda?"

"How the hell should I know?"

His eyes sharpened. "Don't lie to me."

Her throat tightened, and it was hard to push "never" from between numb lips. What was wrong with people? Did they view everyone they met with suspicion? Was that what the world had come to, a lack of trust?

More than a dozen heartbeats later, albeit fast ones on her part, he nodded once. "Let's go get some breakfast."

"WHY DON'T you tell me why you think someone would break into your room and not take anything?"

Mason didn't wait for Shonda to get comfortable. Catching her off guard was the point, and judging by the flush creeping into her cheeks, she wasn't happy about it. Too bad. He needed to know what kind of mess he'd walked into by agreeing to play pretend-boyfriend.

"I told you back in the room. I have no idea."

He wanted to believe her. God, did he ever. But in his experience, women danced around the truth.

Wide, earnest eyes stared at him, and her lips parted as if she might spill secrets if pressed. Even the slight lean of her body toward him screamed honesty. Which meant this situation just went from bad to worse.

"Technically, you said, 'How the hell should I know?' Which, if we're being honest, speaks of avoidance," he countered.

She opened her mouth to argue, but he cut her off with a sigh.

"Okay, love, let's say I believe you. That gives us two options." He ticked them off on his fingers. "You've either picked up a stalker, or someone was searching for valuables. Let's rule out a stalker for the moment. You're too far from home, and it feels too fast to attract one here. Which leaves us with a B&E and a very important question: did they find what they were looking for?"

"Again, I don't know," she said, clearly exasperated. "I don't have anything anyone would want. I know better than to travel with valuables."

She tossed the half-eaten strip of bacon onto her plate.

"Think," Mason pressed, snagging the piece she discarded. "There must be something. A stalker would've taken a trophy or maybe left a message for you."

She paled.

He instantly regretted pushing so hard, not wanting to

frighten her worse than she already was. Yet they didn't have the luxury of pretending this was nothing. The police had brushed it off as her imagination when they both knew it wasn't.

"Mason, I swear to you, I don't know. Assuming someone's after me, why wait until I'm here? Why not attempt to break into my home or office? It doesn't make any sense," she reasoned.

He sighed. She wasn't wrong.

"So what? Assume it was a fluke and double our guard just in case?" he asked.

"This isn't your issue. You didn't sign up for all this drama. I understand if you want to walk away."

Her voice was small and achingly vulnerable. She was holding it together by sheer will, pretending she wasn't shaken to her core.

"I'm not walking away, Shonda," he assured her quietly. "We'll get to the bottom of this."

Expression tight, she gave a slight nod. Worry was etched in every line of her face.

"We will," he promised, lacing his fingers through hers.

Her helpless stare was broken by the server who slipped the check onto the table. Mason signed it and helped Shonda to her feet.

"Now let's go do what we came here for and soak up the sun," he suggested.

A reluctant smile curled her lips.

He'd take it.

FROM HIS TOWEL, Mason watched Shonda at the water's edge, wind teasing her hair, her expression distant, as if caught up in last night's break-in.

She wasn't faking it.

No one wore anxiety like hers unless it was real, and besides, his gut trusted her. Past incidents, however, warned him not to.

A few brave souls ignored his warning glower and ventured closer in hopes of charming her. It was time to remind the crowd she wasn't on the market, even if their arrangement was as fake as a ten-dollar tan.

Mason jogged down the sand, cut between them, and swept her into his arms. He charged headlong into the aqua water, not stopping until they were waist-deep in the surf. An unexpected wave crashed into them, and he twisted as they fell, his body taking the impact as they both went under.

She surfaced sputtering mad, absolutely soaked, and utterly breathtaking.

"God, you are such an asshole!" she snapped.

He couldn't help the grin. "Don't be mad. Come here, I'll let you sniff me."

With narrowed eyes, she slapped water in his direction.

Christ, he adored the fuck out of her fire. His thoughts turned to all the things he could do with her passion, all the heights he could take her.

"Come here," he commanded.

Her mossy-green eyes went wide as her gaze dipped below the water's surface. When she looked up, intrigue had replaced annoyance.

He quirked a brow in challenge.

She waded closer, but stopped a foot shy of touching him. "If this is a game and you dunk me again, I swear, I'll kick your—"

Lunging forward, he caught her around the waist, pulling her to him.

"Does this feel like a game?"

"N-no."

"I want to touch you, Shonda," he murmured against her ear. "Are you willing?"

Her answer was a nod, slight but unmistakable.

His hand slid below the surface, gliding beneath the edge of her suit. When he reached her, he found her slick and warm. "Mmm, seems like the ocean isn't the only thing that's made you wet."

"Mason…" Her voice cracked on his name when he peeled off her swimsuit bottom, tucking it into the back of his waistband. The flush on her cheeks wasn't just the result of the sun's tropical rays, and she cast an uncertain glance over his shoulder. Her voice was breathless as she said, "People are watching."

"Let them. What will they see? A couple enjoying a bit of necking?"

He trailed kisses down the side of her throat, nipping the soft skin. Sinking lower, he drew her closer. When she wrapped her long legs around him and pressed her core against his erection, he groaned and inched her hips away.

"None of that. Not yet," he said regretfully.

With his thumb, he teased her, circling her clit while his fingers moved in gentle, deliberate strokes. She shivered, melting into him, arms encircling his neck as she pressed her face into the crook of his shoulder.

"I've got you," he assured her, sliding his finger inside her warmth. "Let go and enjoy, love."

She clutched his back, her muscles tensing as her thighs crushed his sides. A sharp gasp escaped her lips, followed by a breathless moan. She clenched down hard as he pleasured her and came undone right there in his arms. He held her through the silent trembling, capturing her mouth in a demanding kiss that stole her cry before it escaped. And as she calmed, relaxing her grip, he brushed his lips against her temple, across her cheekbone.

Her eyes were glassy, her lips swollen, and she was positively wanton-looking.

"You okay, love?"

She nodded, gracing him with a languid smile. "Why didn't you…?"

"Because this time was for you," he said, lips quirking.

"Is that all we're doing?" she asked, as she stroked him through his suit.

Mason held himself back from grinding against her hand, wishing to hell they had privacy with the barrier of clothes gone. He wove his fingers through her damp hair and gently tugged her head back so they were face-to-face.

"For now, but you need to know I don't do long-term. If you want to continue this, know it's only for the duration of our stay." Her frown disappointed him, but he had to drive the point home. "You cool with the terms?"

She paused for what seemed like forever, and his heart raced like he'd been the one to experience the orgasm.

"Yes," she eventually agreed.

He shut his eyes in relief. Had she said no, his disappointment would've been keen. His desire for this woman was more than he'd felt for all the women he'd been with in the last five years combined. That alone should have him running in the opposite direction. But he was quickly becoming addicted to the taste of her mouth and the feel of her skin against his.

"Good. That's good," he said on an exhale, sounding winded and embarrassingly glad. "When I get off with you, it's not going to be half hidden in the water with a resort full of people nearby."

She stared at him like she couldn't quite figure him out.

He told himself he preferred it that way. Better to remain mysterious and detached, if only to prove to himself he could be. Closeness equaled eventual betrayal and pain. He'd avoid both if possible.

"Okay, give me back my bikini bottom." She held out a hand, and her expectant air amused him.

Mason flared his eyes. "Oh, crap."

"Don't you *dare* tell me you dropped it," she growled. "I swear to God—"

He produced the tiny scrap of material with a flourish and a laugh.

"You are such an assh—"

Before the end of the sentence was out of her mouth, he kissed her again, eliciting her moan.

"Asshole," he finished the insult with a grin. "Yeah, I know. I saw a kayak kiosk down the beach. Want to go?"

CHAPTER

FIVE

The day was vacation perfection. A hot guy, a toe-curling orgasm, and adventure-filled jaunts. When Mason dropped Shonda back at her suite, she couldn't envision a better time with anyone, past or future.

Bobbing on the high seas in their two-person kayak, he'd turned up the charm, and she'd been powerless to resist.

Not that she'd been the only captivated one.

With a flash of a wicked grin, the teasing sparkle in his eye, and the occasional glimpse of a dimple, people bent over backwards to please him. Men wanted to be him, and women wanted to be taken by him. The guy was a walking fantasy, and no one stood a chance.

Especially not Shonda.

"I'm going to grab a quick shower, and then we can head out for dinner," he said.

"Or we can shower together and order in." She was bold to suggest it, and when Mason gave her a knowing smirk, she was glad she did.

They leaped toward each other with intent. Shirts, shorts, and shoes flew in every direction. Mouths melded and tongues tangled. Exactly how they ended up under the hot spray was beyond her ability to recall.

An hour later, they surfaced, weak-kneed but highly satisfied.

"I'll order us something," she offered, reaching for her phone. "Pizza sound good? A friend told me about a local place. He claimed it's the best on the island."

"He?" Mason's inquiry possessed more than idle curiosity. If she didn't know any better, Shonda would believe he was jealous. Yet, he'd already set the rules of their island fling, and she assumed she was wrong.

"A guy I work with," she clarified as she scrolled through her phone.

"Shonda, how many people knew you were coming here, to this resort?" His voice was measured and caught her attention.

"Why?"

"I'm still bothered by the break-in," he admitted.

His stance was deceptively relaxed, but his eyes were alert as he watched her. Throughout the day, he'd poked at the seams of her story, as if testing for a tear, and she didn't appreciate it. Did he suspect her of lying? At times, she believed he did, and it was off-putting.

"I don't know," she said. "Maybe four, including my boss."

"Do you think any of them would have a reason to harm you?"

"No," she stated emphatically.

He lifted a brow, encouraging further speculation. And after giving it due consideration, she wasn't so certain.

"Yeah, okay. Possibly," she said with a shrug.

"Care to explain?"

Revealing the details was embarrassing. She wasn't the only one who'd taken a romantic dip in the work pool, but confessing to her stupidity wasn't so comfortable.

"When I was first hired on, I dated one of my colleagues. I didn't know he'd been gunning for my position, and he was furious I was promoted over him."

"Dated? As in slept with?" Mason asked.

"Yes." A rush of warmth infused her face. Discussing an old boyfriend with a new lover was always awkward as fuck, and normally, she'd avoid it.

Ducking her head, she busied herself with finding the restaurant's number.

"That's not the whole story," Mason stated flatly.

He shifted closer, and she could practically feel the tension rolling off him.

"Shonda, look at me."

The command, issued in his deep, no-nonsense voice, left no room for refusal. Like a marionette, she jerked to attention and pivoted until they were face-to-face.

"What's his name?" he demanded.

"What does it matter? It was years ago."

"I intend to have a friend check his whereabouts. Let's make sure he's somewhere other than St. Thomas."

What she'd taken for arrogance was Mason's way of keeping her safe. Despite how domineering his request came across, she couldn't fault him for it.

"Do you honestly believe a guy I slept with once, three years ago, tracked me down and broke into my hotel room?" she asked skeptically. "For what purpose? Nothing was taken, remember?"

"His name. Now."

"Who the hell do you think you are?" And what made her so reluctant to tell him Samuel's name?

A chill settled in his eyes, and he stepped back. "My mistake. I assumed you wanted to get to the bottom of this."

"No. *You* want to get to the bottom of something, which may or may not be a simple break-in. You're chasing shadows, and before this is through, you'll have me paranoid of all my co-workers over a random incident."

As he studied her, he seemed to weigh her response. Coming to a decision, he relaxed and cracked a wry smile. "All right. Fair enough. We can shelve the discussion for the time being. Please order our pizza."

His mood shifts were dizzying. One second, he was an icy detective determined to ferret out all her secrets, and the next, a charming rogue willing to enjoy her company. But she'd be damned if she could tell him to get lost. Whatever magic he possessed drew her in until she didn't know up from down. Perhaps after a couple of nights, once he was out of her system, she'd be able to think clearly again. As it stood, she spent ninety percent of her time breathless and off-balance.

"RISE AND SHINE," Shonda called, sailing into the room with two cups of coffee. "Oh, I see you've already done that."

Mason chuckled at her bawdy humor and the way her eyes locked on his morning wood.

"What's on the agenda today?" he asked innocently.

"Uh..." Her focus refused to shift from his half-naked form, and he struggled not to laugh.

"Shonda." When her gaze inched above his waist to meet his, he grinned. "Put the coffee down and come here."

Her eyes widened, but she didn't waste a beat. She set the cup carrier aside and stripped on the way to bed. As she climbed on board the sex train, he had to admit to appreciating a woman with her level of enthusiasm.

Later, barely covered by tangled sheets, with lukewarm lattes in hand, Mason released a sigh of contentment. Did life get better than a moment like this? A flavorful mocha, a beautiful blonde tucked against his side, and insanely hot sex in paradise made it hard to imagine.

"Beach, snorkeling, or hiking," she said out of the blue.

"What?"

"Earlier, you asked what was on the agenda. I'm offering suggestions. Granted, we've done all of those this week, but we can head to the other side of the island."

"Hm. Well, I'd say beach, but I don't know if I've got the energy to fend off the island's male population. They're relentless."

"You really think you're that attractive?" she quipped, flicking his nipple.

Chuckling, he set his cup aside. Ever so carefully, he removed hers and placed it next to his.

"I think you are," he said after they kissed, all traces of humor gone.

She sucked in a breath and gazed up at him, stars forming in her eyes.

Unease unfurled in his stomach. What the hell had gotten into him? He knew good and well not to go there. Attempting to recover, he withdrew his arm and rolled off the bed, tugging her with him.

"I need a shower and a shave. So do you. Those cactus plants you call legs have drawn blood."

"You did *not* just go there!"

"Yep, I'm pretty sure I did." He ducked the pillow she launched at his head. "You should consider how important honesty is in a fake relationship, love."

"Bite me."

A long look at her gorgeous, naked body had him seriously considering it.

"Oh, no, you don't," she growled, her eyes narrowing in a

threatening glare. "Get that look off your face. I came here to see the island, not spend my vacation in bed."

"Ouch! That hurt." Pasting on a mock-wounded expression, he pressed a hand to his heart.

"Right." She failed to hide her smile. "I'll see you downstairs in twenty minutes."

"When did you get so bossy?" he asked with a swat on her ass. "Remember who's in charge here."

"As if."

Laughing, Mason dropped a quick kiss on her lips and reminded her to lock the door behind him.

As he headed back to his suite, he couldn't shake the feeling he might be making a mistake. Their last five days together had been pure bliss. Shonda was open, easy to be with, and hotter than Satan's house cat. But whenever unguarded, there was a glimmer of deeper emotion in her eyes, and it scared the bejeezus out of him.

Under the steaming stream of water, he rolled his neck, hoping to dispel the building tension. They needed another talk to clarify the rules. A simple reminder he wasn't happily-ever-after material.

Armed with a plan, he returned to her room, but the sight of her sleek body and shining face derailed his intentions.

"What did you decide?" she asked expectantly.

"Snorkeling at Secret Harbor?"

Shonda smiled approvingly. "Perfect."

As the day wore on, Mason found it a joy to watch her fascination with every sea creature: urchins, stingrays, and even curious fish. His GoPro caught her wide-eyed delight and was better viewing than any reef. Later, on the ride back to the resort, they laughed over her nearly drowning herself in her excitement.

"Don't tell me you caught it on camera," she complained with a mock scowl.

"I did, indeed." Yeah, he was gloating, but she was so much fun to tease. "I'm uploading it to YouTube as soon as we get back."

Good-natured as always, she laughed. "I'm never going to live it down if anyone sees it. Is there anything I can do to change your mind about posting it?" she asked suggestively, fingers trailing across the front of his shorts.

"Maybe." He rained light kisses up her neck and nipped her earlobe. "Tell me what you have in mind?"

"Oh, I don't know. I'm sure we can come to terms."

Her sultry voice, paired with her hand in just the right place, had him hard and ready to release the Kraken. He captured her hand in his and kissed her knuckles before setting it in her lap.

"I'm open to negotiations, but we'll have to continue this discussion in your room."

Her laughter was light and joyful, causing him to grin in response.

"You two here on your honeymoon?" the driver asked with a glance in the rearview.

The assumption pissed him off.

"No," Mason replied, sharper than he meant to.

And just like that, the mood shattered.

Why did everyone insist on a label? His chest tightened. The immediate desire to put distance between him and Shonda was like a tsunami, strong and fast, with a deadly undertow threatening to drown him if he didn't get to safety.

Sweating profusely, with his stomach in knots, he scanned the road ahead and was relieved to spot a bar. Leaning forward, he said, "Can you pull over? I'm getting out right here."

The stunned disbelief on Shonda's face was a donkey kick to the sternum. But almost as quickly, her expression altered, carefully masking her disappointment and making him realize she'd seen through him to the cause of his restlessness.

Unable to offer a proper apology, Mason kissed her compressed lips and shoved a wad of cash in the driver's direction.

"Please see that she gets back to our hotel safely." To her, he said, "I'll call you later."

The vehicle pulled away, and he waited for it to disappear before crossing the street to park his ass on a barstool.

"Scotch," he barked at the bartender. As he sipped his drink, he sat in silence, shaking his head when the lounge lizards and too-friendly patrons ventured a conversation. He needed alone time to process his feelings.

He'd be lucky if Shonda ever spoke to him again. But if she didn't, it was honestly for the best. As an emotionally stunted man, he had nothing worthwhile to offer her.

CHAPTER
SIX

S honda was done.
Finito.

Kaput.

Gonzo.

And *so* fucking over Mason Sharp's moody, mysterious, emotionally stunted man-child behavior. Sure, she understood he had intimacy issues. His boundaries loomed higher and were tougher to climb than Everest in winter. But leaping out of a cab like it was about to explode, all because the driver had asked if they were on their honeymoon?

Pfft. Yeah, next-level jackassery.

She fumed the whole ride back to her room. Once inside, she resisted the urge to hurl things—like maybe one of those over-priced hotel vases serving no purpose except as tacky tropical décor. Instead, she opted for a long, scalding shower and promised herself she was *not* going to cry. Ever.

No, she wasn't that invested.

Or not yet, anyway.

This was her vacation, too. And if Mason wanted to sulk in

some dingy island bar and unravel over an innocent inquiry, it was his prerogative. But she was done tiptoeing around his hair-trigger emotions. Let the pansy-ass mope! She had better things to do than wait around on a guy who couldn't decide if he wanted to kiss her cross-eyed or ghost her.

She slipped into her cutest sundress. A bold floral print, low neckline, with a body-hugging fit screaming, "I may be alone, but about to be far from lonely."

After a swipe of gloss and the slightest spritz of perfume, she headed out the door.

"Mason, you fuckwit! You don't know what you're missing," she muttered, giving him the mental bird.

The steel drums hit her ears long before she stepped onto the tiki bar's patio. They were playing *Day-O*, and her hips knew exactly what to do. She swayed with the rhythm, loose and free, letting the music work out the tension in her shoulders. She flagged a waitress and ordered a Mai Tai. Claiming a seat in the shade, she let the music settle her. This lively but relaxed atmosphere was what vacation was all about, not moody glances and emotionally unavailable gym owners.

A flash of movement caught her attention, and she did a double-take. From the back, the guy looked like her cousin. Same posture, same gait. But when she shifted for a better look, he was already vanishing into the crowd. But Billy hadn't mentioned getting away, and they were close enough to discuss his plans.

Must be a vacation mirage. The chill in her bones was harder to shake, though.

The waitress, a cheeky little thing with a fierce gleam, a wicked smile, and an I've-seen-some-shit attitude, delivered her drink along with a rundown of the bar's male clientele, complete with warnings about who was trolling for a quick hookup and who might be worth five minutes of her time.

The opening notes of *Shake Señora* blasted through the speakers, and a golden-haired Adonis strode up. The guy looked like he'd stepped off the page of a cologne ad. With no hello and zero hesitation, he slipped his hand in hers and laughingly tugged her to the floor.

"No, I don't—"

He waved aside her protest as they joined his group of friends.

Wary, Shonda scanned for her waitress and received the thumbs-up telling her to go with it. And why the hell not? At the very least, it was a story Erica would appreciate. Within a minute, the dance floor was packed. Bodies moved in sync, and laughter filled the air. Spinning and swaying, she found herself swept up in the collective energy, feeling the music and the carefree joy of it all.

Three songs later, winded from laughing, she wove her way back to her table only to be drawn into a tequila-shot lineup. Because, of course, the band was playing *Tequila*, and those were the rules.

Lick. Shoot. Suck.

Repeat.

And repeat again.

Annoying thoughts of Mason evaporated in a haze of lime and salt. Amid endless laughter and spilled booze, Shonda felt at home with her new friends. Before long, they were shouting out songs to be played, dancing, and singing at the top of their lungs.

For the first time in days, she let herself be free. No worrying about who was going to flake or freak out or drop her mid-sentence. Her brain was buzzing, but she didn't want to stop. It felt too good to let her hair down, both literally and figuratively, and consume questionable amounts of rum.

The vibe mellowed as the tempo changed to a slower, sultry tune. Her nameless blond partner considered it his cue to close in, placing his hands on her hips, intent clear in his hot eyes.

Another man's hands brought reality rushing back.

She wasn't ready for another casual fling, not this soon.

Giving him a regretful head shake, she spun to leave and walked right into a wall of muscle. Both hands flew up, bracing against a familiar chest.

Oh no!

She knew those muscles. Her brain had already filed the topography, but her fingers didn't get the memo. They drifted lower, exploring the ridges of his abs beneath his shirt.

Yep. Definitely Mason Sharp!

"Having a good time, love?" he asked, amusement rich in his tone.

"The best!" she gushed. "You should've been here. We did tequila shots."

She waved toward the crowded madness at the bar.

"I arrived as you were downing your second shot."

"You did?" Shonda couldn't recall seeing him, but then again, she hadn't been searching either.

"Hey, man. I saw her first." Her blond friend interrupted them with a scowl.

Neither she nor Mason appreciated his complaint.

"Fuck off." Mason's voice left no room for argument.

"Why don't you ask the lady who she wants to be with?" her ex-dance partner challenged, clearly a few drinks past smart.

"Yes, why don't we?" Mason said silkily, his gaze locked on Shonda. Challenge glinted in his eyes, compelling enough to make her shiver.

There was only one true answer.

"You, Mason," she replied. "I choose you."

His smile was instantaneous, wide, gloating, and downright indecent.

"Good luck, pal," he called over his shoulder, wrapping his arms around her.

They swayed to the rhythm as the sun dipped low, casting a

golden light on everything and creating a romantic haze. The atmosphere was pure magic, as was his embrace.

Shonda refused to worry about tomorrow or his earlier behavior. All that mattered was savoring the moment.

Mason claimed her mouth, kissing her again and again in his sensual, mind-drugging way. Unhurried and dangerously seductive, punctuated with teasing little nips. Every brush of his lips whispered promises she shouldn't believe.

The beat increased with the next song, and Mason spun her out and reeled her back in, making her giggle. Using skills straight out of Dancing With the Stars, he twirled her across the patio, right back to her original table, and drew out her chair with a dramatic flourish.

"Don't pick up any more men while I'm gone," he said in a low warning growl.

"I didn't pick him up. He picked me up."

Her retort earned her a look. The thundercloud formed.

Shit!

"What I meant was… nobody picked anybody up. We were only having fun."

His mouth firmed, and their earlier romantic vibe vanished. Again.

"Stay." He pointed at the table and strode off toward the bar.

"I'm not a dog," she called after his retreating back.

Who the hell did he think he was? Leaving with no explanation, chasing off her dancing partner like an aggressive mongrel, and issuing commands?

None of it sat well, and the anger she'd stuffed down resurfaced in a rush. She grabbed her purse, spun on her heel, and stormed out the side door.

MASON WASN'T sure what demon had possessed him earlier. He was fairly certain it had more to do with how he was starting to feel about Shonda and absolutely nothing to do with the driver's question. The realization that he actually liked her was disconcerting. Added to his insatiable need for her, well, the old hemmed-in feeling had grabbed hold. He'd needed space to get his head back on straight and break the spell she'd cast on him.

When he'd arrived back at her hotel room to apologize and she hadn't answered, he assumed she was either pouting or had set out for the afternoon to find entertainment on her own. Because the latter sounded more plausible, he wandered down to the tiki bar.

He'd lingered in the shadows, sipping a scotch, content to watch her enjoy herself. The face she'd made after each tequila shot was side-splitting funny. When the mood shifted, causing couples to pair up, Surfer Boy's intention became clear. With no other recourse, Mason had stepped in.

A sick sort of relief flooded Mason the instant Shonda chose him. After his disappearing act, he'd been doubtful of the outcome. Had she been a little less intoxicated, he doubted he'd have stood a chance.

As he waited to settle her tab, he observed the people two rows deep, all vying for the bartender's attention. His gaze lit on a blonde opposite him, leaning over the counter to get a better look at the main room.

Shonda?

How the hell had she reached the bar before him?

The woman cast a glance toward the table where they'd been seated, and then spoke to a man on her right. Gold glinted against her neck, and Mason frowned at the wrongness.

Shonda was wearing dangling silver necklaces.

He glanced back toward their table in time to see her loop her purse strap over her neck.

Stunned, he stared at her retreating back. By the time he recovered his wits, the woman on the other side of the room was gone and Shonda was sailing out the door.

Frustrated at the bartender's slowness, he tapped out his temper on the bar. He'd never moved so fast in his life once the bill was settled. As he shoved his way through the thick wall of bodies to give chase, his mind churned with all the possibilities of Shonda's doppelgänger.

CHAPTER

SEVEN

"Shonda, wait!" Mason caught her in the hallway.

"No, I'm sick of you ordering me around," she snapped. "I was right the first day. You're an asshole."

He released her, feeling thoroughly insulted. Other than the cab incident, he'd been there for her in every way, seeing to her safety and comfort.

"I'm an asshole? I find you kissing up to a fucking wannabe surfer dude—less than two hours after I leave you, I might add—and I'm the asshole. That's rich."

"I wasn't kissing up to anyone. I was having a good time. Your twisted mind always makes everything worse than it is," she retorted.

"Really?" he scoffed. He held up his hand, ticking off his points. "So no one broke into your room? You weren't doing shots and dancing all over a stranger? You're really here on the island alone, even though I just saw your twin at the bar?"

She halted in the process of pushing past him. "What the hell are you talking about?"

"Stop pretending," he snapped, over the runaround. The entire situation reeked, and he was thrust back into the head games Melanie loved. "I want to know what's going on, Shonda. Why did you pick me? Do I have patsy tattooed on my fucking forehead?"

"You're crazy, you know that?"

She shoved against his chest and stormed off.

Perhaps he *was* crazy. The intelligent thing would be to walk away, but he couldn't leave without answers. He caught up and cut in front of her.

"I want the truth." Inhaling deeply, Mason met her furious glare. In a voice far calmer than he was feeling, he asked, "Are you playing me?"

"Would you believe me if I said I wasn't?"

She looked sincere. Sounded sincere. Added to both was how much he wanted to believe her. God, he was a gullible fool.

Hauling her close, he buried his nose in her silky hair.

"If you're in trouble, you can tell me, love. I'll help you," he promised.

"Mason." She drew back and cradled his face in her palms. "Look at me. Really look at me."

He did, but she must've seen the smidgeon of lingering distrust. Her bright, searching eyes dulled, and her expression hardened.

"I see. Good night, Mason." Her tone dripped with ice, freezing him out, and it wasn't a place he wanted to be.

"Shonda—"

"I said good night." She ruined her frosty dismissal with a hiccup.

Shoulders back and head held high, she left him, weaving slightly from the alcohol she'd consumed. And because his desire was to hold her, to hold tight to whatever was building between them, he let her go. Yes, he was a contrary bastard, but in past relationships, clinging had cost him dearly.

He was almost one hundred percent certain she spoke the truth, yet a tiny kernel of doubt held him in place.

But only for a heartbeat.

With a savage curse, he jogged to catch up.

"Hold up!" he called.

"Why won't you just go away?" she cried. And perhaps there was a gleam of tears in those solemn eyes to match her frustration.

"I will once I see you safely to your room," he assured her.

He'd have said it wasn't possible for her to stick her nose up so far, and he'd have been wrong. If the hotel sprinkler activated, she'd drown.

"I don't need you," she told him, haughty and proud.

Suddenly, it registered: she was too buzzed to lie. For fuck's sake, sometimes his idiocy was award-winning.

"I know you don't. But will you humor me?" he cajoled, tucking a strand of her hair behind one delicate ear. "I don't want to worry throughout the entire night."

"Fine. Whatever. But none of your sexy-ass bullshit. I'm not caving," she warned with a finger wag.

A bark of laughter escaped. "Sexy-ass bullshit? Will you clarify what you mean, so there's no misunderstanding and all?"

She waved a hand up, down, and all around. "That! Right there. First, you're all Neander-man, practically banging your chest. Now you're all sweet and shit. All, 'let me escort you back to your room.' Don't do that."

"I see," he said, with mock thoughtfulness. Later, when she was less combative, he'd ask what Neander-man meant. He suspected he knew, but clarification was in order.

Holding up his hand, two fingers skyward, he pledged, "I solemnly swear, I will honor my commitment to walk you back to your room without any sexy bullshit. On my oath as a Boy Scout."

Shonda scoffed. "Oh, knock it off. As if any of you Sharps were Boy Scouts," she grumbled. She gripped his hair so tightly he dared not sneeze or he'd have bald spots. Her low, frustrated growl tickled him, and he was on the verge of making a wiseass remark. Jerking his head down, she kissed him, erasing any desire he had to kid.

"The Scouts were a three-finger salute," she informed him, never losing sight of the conversation. With a defeated sigh, she added, "And I'm so glad you weren't. Race you back to my room. First one there gets to be on top."

Mason gave her a ten-second head start for three reasons. One, he wanted to admire her ass. Two, he was more than fine with her taking command of their sexcapades. The third reason? Expending unnecessary energy went against the grain. He fully intended to use all he could muster in making love to her.

Suddenly remembering he didn't like to lose, he quickened his pace.

They arrived at her door together. Technically, it was a tie, but she proudly declared herself the winner, and Mason found no reason not to indulge her.

A single glimpse of her puzzled visage shot any plans for the night straight to hell.

"What is it?"

She gestured toward the slightly ajar door.

"Stay back," he ordered in a low voice.

"This again?" she whispered fiercely.

Done with the nonsense, Mason snaked an arm around her waist and backed her up against the opposite wall. Once they were at a safe distance, he tipped her chin up. In a low voice, he said, "Please go to the reception desk and get security up here." He pressed his forehead to hers. "I'm asking, not telling. Please, Shonda. I only want you safe."

He dropped a soft kiss on her lips, lingering longer than he should've. Time was of the essence if he wanted to catch the culprit terrorizing her.

"Okay." She sighed and cast a worried glance behind him. "But shouldn't I just call them? What about you?"

"I'd prefer you away from the danger. I'll be fine. Promise."

He waited until she rounded the corner before cautiously inching open the door. The air was stale, as if the suite was empty, and his sixth sense told him no one lay in wait. But caution was the theme of the day.

He stopped and swore.

The place was completely trashed. He'd bet his last dollar nothing was missing this time, either, and the break-in was a scare tactic.

Grim determination settled over him.

Whoever was harassing Shonda was going to pay. Dearly.

Two hours later, after the police cleared out, Mason helped Shonda pick up and fold the clothes strewn about.

"Pack your things. You're staying with me for the remainder of our trip."

"No, Mason. I can't impose on you."

"It isn't up for debate, love. We're spending our nights together anyway. Why not move in together?"

"They're re-keying my lock. I'm sure I'll be fine."

His frustration spiked. "And if you aren't? How do you think I'll feel if something happens to you, knowing I could have prevented it?"

"Mason…"

"No!" he shouted, finally losing his temper with her continued stubbornness. "Shonda, there are things at play here you're clueless about."

"Such as?"

"Earlier tonight, I saw a woman who was identical to you at the bar." He ran a hand through his hair and blew out a breath. "My gut tells me she's behind this. Do you honestly believe re-keying a lock will prevent her from obtaining a copy of the new key card? I doubt if she stood in front of the hotel manager at this point, he could tell the difference." Mason fingered her double-strand necklace. "Hell, if it weren't for the fact that this tangled with my button when we were dancing and your dress is a different shade, I'd have believed she was you, too."

"It makes no damn sense," she argued. All traces of her earlier intoxication were gone as she paced. "Are you sure about what you saw? I mean, the bar was dimly lit. How can you be positive?"

He'd never wanted to strangle someone more than he did her right then. Exasperation had him rubbing his palms up and down his face to counter the compulsion. A ten count, then twenty, made him no less irritated.

"I need glasses now?" he growled.

She threw up her hands. "Will you stop taking offense at everything I say? Every time someone questions you, you get angry."

Admittedly, she wasn't wrong. Around her, his emotions were closer to the surface.

Softening her tone and expression, she placed her palm on his chest. "I'm an only child. There is no possible way someone can be identical to me. And what are the odds of two of us being in the same location?"

"First, I do not get angry. I get annoyed. There's a difference," he clarified with exaggerated patience.

A smirk teased her mouth. "I stand corrected."

He ignored her to make his next point. "Second, I'm not mistaken. She was purposely watching you, Shonda."

Stunned into silence, she simply stared.

"Third, the odds would be fairly high that the two of you were in the same location if she happens to know your itinerary and is stalking you."

"Okay."

"Okay, what?" he asked.

Her sudden shift was confusing. And since when did a woman give in to logic? And what exactly was she giving in to?

"Okay, I'll stay with you until my flight home. But you need to agree you won't freak out again like you did today in the cab."

He nodded. "Thank you. But, uh… please don't think—"

"I get it, Mason," she said with a tired sigh. "You don't do long-term."

Shonda returned to sorting her strewn items.

Leaving her to her chore, he stepped out onto the patio. An escape of sorts.

Cowardly? Hell, yeah. But he'd never claimed to be Superman in the face of emotional drama.

The ocean breeze, the stars, and the distant tiki bar music all contributed to calming him. Between their fight, the break-in, and the stress of needing to find out who wanted to terrorize Shonda, he was wound tight. Possibly too tight.

"Mason? I'm ready to go."

He faced her, bracing his hands behind him on the railing.

She hovered in the doorway, still wearing the sundress from earlier. The halter top propped up her breasts, creating a mouth-watering display of cleavage. The desire to hold her overtook him.

"Come here." His voice was hoarse, but they both ignored it.

She moved to stand between his splayed legs.

Using one finger, he trailed the opening of her top.

"You are so fucking beautiful," he said huskily, dipping under the material to caress her skin and toy with her nipple.

Shonda bit her lip on a soft moan, but Mason felt the slight sound throughout his body.

He lowered his head as he skimmed his long fingers along her jaw. Plunging his hands into her hair, he brought her mouth within kissing distance.

Mason closed the gap, but the resistance of her hand against his chest stopped him.

With her other hand, she stroked him through his shorts.

"We should take this indoors," she said, staring at his mouth. "I'll lose all sense of propriety out here, and anyone with a phone—"

"I get it." Before he lost his wits, he clasped her hand and led her inside, stopping only long enough to lock the sliding door. "Should we make use of your bed one last time, love?"

Her smile was deliciously naughty. "Well, it *is* a very comfortable mattress."

CHAPTER

EIGHT

"The driver's downstairs, Shonda. If you don't hustle your ass, we're going to miss our flight," Mason called through the bathroom door.

"Coming! Hold your damn horses," she hollered back.

The handle jiggled.

"Why is it locked?" he asked.

The confusion in his tone was warranted. They hadn't bothered with privacy since spending the bulk of their days wrapped around each other. But today, right this minute, she needed to hide.

She splashed her face with cool water, patted it dry, and meticulously touched up her eyeliner and mascara, using waterproof the second go-around. Given her current emotional state, she wasn't taking chances. Raccoon eyes were never en vogue.

"Shonda?"

After two fortifying breaths, she opened the door.

"What the hell? Are you okay?" Concern laced Mason's voice, but she knew better than to mistake it for anything beyond basic human decency.

"I'm fine. Just bummed about leaving paradise and heading back to a hellish winter," she lied smoothly.

"That's it?" he asked skeptically.

"Mmm." She forced a bright smile and breezed past him to drop her makeup case into her purse.

"Why do I get the feeling it's something else?"

Because you're a perceptive fucker.

"I have no idea. I can assure you it's not." She kept her gaze averted, scanning every drawer, peeking under the bed, and double-checking the bathroom one last time to ensure nothing was left behind. "I think that's it. Javier can take the bags now."

"Shonda—"

She met his gaze squarely, though her smile was tight and strained. "I'm fine. Swear. Please, let it go."

"Are you upset we didn't find the people responsible for breaking into your suite?"

Sure, it would've been convenient to grab hold of the excuse he offered, but she wasn't about to add another lie to the growing pile. The break-ins were unsettling, sure, but she wouldn't heap guilt on his shoulders because they'd come up empty-handed.

"No. Can you please drop it? I'm just tired and not looking forward to the long day of travel. The trip down scarred me for life."

Her excuse appeared to be one Mason could get behind, and he flung an arm across her shoulders. "Fair enough. Let's go."

They didn't speak much during the ride to the airport. There was nothing left to say. Everything meaningful and painful had been said that morning, when he'd calmly reminded her their affair would end the moment they returned to the real world. To his credit, he'd at least appeared remorseful.

Standing in line at bag check, Shonda could practically feel the distance stretching between them. The closer they got to the counter, the more reserved and distant Mason became. When it was finally his turn, he stepped forward, claimed his baggage tag, and, without so much as a goodbye, cast her one last indecipherable look before heading for security.

By the time she stepped up to the counter and handed over her passport, her hands were visibly shaking. Mason's had to be the coldest goodbye in the history of all her relationships. Despite the brief length, it cut the deepest.

Through security, she found a seat near her gate and sank into the chair like an airless balloon. Mason lingered nearby, off to one side, leaning against a column with his nose buried in his phone. If he noticed her presence at all, he gave no indication.

Sadness settled over her like a heavy cloak.

Refusing to spiral, she pulled out her tablet and opened her social media accounts. A soft smile tugged at her lips when she saw Erica's latest post on her wall: a lone "Hello?" followed by a frowning-face emoji.

Curiosity got the better of her, and against her better judgment, Shonda looked up Mason's account. No recent updates. Everything was business-focused and impersonal. Unlike her, he clearly wasn't a social media junkie. For a brief second, she hovered over the "Add Friend" button, but the thought of him ignoring her request made her stomach clench. In the end, she logged out and mindlessly scrolled through shopping sites' daily deals. Retail therapy had its uses.

The boarding announcement called her back to the present. She and Mason reached the same spot in the line simultaneously. Awkward didn't begin to cover it. Wordlessly, he gestured for her to go ahead, and she moved past him without comment. Once on the plane, he helped her stow her bag in the overhead compartment, then slid into his own seat several rows behind her, offering nothing more than a distracted smile.

His dismissal couldn't have been clearer.

And if her eyes burned with unshed tears, at least he couldn't see them from where he sat.

AFTER DISEMBARKING and making her way to the luggage carousel, Shonda stood off to the side to wait. A sense of loss hit her squarely in the chest. Part of her wanted to curl into a ball and grieve. Another part wanted to scream and send Mason detailed directions straight to hell. But the biggest part of her, maybe the most harebrained, wanted to fight for what they'd found in St. Thomas.

Too bad he wouldn't let her.

He'd already said his goodbyes. And now, directly across the conveyor from her, with his eyes glued to his phone, Mason looked every bit the man who'd moved on before she'd even taken off her damned seat belt.

How many messages could one guy have?

"Probably an inbox full of women telling him to suck it," she muttered to herself.

Yeah, she was being petty. She hadn't gone into their fling expecting forever, but she hadn't counted on it hurting so much either. She'd invested more than time. She'd handed him her heart, unbelievably fast and foolhardily.

God, she should've known better at her age.

The carousel motor hummed to life, drawing her attention from her current obsession. Her black-and-white suitcase with its hot-pink ribbon tied to the handle was the first to appear. As she stepped forward to grab it, a kindly man next to her lifted it and set it at her feet.

"Thank you," she said, mustering a warm smile.

She cast one last glance across the distance. Mason still hadn't looked up.

Mentally flipping him the bird, she turned on her heel and headed toward the exit. From just outside the sliding doors, she tapped the remote starter to warm her car, then popped the trunk.

The sight of that gaping empty space stopped her cold.

There she was, thirty-three years old, standing in front of an open trunk, once again alone with no one to greet her with a smile or a kiss. No partner. No children to read stories to and tuck in bed. Nothing but a suitcase and an ache in her chest. She'd been so busy cultivating a career, she hadn't taken time to create anything real.

The one true constant in her life was Erica.

That empty trunk was the perfect metaphor: sleek on the outside, hollow on the inside.

And she was pining after a man who was so far removed from wanting a relationship or family that he could be on another planet. Was it possible to reprogram her brain and heart to stop falling for emotionally unavailable bastards?

"God, I need a life," she said morosely.

Seriously, it was time to get real. Time to find true fulfillment.

Firming her resolve, Shonda reached for the handle of her bag, then froze.

A buzz zipped along her spine, tickling her Spidey senses. Gaze scanning the parking lot, she found nothing out of the ordinary and put it down to her overactive imagination. She shook it off with a self-deprecating laugh and reached for the suitcase again.

And that's when another sensation hit. The one that never lied. Her body's instinctual response whenever Mason was near. That unmistakable awareness settled in her chest, and every nerve stood at attention.

Slowly, she turned.

One row over, he stood by his car, one arm braced against the doorframe, the other on the roof, his gaze locked on her like a missile sighting a target.

Their eyes collided, and her world narrowed.

His expression was pure passion-packed. Every come-hither inch of him radiated unspoken promise. And boy, did she want to come hither.

Her breath hitched.

What was she to think? For someone so hell-bent on walking away, he was throwing off seriously mixed signals. His stare alone nearly buckled her knees.

Then came the slow quirk of his mouth.

It started as a faint twitch, the suggestion of a smirk, then turned into a lazy, confident grin. The kind that made panties self-destruct and women kick caution out the bloody door, bolting it after.

The man was irresistible, and he fucking knew it.

Shonda blew out a breath, girded her loins, straightened her spine, and presented her back, steeling herself against his magnetic pull.

A car door slammed.

Her heart leapt.

She didn't know if he was leaving or coming toward her, but the answer arrived in a wave of heat behind her. He was close. Oh, so close!

His warm breath brushed her ear, and his voice dropped to a husky whisper as he said, "I've changed my mind."

Butterflies woke in her belly, her joy blooming before she could crush it.

He turned her gently and met her gaze with a slow, devastating smile. "I'm not ready to end it… yet. I'd like a few more days, if you're willing."

Her heart ceased its celebration. The happiness bursting to life withered. The hope she hadn't wanted to admit to flared and fizzled in a three-second blip.

Shonda had a choice. Tell him to go pound salt, or create a few more memories for later. The aftermath would be a bitch, though. Only her brain opposed the second alternative. Her heart and body had already cast their votes.

Still, she managed a token protest. "I don't know if it's a good idea…"

He gently traced her lips with the pad of his thumb, spending an inordinately long time regarding his action. When he leveled his gaze on her, the raw longing in those blue eyes nearly unmade her.

"I want you, Shonda. To a degree I've never wanted another woman. For longer, too. Can't we just leave it there and enjoy a few more days?"

She should say no. Hell, she knew better. But agreement fell from her lips anyway.

"Yes," she whispered.

God, she was seriously going to regret her madness.

He leaned in, resting his forehead against hers with a quiet sigh of relief.

What the hell did his action mean? She refused to examine it too closely.

"I'll follow you to your place," he said, brushing a soft kiss over her mouth. "Drive carefully. The roads might be icy from the last snowfall."

During the car ride home, she berated herself. Why had she relented so easily? What manner of sorcery did he possess to bend her to his will? No protests had been anywhere near falling out of her mouth. Where was her self-preservation?

Her brain suggested she beat her head against the steering wheel. It might be the only way to knock some damn sense into it.

NINE

Shonda greeted her cat and skimmed the note from her pet sitter.

"Jannaya said you were a good boy and no trouble at all," she praised, scooping him into a hug. "That's my sweet boy."

From across the room, Mason was vaguely irritated by the amount of affection she lavished on the cat, but refused to comment. Maybe it was the smug look on the beast's face as it stared him down. The one that said, "She's mine, asshole."

"Dinner at Luigi's sound good to you tonight?" Mason asked, attempting to redirect her attention.

"Luigi's? Over in Springdale? How do you plan to get a reservation this late?"

Fair question. He hadn't thought past the incredible food after the slim pickings all day, but a smile and a fifty could usually move mountains.

"I have my ways," he said with a cocky grin. "How about a quick shower before we head out?"

She snorted. "Since when have our showers been short?"

He laughed. She wasn't wrong. On vacation, they'd only managed to leave the bathroom because the hot water gave out.

"We'll set a timer," he assured her.

As he stepped forward to pluck the cat from her arms, the little gremlin hissed and swatted at him. Unfazed, Mason reached for the scruff of its neck.

"No!" Shonda snapped. "Don't even think about picking Loki up that way. What's wrong with you?"

He raised a brow but said nothing. While he knew next to nothing about cats, he was pretty sure he'd seen a mother cat pick up her kittens in the same fashion. He kept quiet as she soothed Loki's hurt pride.

With a roll of his eyes, Mason hauled their suitcases to the larger of the two bedrooms with the assumption it was the primary. He didn't see himself making fast friends with her pet.

Correction, *pets*.

At the center of the queen-sized bed lounged another feline. One decidedly bigger and clearly more pissed off than the first. The malevolent glare could've turned a lesser man to stone.

Jesus. How many of them were there?

The beast was enormous, thirty pounds if an ounce.

Mason half worried it might attack him in his sleep. Or sit on his chest and crush him.

What the hell was she feeding these animals?

He dropped his garment bag on the chest at the end of the bed and unzipped it, pulling out a pair of black trousers and a white button-down. He considered placing them on the mattress, but one look at the abnormally round menace nixed his idea. The monster cat had an air of ownership about its surroundings, and Mason's clothes didn't stand a chance.

Assuming steam would smooth the worst of the wrinkles, Mason started the shower, adjusted the temperature, and stepped under the spray. As hot water streamed down his back, he questioned why he chose to continue their affair. Not being a complete and clueless tool, he saw the way Shonda looked at him. She'd caught feelings. And he wasn't able to handle that aspect of a relationship. He'd been prepared to walk away. Had spent the entire flight staring at the back of her glossy blonde head and telling himself it was better to end it cleanly.

Yet hearing her car start and watching her prepare to leave had triggered a panicked reaction.

Mason scrubbed a soapy hand over his scalp and blew out a cleansing breath. Yeah, a closer examination of his deeper emotions wasn't going to happen. He'd give them a few extra days, max, intending to enjoy them to the fullest.

Shonda knew the score and wouldn't push. It counted for a helluva lot, allowing him to remain and draw this, whatever *this* was, out.

But in the unguarded moments when he caught her speculative look, the one debating if she could change his mind, he grew worried. If things became sticky, he'd bolt. He'd have no choice.

He was so distracted, he jolted when her hand landed on his back.

"Christ!" he swore.

"Sorry. You looked so serious." She laughed.

"Yeah. I have a lot on my mind." He shifted to make room.

"Anything you care to talk about?"

He smoothed the small furrow between her brows and gave her a lackluster smile. "No."

Thankfully, she let it go. Had she pressed, he'd have high-tailed it out of there faster than a lazy cat blinks. Mason didn't exactly fear honesty, but getting all touchy-feely about his emotions was a big nope.

"In that case, let's get this show on the road," she purred, cupping him.

Her take-charge attitude triggered an immediate response, and

Shonda laughed softly at the effect on his body. The deep, throaty sound made him harder.

Mason needed space.

Needed to not stare into her soulful eyes and lose what little detachment he still had.

"Face the tile and spread your legs," he ordered, voice gravel-low.

She complied with a slow toss of her head, sensual and unhurried.

The liquid soap in his hands became a tool of seduction. He smoothed it over her curves and slicked his palms across her hips, her thighs, her breasts. Her moans echoed off the tile.

Mason bent, lifted one of her legs to the shower bench, and stepped in behind her. He teased her entrance with the head of his cock, coaxing out another breathy moan.

Her head dropped back to rest on his shoulder, and he seized the moment to nip at her throat. His tongue traced the line of her collarbone, his hands working over her breasts, teasing until her nipples were tight little peaks.

"Please. Now," she panted.

God, he loved how responsive she was. But the devil in him wasn't about to give in easily. He bent her forward slightly, hands roaming over the swell of her ass. He found her folds, slick and ready, then ran one finger in tight circles over her clit.

Her moan turned into a strangled cry, and as he inserted his fingers into the welcoming heat of her vagina, her climax hit. He felt her contract around him, her thighs shaking with the force of it.

Before she recovered, he entered her. Slow. Deep. Thrusting on repeat until she whimpered, with her body arching back against him. His steady rhythm drove them higher, and she braced her hands on the marbled wall.

Mason tightened his grip on her hips, pausing for the slightest moment to catch his breath and appreciate the beautiful sight she presented. The glorious, graceful curve of her back and neck, the soft, creamy skin, pink from the water's warmth.

He drew back before sinking into her, pushing as much as she could take. She came again, gasping and chanting "yes" with each thrust. Her screamed release shattered what little control remained, and he followed her over the edge.

They washed quickly, panting and spent.

As they stepped out, she asked, "Still interested in dinner, or would you prefer to order in? There's a great little Chinese place not far from here that delivers."

The part of him trying to avoid anything intimate—like dinner at her place—overruled her suggestion. "Go ahead and get dressed. If it's all the same to you, I'd like to take you out."

She gave him a small, flickering smile, and he couldn't help noticing the hesitation.

He wondered at her lack of enthusiasm. Most women he knew would be giddy over a reservation at Luigi's, but Shonda just looked… tired.

"Or I can go if you're too exhausted," he offered.

"Nope. All good. Give me a few minutes to recover and dress."

———

BY THE TIME she emerged from the bedroom, Mason was buttoning the cuffs of his shirt, his hair damp and tousled.

Shonda had selected a fitted burgundy sweater dress and dark hose, keeping her makeup minimal. Adding only enough to hide the red tinge around her eyes. Expensive jewelry elevated the look, enhancing her natural, yet classy appeal.

"You ready?" he asked, slipping his watch on.

"As I'll ever be," she replied, fusing a chipperness he suspected wasn't real.

The drive to Springdale was quiet. Not the awkward, tension-filled silence of people who'd fought, but something closer to two people walking a high wire, afraid any unbalance would send them tumbling.

And again, he wasn't clueless. Simply cautious.

They arrived at the restaurant and pulled up to the valet station at the front entrance. Mason circled around the front of his car, tossed the keys to the attendant, and opened the passenger door for Shonda. A smiling employee gave her a respectful nod, indicating she must be a regular.

Inside the grandiose restaurant, they pushed through the throng of would-be diners to reach the host stand. The man behind it studied them for a moment too long, as if sizing them up. "I'm sorry, sir. There's a two-hour wait."

Mason slid him a fifty. "You sure? Will you check again?"

The host glanced down, then said, "I may have been mistaken. The wait is only an hour and a half."

Irritation surged. The fucker was an extortionist!

Shonda was biting her lower lip to keep from laughing.

With a resigned sigh, Mason slid another fifty across the stand. "And now?"

"Yes, I see. Here, I can seat you in approximately one hour."

He was ready to reach across the podium when a distinguished older gentleman approached, his eyes locked on Shonda. A warm smile lit his face.

"Hello, Bella. When did you get back in town?"

"Hello, Papa." Shonda stepped into the bear hug he offered, while Mason stood frozen. "I arrived this afternoon," she added.

"You should've called. I would've had a table waiting," her father said with mock sternness.

"I thought it would be more fun for Nico to play with my date." She laughed.

There was an unapologetic glint in Nico's eye.

"You'll never find a husband if you torment the men you date," her father scolded. "Come, I'll take you to the private dining area."

Color rushed to Shonda's cheeks. "I'm not looking for a husband, Papa."

Given her blush and her father's skeptical expression, Mason wasn't sure he believed her. The room grew hot, and he stopped himself from loosening his collar.

"Nico, give his money back," Shonda ordered.

"No." Mason lifted a hand. "He earned it."

The sparkle in her eyes made it worth every dollar. He placed a hand on her lower back as they followed Luigi through the restaurant.

Their meal was extraordinary. One masterful dish after another arrived at their table. And Mason, a devoted foodie, couldn't get enough. Italian cuisine happened to be a favorite, and tonight, the flavors practically brought tears to his eyes.

The dessert sampler was clearly Shonda's favorite. The noises she made rivaled those from their earlier shower. He sipped his wine, mesmerized as she spooned a bite of tiramisu between her lips and closed her eyes in bliss. Next came the dark-chocolate gelato. Each of her reactions heightened his arousal. There probably wasn't anything about her that didn't turn him on.

Mason was so caught up in his Shonda Dessert Porn Fantasy, he didn't register Luigi's approach.

A firm hand clamped down on his shoulder, and he instinctively adjusted his napkin. Luigi's booming laugh told him the move hadn't gone unnoticed.

"What are your intentions toward my daughter?"

Mason sputtered wine across the table.

"Papa!" Shonda groaned, jumping in. "We've known each other for less than two weeks. Please don't."

Luigi narrowed his gaze. "Two weeks? But you only returned today."

"We met on the plane," she said quickly.

Although she wasn't technically lying, she was clearly attempting to make their connection sound more innocent than it was.

The twisted troublemaker in Mason couldn't help it.

"We were seated together on the flight to St. Thomas, shared dinner that night, and spent most of the next week enjoying… the island."

Why he felt compelled to force her to acknowledge their time together, he couldn't say.

Horror dawned in Shonda's eyes before they narrowed with promised retribution.

"I suppose your mother is all right with this… this…" Luigi flailed for words, his face becoming a concerning shade of red.

"Mason, please excuse us." Shonda hauled her father toward the back of the restaurant. When she returned five minutes later, her expression was pinched and her lips thinned. "We should go."

"Shonda…" He was unsure what to say, but figured it had to start with an apology.

"We should go," she repeated firmly as she gathered her things.

Regretful, Mason climbed to his feet and tossed cash on the table. But she was quick to shove the bills back into his hand.

"He'll be offended," she said by way of explanation.

On the drive home, he couldn't help but try. "Want to talk about it?"

"No."

"For what it's worth, I'm sorry."

"I don't know why you did what you did, Mason, but it was a dick move."

"I know." He shifted tactics, hoping she'd open up or soften. "How is it you're Luigi De Vitis's daughter but your last name is Grant?"

"My mother left him and married Nolan Andrews when I was a baby. She wanted Nolan to adopt me, but Papa refused, insisting I keep his surname. He felt it was good enough for generations of De Vitis, and so it was good enough for me." Shonda scoffed. "Of course, Mama had to thwart him and used her maiden name on my school records. Afterward, changing it was too much of a hassle."

"That's right! I remember now. Luigi was married to…" He did a double-take, gaping. "Wait, your mom was Eva Grant? *The* Eva Grant? Centerfold and supermodel?"

"The one and only."

She clearly wasn't thrilled about it.

Darting quick looks between her and the road, he cataloged all the similarities.

"The resemblance is definitely there. Her hair is redder than yours, but the features are the same. And the body…" He trailed off, suddenly recalling exactly how familiar his teenage self had once been with the swimsuit spread featuring her mother. Awkward didn't begin to cover it.

Shonda's arch look said she knew exactly what memory he'd tripped over.

He barely managed not to squirm in his seat.

They fell into awkward silence for the rest of the drive, but as soon as they arrived at her apartment, Mason halted her escape.

"You're far more stunning than your mother," he said, meaning it and willing her to believe him.

Her eyes locked with his, and whatever she'd been stewing over during the ride vanished.

"Thank you," she whispered. "Now take me upstairs and do what you do best."

CHAPTER

TEN

"We have to go back to the real world, love."

True, but Shonda didn't want to. Their last three days had far surpassed their entire trip. The passion burned hotter, the connection deeper, and the sex was soul-transforming. How Mason could walk away from what they'd shared without a backward glance defied logic.

"Same rules apply?" she asked quietly, already well aware of the answer. Pushing would only lead to an ugly blowup.

He was quiet too long for her comfort. Her emotional flight was about to nosedive, and she braced for impact.

"Yes. Nothing's changed," he eventually said, firm and detached.

No, not for him in any case.

But for her, everything had.

She loved him. Completely, stupidly.

His casual rejection of what they'd shared was brutal, and the pain she'd experienced at the airport was nothing close to how she was feeling as he climbed from her bed. Once again, she'd mistaken a man's true intentions, reading more into his deeds than was wise. She'd shamelessly fallen into her old pattern of equating sex with love.

Crikey, she needed her head examined.

"Want a cup of coffee before you go?" The casual offer took everything she had.

"Actually, I'm running late. I'll grab one at work."

Could it get more stilted and embarrassing? How had they gone from last night's tangled limbs to a frosty morning-after?

"Thank you." His softly spoken gratitude halted her mid-sugar scoop.

"For what?" she asked.

"From the beginning, I knew a casual affair wasn't your thing. I hesitated to take it further than our first dinner date. But you haven't made it weird or awkward by getting clingy. I appreciate that."

A startled laugh burst from her.

He meant well, but could a man be more oblivious? The absurdity of it gave her spine the much-needed steel. She'd not beg Mason to see her worth.

"Think nothing of it," she replied, dry as unbuttered toast.

Judging by his faint frown, he'd caught her sarcasm. And instead of giving him a chance to comment, she keyed in the alarm code, removed her handy new security stick, and whipped open the door for his grand exit.

Suitcase handle fisted tightly, Mason paused.

Their gazes locked.

With his free hand, he tucked a stray strand of hair behind her ear, then stared at it for a long beat, as if he might find answers he didn't have there. His pale gaze flicked to her lips, eyes flashing with indecipherable emotion. A curtain came down over his expression, and he ruthlessly shut it all down.

"Goodbye." Mason pressed a hard kiss to her mouth and strode out.

Body trembling, Shonda leaned back against the closed door as the dam broke. He'd never know the devastation he'd left in his wake. Unrequited love like hers required recovery time, and she headed straight back to bed, hiding under the covers to mourn.

Time lost all meaning. It might've been two hours or twenty. She didn't care. All she wanted was to wallow. But the universe had other plans.

Her phone rang.

And rang three additional times in under five minutes.

On her persistent caller's fourth attempt, Shonda answered.

"Ms. Grant? This is Nancy from Stonebrooke Memorial Hospital."

"Yes, I'm Shonda Grant. How may I help you, Nancy?"

"You're listed as the emergency contact for Erica Sutton. Is that correct?"

Her stomach plunged through all three floors of her apartment building to the ground below.

"What happened to Erica?" Her voice cracked, and her lungs threatened rebellion.

"Ma'am, I hate to inform you this way, but Ms. Sutton was injured in an attack. She's being prepped for emergency surgery. Do we have your verbal consent to proceed?"

"What? Oh, y-yes. Of course." She was babbling, but the shock was great. "Do whatever you have to. Can you tell me how bad it is? Is she going to be okay?"

"I'm sorry, but I can't give any more information over the phone." Nancy was kind but firm. "We'll need you to sign paperwork in person, and we'll be happy to answer any questions at that time."

"I'll be there in ten minutes."

Erica.

Attacked!

Of all the things to happen in sleepy Stonebrooke!

Her mind struggled to make sense of it as she yanked on jeans. Sending up a frantic prayer for Erica's successful surgery, Shonda grabbed her keys and ran for the parking garage. Traffic was light, and fortunately, she arrived at the hospital in under nine minutes, securing a front-row spot.

Hopefully, it was a sign from the universe that everything would be okay. She bolted for the entrance with nothing on her mind but finding out Erica's current condition.

"Shonda?"

She skidded to a halt and whirled around.

Mason.

"What…? Why are you…?" Shaking her head, she pressed a finger to her gathered brows.

He must've read her confusion, elaborating without her needing to.

"My brother Zack's girlfriend was admitted," he said.

Her mouth opened and closed again, unable to process anything but her driving need to find Erica.

Another man appeared, jogging up beside him. By his resemblance, he was obviously Dane, the youngest of the Sharp brothers.

Suddenly, it was too much. If she didn't discover what was happening with Erica, she'd have a meltdown on the spot.

"I've got to go," she blurted.

"Hey." Dane held up a hand. "You're looking for Erica, right? Come on. I know where she was taken."

How he knew didn't matter. If he could lead her to Erica, she'd follow him anywhere.

"Thank you," she replied, grateful for the assistance.

Together, the three of them raced down the corridor toward the O.R. waiting area.

***

"What happened to Erica? Is she all right?" Shonda blurted the second they entered the room.

Mason pressed a hand to her lower back, hoping to provide support.

"I'm sorry. Who are you?" Zack asked, distracted and on the rough side of ragged.

"Shonda. I'm Erica's best—" she began.

He cut her off with an impatient wave. "How the hell did you learn about her attack? Did the hospital call you?"

"Yes. She asked me to be her emergency contact since her parents are in Florida."

In the face of Zack's scowl, Shonda burst into tears. But when he moved to touch her shoulder, Mason cut him off with a nudge and pulled her into his arms.

"Don't cry, love. She's going to be fine. Promise."

"How is it that you're here?" she had the presence of mind to ask. "I didn't expect to see you again so soon."

There was no good answer. The truth was, he hadn't planned on it either. He'd thought their goodbye this morning was final.

His brothers' twin looks of astonishment grated. Honestly, one would believe he was celibate the way they gawked, as if showing up with a woman or offering comfort was outside his wheelhouse. It wasn't as if compassion was a dreaded disease, right? If caring were communicable, Mason would've made damn sure to get inoculated long ago.

But holding Shonda soothed Mason in a way he hadn't expected. A few hours earlier, he'd returned home feeling ancient and morose. He'd meant to check in at the office, but his shitty mood sapped his energy. Instead of unpacking, he'd collapsed into bed for a nap, blaming his funk on jet lag. Hell, anything but the obvious. Yet seeing her so distraught twisted his insides.

Once Erica was out of danger, Mason would put real distance between them. Maybe he'd flip through his little black book, call up a worldly friend from his past, and grab a drink with her to remind himself there were plenty of women who didn't rattle him. Yet Shonda's warm body against his made the prospect feel hollow.

Unsettled, he eased back and guided her to the nearest chair.

"Anyone need coffee? I was about to hit the kiosk in the lobby," Zack offered.

"I'll go with you," Dane chimed in.

"We'll take coffee. One black, one with two creams, no sugar," Mason said.

"You know how she takes hers?" Dane blurted, lacking tact.

Mason glared, relaying the clear warning that his little brother was about to get a beatdown. Zack, smart enough to catch the cue, grabbed Dane's arm and hustled him from the room before Mason tore a strip from his ass.

Shaking off his irritation, he faced Shonda. "Are there other family members of Erica's we should call?"

Her mouth formed a silent "oh, shit," and she scrunched her eyes shut.

"Do you want me to do it?" he asked, gentler.

"No, I can. Thank you for reminding me. I…" She swallowed audibly. "I need to."

Her resolve was a testament to her quiet strength. Stubborn pride refused to allow her to fall apart completely. No damsel-in-distress routine here, which was both admirable and gut-wrenching. It knocked the wind out of him every time.

When she left to make the call, Mason reflected on what it all meant. Funny, really. The minute he wanted to step up, she pulled away to stand on her own. Proof women were the contrary creatures he believed them to be and why it was best to keep things hassle-free. If those like Shonda couldn't accept his terms, well… it was on them, not him.

He shoved down the warmth he'd experienced by spending time with her. So what if he enjoyed waking up with her curled against him? Such feelings eventually led to heartbreak. And odds were, she'd be the brokenhearted one, because he wasn't built to give his whole self to anyone.

Ten minutes later, his brothers and Shonda returned, but they all sat in tense silence, lost in their own versions of hell.

For Zack and Shonda, it was worry.

For Mason, it was the creeping realization he might be in over his head.

An hour later, a man in surgical scrubs stepped into the waiting room. The doctor's eyes immediately sought out Zack, who shot to his feet.

"How is she? When can I see her?" he asked.

The barely leashed panic in his brother's voice indicated Zack had it bad.

"The surgery went well. Erica was lucky to find help as quickly as she did. She's in recovery for the next half hour, then we'll move her to a private room. You'll be able to see her after she's settled."

"How soon before she's able to go home?" Shonda asked.

"I'd like to keep her for the next day or two. I want to be sure she doesn't experience a fever or infection. If everything looks good in a few days, she'll be discharged," the doctor explained. "She's going to need to rest for the next ten days. We'll go over everything when we discharge her, but I expect Erica to make a full recovery."

Overcome, Zack could only nod and pump the man's hand in gratitude.

"She's going to be fine, Mr. Sharp."

"Thanks."

"If any of you plan to hang around, the cafeteria food isn't half bad."

"Are there donuts?" Zack asked.

"Excuse me?"

"Erica's going to want donuts when she wakes. It's her go-to food for stress."

Dr. Montgomery, as Mason learned his name was, chuckled and shook his head as he exited.

"I can make a donut run," Dane offered. "Text me what everyone wants."

"You guys don't have to stay."

"Three musketeers, remember?" was Mason's low-voiced reply.

"The three musketeers," Zack concurred. "In that case, you can pick up a dozen. Four need to be lemon-filled. The rest can be whatever you guys want."

"You know Erica's favorite flavor?" Shonda asked. And glee followed her amazement, lighting her eyes from within.

"It's not like she's kept her donut addiction a secret," Zack hedged.

Mason smirked at his uncomfortable expression. Enjoyment over his brother's predicament kept him quiet while Shonda continued her special brand of torture.

"Uh, yeah, she normally does," she informed Zack.

"Right. The woman is all about the carbs and would kill for a slice of cake, pie, or pizza. I hardly think that's something she'd be able to hide for long."

"You don't understand. Not even her last boyfriend knew what she liked. She's actually a very private person." Shonda shook her head. "She rarely speaks up for herself."

"Are we talking about the same Erica here? She swears like a sailor and grumbles every time she has to go to the gym. Once, she threatened my life because I couldn't produce coffee fast enough."

"She only gets testy about coffee when she first wakes up… Oh!"

"Oh? Oh, what?" Zack was getting testy, and it was a joy to witness.

"You're sleeping together. It's the only way you would know that."

His neck turned red. "She's been living in my house since hers burned down two weeks ago."

"*What?* Her house… Oh, God! She loved that house." Shonda clutched his wrist. "How did it happen?"

"A screwball fire-starter who seems to have a hard-on for hurting Erica," Zack said, anger heavy in his voice. "It's why she's here."

"How—"

"Look, I'm sure she would've explained it if you'd bothered to return her calls. As it is, you'll have to wait to talk to her. I don't care to go into it right now."

"Zack!" Mason barked, furious at his brother's rude comment. "Don't speak to her like that. She's not done anything wrong."

"No, nothing you didn't do, right?" Zack snapped. "You've avoided me for the last three days. If you'd have returned a goddamned text or call, this might have been prevented. I could've been with Erica today while you ran the office." The rage, which had come upon him suddenly, left as abruptly. Shaken, he ran a hand through his hair and blew out a breath. "I'm sorry, Mason. I…"

Mason felt like a complete shit. "No. You're right. There's no excuse to avoid responsibility. It won't happen again."

The waiting room was relatively silent after Dane left, leaving each to their tumultuous thoughts.

"Mr. Sharp?" They shot to their feet as a recovery-room nurse entered the room. She directed the next words to Zack as he rushed forward. "Ms. Sutton is being wheeled to her room, two-twenty-three. You can head there now. We ask you keep it to only two visitors at a time."

"Thank you." He turned to Shonda. "Do you mind if I see her alone first?"

Shonda's agreement was a soft smile, and Zack returned it with a broad one of his own before giving her a tight hug. Bending, he spoke directly into her ear. The slight blush staining her cheeks put Mason's back up.

Zack followed up with a hard, fast kiss on her lips. His grin widened the instant Mason objected, and with a wink for Shonda, Zack dashed toward the elevators.

Left to stew in his own juices, Mason grew increasingly pissed at how friendly his brother had gotten with Shonda, and worse, how receptive she'd been to Zack's friendliness.

When he couldn't take it a second longer, he snapped. "What the hell was that?"

"What?" Her puzzled expression might've been adorable if he wasn't seething.

"That." He gestured wildly toward the door. "The scene with my brother."

"Mason, I honestly have no idea what you're talking about."

And likely she didn't. He'd been silently spiraling for a good fifteen minutes before working up the nerve to call her out.

"The flirting with my brother," he ground out.

"Dude. Are you insane?" Her incredulous glare was backed by fire and fury. Her righteousness sent all his petty little demons straight back to hell. "My best friend—who is your brother's new girlfriend—was stabbed and is lying in recovery. Do you really think so little of me to believe I'd make a move on her man?"

Well, no, not when she put it that way.

Christ, what was going on with him?

"Asshole!" Her scathing comment cut.

"I guess sniffing me is out of the question?" he offered, managing a sheepish grin.

She stormed from the room as if she couldn't bear to look at him. And honestly, he didn't blame her.

He *was* a total asshole.

CHAPTER

ELEVEN

Shonda wandered the halls until she stumbled across Dr. Montgomery. In the back of her mind, she registered he was high on the yumminess scale. Erica would appreciate hearing her opinion when she was awake and lucid. She always knew how to admire a hot guy.

After thanking him for his help, Shonda followed his directions to Erica's room. Pushing through the door, she came upon Zack perched on the bed, waving a bag of donuts under Erica's nose while they grinned like fools at each other.

Their undeniable love was a boxer's jab to the chin, and she felt out of place, the intruder in her best friend's life. She almost left them to their privacy, but her need to connect with Erica propelled her closer.

"Erica?"

"Well, if it isn't my long-lost friend. You don't call. You don't write," Erica joked tearfully.

The emotions were catching, and Shonda's eyes filled, too.

"Can I hug you?" she croaked.

"Yes, if you're careful of my right side."

As they embraced gently, Zack offered up a quick excuse and left them to reconnect.

The next thirty minutes were all Erica and what had happened, how she was feeling, and everything else Shonda had missed.

But the conversational table turned, and vulnerability gripped her.

"So, where the hell have you been? I thought you were only going for a week?" Erica asked.

"Ten days," Shonda corrected with a weak smile.

"Okay, ten days. It's been fourteen. You couldn't shoot me a text to say you were still alive?"

"I'm sorry, E. I met someone. He's amazing."

"I sense a *but* coming on. What's up?"

Leave it to Erica to zero in. Maybe it was her writer brain always scanning people for emotional nuances. Or maybe it was just because they'd known each other forever.

"He's a player. I'm crazy about him, but I can't say he didn't clarify from the get-go he wanted nothing more than a holiday fling."

"So, you're pining away for a guy you met in the islands? It should help that you're home, right?"

"It should," Shonda agreed glumly.

"But it doesn't," Erica concluded, reading her like a book.

"He lives in Stonebrooke."

"You're shitting me!"

"No. And should I mention he is the brother of your new boyfriend?"

"What? Which one?"

"Mason," Shonda said.

"Ah."

"'Ah'? What do you mean by 'ah'?" Shonda demanded hotly. She'd jumped up to pace, then stopped cold at the foot of the bed, scowling. "What do you know?"

"Don't you remember him from school? He was actually the most serious one of all the Sharp brothers. If I recall correctly, he was dating Melanie Simms," Erica explained.

Shonda blinked, trying to summon the face to match the name. "Melanie Simms? You mean the girl who died in the car accident up by Makeout Point? But wasn't she there with Tommy Travers?"

"Yep. Can you imagine discovering your one true love was cheating on you, because she died in a wreck with another guy?" Erica asked with an eye flare and grimace. "Zack told me that, after finding out, Mason developed a devil-may-care attitude. The only thing he doesn't play at is business. Supposedly, he is phenomenal at marketing."

The air whooshed from Shonda's lungs. The sinking feeling she'd been ignoring all morning returned with a vengeance.

Mason would never love her. He wouldn't let himself be vulnerable to hurt again. The certainty attached to her conclusion was inescapable.

Erica reached out and gripped her hand, anchoring her. No words were necessary. They never were. Their friendship had always operated on an unspoken frequency, similar to twins. They knew when to give space, when to circle the wagons, and when to simply sit in silence, absorbing situational shock.

"Are you planning to stay with me?" Shonda asked after clearing the lump from her throat.

Erica turned to the window, displaying a flicker of vulnerability before she could mask it.

"It's like that, huh?" Although amused by the sudden shyness, she offered Erica quiet understanding.

"Like what?"

She snorted. "Don't try to pretend with me. I know you better than I know myself. You're the queen of avoidance if you don't want to answer."

Erica sighed, tossed her a helpless look, and then leaned forward to ensure the door was closed.

"I'm completely and hopelessly in love with Zack," she admitted. "I should move out, I know that, but I want to stay."

Shonda arched a brow. "Do you think it's wise? How does he feel about you?"

But really, who was she to judge, especially when her own situation was a mess?

"That's just it. I'm not sure. The way he acts toward me, how caring he can be, how protective, leads me to believe he sees me as more than a convenient lay."

"I suspected, but ohmygod! You've been sleeping with him? With Zack Sharp? Mr. All-Star Jock? You?" Shonda's voice climbed higher with every syllable, reaching a screech and triggering Zack's alarm bells. He burst through the door, his expression full of panic.

Any man charging into a room without knowing the threat and sans a weapon earned major points.

When he was assured they were safe, he swiped the remaining half of Erica's donut, blithely dropped a kiss on her mouth, and saluted Shonda on his way out.

Mouth twitching to suppress her amusement, Shonda beat a hasty retreat. A promised visit, a quick hug, and she was gone, lighter in spirit than she had been.

Until she walked straight into the tail end of a conversation not meant for her ears.

Outside the door, she couldn't help but overhear the brothers' voices. She debated entering, not wanting to interrupt what sounded like a serious conversation.

"Should I be concerned?" Mason was asking.

"I don't know. You tell me. What's going on there?" Zack demanded.

"Nothing," Mason snapped. "Jesus. First Dane, now you. It's called a *private* life for a reason."

"Don't break her heart, man. I don't need the fallout. I have enough shit on my plate right now," Zack warned.

"Look, she knew the score going in." Mason's caustic reply caused her heart to hammer painfully. "We met on the plane, had fucking mind-blowing sex, and parted company at the airport when we got home. No hearts were involved."

"Bullshit. You're looking everywhere but at me. If that's the case, where were you these last three days?"

The slap of hands against his jeans expressed Mason's frustration. "Fine, we may not have parted ways at the airport. I followed her home for another few nights together. That's it."

"That doesn't explain why you're both here together," Dane interjected.

"Actually, I was sleeping off the aftereffects when you called. I met Shonda again in the parking lot," Mason said. "I didn't expect to see her again, but she came walking up at the same time we did." To Zack, he said, "Dane was the one who picked me up this afternoon."

Zack groaned. "Erica is going to hate you, and maybe me, because you're an ass."

"Her friend is an adult who knew the score," Mason countered with attitude.

Shonda stepped into the doorway. The need to see Mason's expression was overpowering. If she could burn his arrogant dismissal into her memory banks, maybe she could learn her lesson and move on. He didn't notice her right away, which was fine. She intended to give him enough rope to hang himself.

"I'm not taking the rap for someone reading more into a casual fuck—" His face paled as he bit off his retort.

Both Zack and Dane pivoted in her direction.

Hot and cold flooded her body. The shock threatened to shut

down her system, but the heat from her humiliation kept her alive and anchored in the moment.

She wasn't embarrassed to be spoken about so rudely. No, that was on Mason. But mortification for being so blind to what an arrogant son of a bitch he was stained her cheeks and was harder to brush off.

"Idiot," Dane growled before stalking out.

Head high and heart dead in her chest, Shonda walked woodenly to the chair she'd occupied earlier. "Excuse the interruption, fellas. I left my jacket here. Please, carry on."

At least her voice was smooth and cool. Thank God for small favors.

"Shonda, please let me explain." Mason shifted to block her exit. Right when he would've invaded her personal space, she stopped him with an outstretched arm.

"No need. I'm 'an adult who knew the score,'" she said evenly, amazed at the calmness settling over her. "I promise you, I'm not reading our last two weeks as anything but your casual fuck. Now, if you'll excuse me, I'll be leaving."

Zack, who Shonda considered the wiser of the brothers, left Mason to face the music. And Mason, who was as sharp as a pebble, didn't know when to quit. "No. Please, you don't understand."

"Oh, I think I understand perfectly well. You've gone out of your way to tell me, and anyone who will listen, how *casual* our *fuck* was." Yes, she was repeating herself, but who really gave a damn? Not her, and certainly not him. He'd have to possess a human heart to care. "Goodbye, Mason."

He grabbed her arm as she passed. "Shonda, don't."

"If you don't let go of my arm right this instant, I will scream this goddamn hospital down around your ears," she threatened. "Let. Go."

"Love, if you would just list—"

"Don't you ever call me 'love' again. It makes me *sick*." She peeled his fingers from her arm and flung his hand away.

She held it together all the way home, but once the door was shut and locked, Shonda broke. What was it about her that was so damn unlovable? Her mother had never truly cared if she was alive, other than as a tool to control her father. Her father cared about her to some degree. Although for him, it would have been better had she been a boy. Stupidly, she always dreamed of the day Luigi would storm her mother's five-thousand-square-foot mansion and snatch her away to live with him.

He never did.

And Nolan only ever considered her a nuisance.

Over the years, not a single boyfriend had ever uttered the words "I love you." Nope, she was the moron who always poured out her feelings, only to have guys run for the door before the final word left her mouth.

Erica was different, but now their relationship was tainted for Shonda, too. If she stayed with Zack—and it sure looked like she would—Shonda would constantly be reminded of this horrible time.

What a piss-poor judge of character she was! Her good-guy radar needed new parts. Perhaps she should do research on "How to pick the proper guy for your unlovable personality type."

Her smartphone dinged.

Erica.

Of course, Zack must've tattled to her about what went down with Mason, and being the incredible friend she was, Erica was required to check on her. Girl code.

"Are you okay?"

"It's all good. You concentrate on getting better. I'm fine."

Shonda hoped her reply was convincing.

"Liar."

Well, Erica wasn't wrong, but she didn't want it to get back to Mason that she was upset in the least.

"LOL. You only want something to take your mind off your boredom. I'll bring more donuts tomorrow. Love ya. TTYS."

"Love you, too. Remember, I like the lemon."

Shonda snort-sobbed.

As if Erica would ever let her forget.

"I think I can remember after twenty-something years of friendship."

"You must be okay, since you are your normal wiseass self."

No, she was so far from it, it wasn't funny. But Erica already had enough to deal with.

CHAPTER

TWELVE

"So, what's going on with you and Mason?"

Shonda didn't pause in brushing Erica's glossy auburn hair. Truthfully, she'd been expecting the fifth degree for the last two and a half days. Honestly, it was shocking Erica had taken as long as she did. Her friend had never known a second's restraint in her life.

"Not a thing," Shonda replied smoothly.

"I'd turn around and call bullshit, but it hurts to move," Erica muttered.

And it was a good thing she couldn't see her expression, or she'd call Shonda out for a liar again.

"Take it at face value and move on," she suggested.

Erica caught her hand and gave a gentle tug, a silent order to shift into view. Worried brown eyes met Shonda's carefully neutral gaze.

"Shonda, it's me. Whatever's going on doesn't have to go any further. Just… don't shut me out."

"I'm not."

"You are," Erica insisted. "Three days ago at the hospital, you were on the verge of telling me Mason was the one. And now you're sitting here with the soul sucked out of you." Her voice softened with her concern. "I'm worried about you."

"Don't be. I'm fine."

"You're *not* fine. And if you don't start talking, I swear, the second I'm able, I'm kicking your ass."

Zack appeared in the doorway, to-go coffees in hand and a box of donuts under one arm. "Everything okay in here?"

"Peachy." Shonda handed him the brush in exchange for a coffee. "I was just heading out."

"Oh, hell no! You don't get to leave when I can't chase you down and yell at you," Erica called after her. As always, even livid, she was hilarious. Her first real smile in two days tugged at Shonda's mouth. Reaching into the box, she grabbed a donut and stuffed it halfway into Erica's gaping pie hole.

"Later," she sang, giving a finger wave on her way out.

Erica's sputtered outrage and Zack's chuckle followed her.

"She's going to murder you in her next novel, you know that, right?" Zack said, falling into step beside her.

The twinkle in his eye was unmistakable. "I don't know if you've ever read her books, but one in every four murdered women bears a striking resemblance to me."

His bark of laughter, a twin to Mason's, had her placing a hand over her heart and rubbing.

"You okay?" he asked, gesturing to her chest.

Leave it to Mr. Perceptive.

"Heartburn," she lied.

His brows shot up, but he let it go. Instead, he lowered his voice and leaned in conspiratorially. "I'm throwing a surprise party for Erica tomorrow."

Shonda choked on her next sip.

"Dude, she hates surprises. Tell her people are coming and to act surprised, or she'll stab you in your sleep."

The blood drained from Zack's face, leaving him ghostly.

"Oh, shit! I'm sorry!" she blurted, horrified by the faux pas.

"Can we shelve the word 'stab' for a bit?" he asked wryly.

"Abso-fucking-lutely," she agreed, full of remorse. "Zack, I really am sorry."

"You can make it up to me by being here tomorrow, eleven a.m. sharp."

She grinned at how easily he manipulated her.

"I'll be here," she assured him. "Can I bring anything?"

"Nope. Just yourself." Zack kissed her cheek. "See you tomorrow."

With one hand on the door, she paused for a deep breath and to shove down the sudden wave of envy.

"For what it's worth, I think you're the best thing that's ever happened to her, Zack." She patted his arm, wishing she could ease his mind. "She told me you're blaming yourself for the attacks. Don't. You're not responsible for all the crazies out in the world."

He didn't appear to believe her.

"Speaking of dastardly deeds, Mason told me about the break-ins down in St. Thomas. Any trouble since you've been home?" he asked.

"Dastardly deeds?" she echoed with a laugh, doing her best to ignore the surge of annoyance at Mason for sharing her business. "I can tell you've been hanging around an author."

He didn't crack a smile.

Okay, no deflecting this one.

"No, Zack. No dastardly deeds since I've been home. Either perpetrated by me or against me. Happy?"

With a grin, he nodded. "Tomorrow. Eleven."

"Oh, and tell your brother I'm going to kick his ass for gossiping like an old woman," she said with saccharine sweetness.

His grin widened. "You got it. And I can't wait to see it."

She stomped through the dusting of snow to her car.

"And shovel your damned sidewalk," she called over her shoulder.

"Nag, nag, nag," he hollered back. "Drive safe!"

Yep, Erica had definitely found herself a good one. The non-jealous part of her was genuinely thrilled for her friend.

Sliding into the driver's seat, Shonda started the engine and turned toward the grocery store. She'd wallowed long enough. If she didn't buy cat food soon, her little fatties might start sizing her up for dinner.

Happy the store wasn't crowded at this time of day, Shonda leisurely wandered the aisles. Peanut butter and jelly were added to her cart, followed by chocolate and cheese puffs. A trip down the pet aisle secured enough food to keep her beasties satisfied for at least three weeks. She ended her tour in the wine section, contemplating the best pairing for cheese puffs and chocolate. One contender went into the basket, and she picked up another to read the label.

A high-pitched giggle made her tense. It was familiar and as grating as nails on a chalkboard.

Rachel Westington.

Linked arm in arm with the very last man Shonda wanted to see.

Just her fucking luck.

Ducking behind a display, she crouched low.

Too late.

Mason's jean-clad legs came into view. Dammit.

"Want to tell me why you're hiding, love?"

She closed her eyes and counted to ten before cracking one open. Unfortunately, he wasn't a mirage.

"I'm not," she lied, slowly rising and wincing when her joints argued aloud. "I was studying this display." With an arched brow, she pretended great interest in the back of the card-board cutout.

Mason's voice dipped, meant only for her. "You never struck me as the type to avoid confrontation."

Her spine snapped straight. "If you'll excuse me, I'm done here."

Rachel eyed Shonda's bounty, and her disdainful sneer screamed personal offense.

"Really, Sondra? Could you advertise 'single' any louder?" she asked in her fake upper-class accent.

"It's *Shonda*, as you well remember. And you can kiss m—"

"Actually," Mason cut in smoothly, stepping in behind her. "Shonda and I are here together." He dropped his basket into her cart and wrapped one arm snugly around her waist. "She sent me to get the salad fixings for dinner tonight." He tucked his head next to hers to get a better view of her choices. "You forgot the popcorn for our movie, love, but thanks for remembering the cheese puffs. My favorite, as you well know."

Yes, he'd laid it on thick, but convincingly enough to annoy Rachel.

"You turned me down… for *her*?"

Never one to gloat, Shonda nevertheless gave her a smug smile. "Sucks for you, doesn't it, Regina?"

"Rachel!" her nemesis snapped before storming off, her stilettos clacking a furious rhythm.

After letting herself enjoy the solid feel of Mason's arms for a heartbeat longer, Shonda got hold of herself.

"You didn't need to do that," she said, drawing away.

"She's a bitch," he countered with a shrug. "And she's been sniffing around since high school. You did me a favor."

"Fair enough." She handed him his basket with a small pang. "Here."

Instead of taking it, he draped himself across the cart's handle.

"Cheese puffs really are my favorite. I can grab some beer, and we can head to your place."

The suggestion in his voice awakened an unwelcome response inside her. One she should've built defenses against. But she hadn't.

His troublemaker grin flashed, promising sin and regret in equal measure. But it was his cool satisfaction, his assumption she'd cave, that firmed her resolve. For once, her brain and heart were in perfect accord, preparing a defense against him.

"Sorry. I'm catching up on work stuff," she said.

She set his basket on the ground and yanked the shopping cart at the opposite end, causing him to stumble. It was difficult to determine if his frown was one of disbelief because his charm didn't work or because she'd knocked him off balance.

"Besides, I'm done with *casual* fucks," she added with a stone-hard stare.

Splendid as far as exit lines went, but her timing was straight-up cursed.

Rachel's grating giggle froze them in place, and they shared a horrified glance.

Shonda rotated, meeting her triumphant gaze.

"I was halfway out the door before I realized Mason had to be toying with you," Rachel said, voice dripping with sugar and a hint of pity. "He likes to make me jealous."

Was this really her life? Dealing with ex-hometown cheerleaders fueled by pettiness and spite? Why couldn't this suck-ass week just end already? And why couldn't she just leave without saying a word?

Yeah, not going to happen.

"Oh, honey, get a clue," Shonda said, pulling no punches. "The man breaks out in hives within a foot of you."

Mic drop! Now *that* was a splendid exit line!

Giving herself a mental fist bump, she grabbed a bottle of wine from beside Rachel's head and swept away, patting herself on the back when Mason's laughter echoed behind her.

In the checkout line, Shonda kept her eyes straight ahead, ignoring the buzzing along her nerve endings announcing Mason's proximity. His scent, *Eau de Damn Him*, sealed the deal.

She was one customer away from freedom when the cashier's light blinked off.

A price check delay.

Naturally.

A second later, he pressed in behind her.

Unless she wanted to mow down the eighty-year-old in front of her, she was cornered.

"I didn't get a chance to say it earlier, but you smell amazing," Mason murmured, lips against her ear.

A delightful shiver danced along her spine.

She threw an elbow toward his stomach and missed.

"No means no, asshole," she muttered through gritted teeth.

"I'll let you sniff me," he teased. "I know it's your favorite thing."

True, but she'd rather lick a porcupine than admit it.

"Your line is getting old."

"So is you calling me an asshole," he countered.

She lobbed the verbal tennis ball back. "If the shoe fits."

"I thought you liked the size of my… shoe."

"Dear God, do these stupid lines actually work on women?" she asked with a glare.

"They worked on you well enough."

"I thought I was going to die in a plane crash. Here"—she slammed the cheese puff package against his chest—"your cheesy pickup lines need work." The bag burst, and the stunned expression on his orange-powdered face was too much.

She giggled.

Unable to help herself, she raised her cellphone and snapped a picture. Taking a second to capture the forming thundercloud.

"Give me the damn phone," he growled.

"Nope!" She laughed and tucked it safely into her bra.

"Shonda, you are—"

"Next!" the cashier called.

"Gotta run," she said. "And don't worry, Mason. Those cheesy puffs you love are on me. Well..." Her gaze dipped pointedly to his shirt. "Technically, they're on *you*, but I'll pay for them."

Epic! And she grinned all the way to her car.

Groceries loaded and keys in hand, she reached for the ignition.

Her door flew open, and Mason yanked her out.

"Stop man-handling me," she snapped. "I don't like it."

"We need to talk."

"The hell we do."

As he dragged her toward the warmth of the shop, an explosion rocked the air and slammed her into his back, sending them both sprawling on the ground. Instinct took over, and he rolled, shielding her head with his arms. They lay unmoving for a few minutes until the initial shock wore off.

Once the ringing in her ears faded, she shoved at his chest.

Mason's movements were stiff as he pushed to his feet and held out a hand to her.

"Are you okay?" she asked, checking him for injury.

"I'll live," he replied darkly, brushing dirt from his jeans. "Really, Shonda, stop. I slammed my knee on the way down, but it's fine. But your car, though..."

"My car?"

She whirled just in time to see her white Maxima fully engulfed in flames.

"What the fuck?" she cried, unable to wrap her head around the loss or why it would explode. "Do you think it was a faulty wire? Why would a car just blow up?"

"It wouldn't," he said grimly.

CHAPTER

THIRTEEN

"The fire marshal called. It was definitely an incendiary device," Mason informed her, striding into the kitchen.

"A bomb, Mason. You can call it a bomb." Shonda's voice wobbled.

He fought his desire to gather her close and assure her he'd keep her safe. But his arms remained at his sides. His protective instinct didn't mean a damn thing when safety wasn't something he could guarantee. The only reason she wasn't in a body bag was because he'd stopped her from driving off. If his anger hadn't gotten the better of him, she'd be ash and bone right now. And her death would've wrecked him in ways he couldn't admit out loud.

Too many puzzle pieces didn't fit. Was it a warning, like the break-ins in St. Thomas? Or was it intended to finish her this time? Maybe she'd unknowingly witnessed what she shouldn't have, and someone wanted her silenced. But how did her doppelgänger play into this? The questions came fast, stacking like bricks in his mind.

"I'm worried for your safety, love."

"Me, too. I don't know who's doing this, making it impossible to put safeguards in place. Stonebrooke's tiny police force is stretched thin, looking for the person terrorizing Erica and Zack." She couldn't hide her rising panic. "Oh, crap! Will you call your brother and make sure Erica doesn't watch the local news? She doesn't need to worry about me. Not with all they have going on."

His mouth tightened, giving him away. He hated secrets and half-truths. And her pleading don't-make-this-worse expression twisted him up. But he couldn't find a single reason to argue against it. With a few quick taps, he sent Zack a heads-up.

"You might want to give your parents a call, too," he said.

"Fuck! You're right. Papa will have a meltdown. I'll contact Nico."

"Nico?" The handsome maitre d' from the restaurant? "Why not your father?"

Her silence was suspect.

"Shonda, why don't you want to speak to your father?"

The casual shrug didn't fool him.

"Is he still upset with you from the night we had dinner there?" Mason asked.

"Can you please drop it?" She rubbed the spot between her brows and sighed. "I can't see where it's any of your business anyway."

"It damn well is if I caused a permanent rift between you and your dad."

"You didn't. I did when I told him whoever I chose to have an affair with was none of his concern. He wasn't invested in being a parent during my formative years. Starting at thirty-three is too little, too late."

Her words were cavalier, but the crack in her voice betrayed her. Luigi wasn't simply late in caring; he had never started, not the way a father should.

"Is there anything I can do to help?" Mason asked.

Her snort wasn't polite or delicate. It was an ugly bark of disbelief.

He scowled. "Why is that funny?"

"Seriously, dude?"

"Seriously."

"Fine. If you want the truth, I'm more than happy to lay it out for you." Arms crossed, chin lifted, she was a woman ready to wage war.

And he already knew the coming speech wasn't going to be flattering.

"You want one thing from me. Every time we're together, you're either insulting me or trying to get in my pants. You don't give two shits about me or my problems. Stop acting like you do."

The impact landed low and hard. Brutal. And he couldn't deny it. She had every right to view his behavior through bitter glasses. But it wasn't entirely accurate.

The truth was, he did care. Only not the way she wanted.

"Why can't we remain friends? Why does there have to be hostility between us or every conversation turn into a minefield?" he asked, despising his wheedling tone.

Mason closed the distance and braced his hands on the counter beside her hips. Her breath hitched as he filled the space between her thighs. Their eyes met, level for once, and the bottom dropped out of his stomach.

The faint dilation of her pupils, the shift of energy between them. Yeah, he recognized desire the second it hit. It was as familiar to him as his name, because his own blood surged with it whenever he was around her.

His mouth hovered inches from hers, waiting, giving her the chance to pull back.

She didn't.

Her tiny lean forward sealed their fate. His mouth crashed onto hers with the desperation of a man making up for lost time.

Three days of separation burned away in an instant. She whimpered and wrapped her legs around his waist, arms climbing under his shirt as her fingers dug into his back to pull him closer. Her hands left nothing untouched, matching his in intensity, clutching, stroking, claiming.

Her sweater made it halfway over her head when the first knock came.

"You've got to be kidding me," Mason growled, breaking the kiss. His chest rose and fell in harsh, broken bursts. "Stop and answer the door, or ignore them?"

Another knock, louder and more insistent, decided it.

"Bella!" Luigi's frantic voice boomed. "Bella, it's Papa."

They exchanged a wary glance.

Mason stepped back.

"Well, I guess it's option one," she said, not moving.

"Think he has a gun?"

Laughter sounded through the layers of the sweater she was putting back on. Before she could finish, Mason caught her hands and held them high.

"One last glimpse," he murmured with deep regret.

"You're such a sweet talker."

"I'll remain behind the island until I get my situation under control."

Her light giggle softened the existing tension between them. He helped her down and kissed her tenderly. "Signal me if I should intervene. Eye twitch. Flip of the bird. You know, our standard code."

"Thanks, but your smoothing-over techniques suck."

"I'm wounded."

Her snort followed her to the door.

Luigi entered faster than a Florida storm front. The air around him shifted, becoming sharp, electric, and commanding.

"Sit down, Bella. I have bad news."

"What's going on?" Shonda asked, apprehension in her tone. Mason joined them.

"Your mother's house burned down earlier today," Luigi said grimly.

"WHAT?" Her hand flew to her mouth as Mason dropped beside her, fingers curling around hers. Her shock gave way to her panic.

"Is Eva… is she…?"

"She's fine. She was in Malta for a few weeks, but is flying back soon. The house is still in my name, so I'll handle the paperwork."

"Wait! You came to tell me about Eva. So, you haven't heard about my car?"

Luigi stiffened. "What about your car?"

She gave the short version.

Her father paled, and worry built behind his expression, layer by layer.

"Mr. De Vitis, may I pose a delicate question?" Mason asked.

"Yes."

"In St. Thomas, I saw a woman who was identical to your daughter. Did you or your wife ever have another child before or after Shonda? Maybe one who might've been put up for adoption?"

"No!" Luigi's voice boomed with outrage. "I would never agree to give away my own flesh and blood."

"I already told you I was an only child, Mason. Why would you ask such a thing?" The anger vibrating in Shonda's voice didn't bode well for him. He suddenly had father *and* daughter to contend with. "My parents have always had the money to care for another kid. What reason would they have for giving up a child?"

He ignored her and kept his gaze locked on Luigi.

The man's scowl transformed into an expression of confusion, or perhaps realization.

"Did you remember something, sir?"

There was a weighted pause.

"Shonda was a twin," Luigi said, his voice filled with remembered grief. "Her sister was stillborn."

Shonda gasped. "Papa, I never knew that."

"Eva went into labor two months early. I was in Italy, and by the time I returned, your sister was gone. Your mother blamed me. Perhaps the death was brought on by the stress of my absence. It was the beginning of the end for us."

Tears glistened in his eyes before one dropped to travel along his leathery cheek. Shonda jumped up and wrapped him in a comforting hug.

"I'm sorry," Mason said, meaning it. A loss like theirs was hard to comprehend. "I didn't intend to dredge up the past. I just…"

Luigi waved him off. "These memories sit close to the surface when you're my age, and it doesn't take a lot to stir them."

"To clarify, Eva was never pregnant before or after?" Mason probed gently, wishing he didn't have to.

"No. Not with my child. If she and Nolan…" He shrugged.

"When she married Nolan, I was seven," Shonda offered. "I would've noticed."

Mason nodded. "Which side of the family carries twins?"

"Eva's," Luigi replied.

"What are you thinking, Mason?" she asked, her frown deepening with confusion.

He hesitated, weighing the damage truth might bring. If he was wrong, it could cause undue pain. If he was correct, well, he'd open up a whole other world of problems for her.

"Mason."

Glancing between them, he came to a decision. "I think we

need to review your family's life insurance policies, especially your mother's."

"You think someone wants to kill her?" Her voice rose.

"Take a step back and look at what's happened, love." Mason stayed calm in the face of her disbelief. "Eva's house went up in flames. Your car exploded. These aren't coincidences. My guess is revenge or financial payout, or both."

She turned to her father, pale and shaken. Together, they absorbed the full gravity of what he'd suggested.

"But why?" she asked. "I don't get why anyone would want to harm either of us."

Luigi gripped her hand and met Mason's gaze. "I agree with Shonda. Eva's wealth was substantial at one time, but her fortune has evaporated over the years under the weight of indulgence and pretense."

"To an outsider, her financial status might not be as obvious," Mason concluded. "She continues an elaborate lifestyle by anyone's standard, doesn't she?"

Shonda nodded. "Okay, I'll give you that, but why me?"

"I haven't quite unraveled the reason yet." He had. Truth hovered on the edge of his tongue, but without proof, he wasn't ready to mention it aloud.

"I can obtain the financials and life insurance policy for Eva. There is one for Shonda as well," Luigi offered.

"Thanks," Mason said.

"Papa, Eva… she…"

"It's okay, child. You can tell me. I'm well past being hurt by her insults."

"She said you had multiple affairs during your marriage to her. Did you father any other children?"

No amount of control could mask Luigi's flare of fury. He was nowhere near past hurt.

Mason immediately recognized the direction in which Shonda was headed. It aligned too well with his own suspicions.

"You think maybe a bastardized child is seeking revenge against you and your mother because they missed out on the whole perfect family gig?" he asked.

Eyes locked on her father, she gave a sharp nod.

Luigi's voice dropped to a ragged whisper. "She was wrong. You and your mother were my whole world, Bella. You've never believed me before, but you need to believe me now. I love you."

Unwilling to intrude on their tender moment, Mason slipped outside and onto the balcony.

His chest squeezed tight.

Witnessing a father love his daughter as fiercely as Luigi did Shonda had triggered a long-buried ache. Mason was only five when James Sharp walked out. No note. No warning. No goodbye. Dear ol' Dad left his kid standing in the backyard, glove in hand, waiting for a bonding moment that never happened. The coward had snuck out as Mason waited over forty minutes. Crushed.

Anger surged, familiar and corrosive. What kind of man promised a game of catch, then ducked out the front door? The bastard didn't deserve the space he'd ever taken up in Mason's heart or mind. And if he ever dared show his face again, well…

The front door opened and closed behind him, signaling Luigi's departure.

"Mason?" Shonda's voice floated to him.

"What?" Eyes fixed on the woods beyond her property, the word fired out before he could pull it back.

A frown creased her brow. "Why are you suddenly upset?"

No way in hell could he admit the truth. Seeing her receive the love he never received opened a canyon inside him, and he didn't know how to bridge the gap.

"Not a damn thing other than the fact someone's trying to kill you. And although I have a million and one things I should be doing, I'm stuck here."

She flinched.

Shit.

His ugliness echoed back in the worst possible way.

Her recoil was like a slap, and his regret was instantaneous. "Ah, love. I didn't mean that the way it sounded."

Too late. She was having none of it. Her expression shuttered.

"I'd like you to go," she said stiffly.

"You're cracked in the head if you think I'm leaving you here alone with a potential killer on the loose." He jabbed a finger toward her, emphasizing his point. "Not happening."

"I won't be alone. I'll call Samuel to come stay."

His blood turned to fire. "Who the hell is Samuel?"

"I've offered a solution. You're free to hightail it back to your bachelor pad and carry on with a clear conscience. I don't need you."

Oh, but the idea of her calling another man caused sweat to break out on his upper lip and his hands to shake.

"You damn well *do* need me," he bit out, unsure why he was fighting to stay when all he'd wanted minutes ago was distance. "The one thing we do know in this whole mess is that I'm the only one not trying to kill you."

"Wrong."

He blinked. "Excuse me?"

"You know one other person who isn't trying to kill me. Your brother, Dane."

His stomach flipped.

"You can ask if he'll babysit me while you go handle your million and one things."

He wasn't mistaking her tone or the sneer wrapped in silk.

"Whatever. I'm the one trying to help here, but I didn't sign up for you to bust my balls," he replied, annoyed by her refusal to accept his apology.

"Really, Mason? You view the situation as me out to bust your balls? Not as you insulting me?" Her voice sharpened, making his heart thud. "Well, I'm so glad we cleared it all up. Call your brother, or I'll get the number from Erica. Either way, I want you gone." She pivoted and stormed toward the slider like she couldn't get away fast enough.

Panic hugged his chest, and he gave chase.

"We aren't finished! Get back here!"

"Oh, I'd say we damn well are," she shouted over her shoulder, snatching her purse from the coat rack. "You have exactly one minute to get the hell out of my apartment before I call the police and have you arrested for trespassing."

A blood vessel throbbed at his temple, the pressure building behind his eyes and teeth.

"You're crazy, you know that?" He grabbed his coat and stomped toward the door. "I'll be outside until you come to your senses."

"Bundle up. It's going to be a long-ass night."

CHAPTER

FOURTEEN

Alarm set and locks engaged, Shonda descended the stairs to meet the Uber waiting out front. One glance at the parking lot confirmed Mason's Lexus hadn't moved since yesterday. Holding up a single finger to stall the driver, she veered toward the familiar vehicle and leaned down to peer through the tinted glass.

Empty.

"Looking for me?"

A scream tore from her throat.

"Asshole!"

"I'll—" Mason began.

"Don't you even *think* about saying you'll let me sniff you. Not if you want to live."

"Sorry. I forgot you're not much of a morning person."

He leaned casually against the car, sipping from a to-go cup as if her near-heart attack amused him. Caffeine remained elusive this morning, and his steaming cup practically called her name.

She reached for it.

Of course, being the contrary bastard that he was, he held it up and away as he waved a finger. "Uh, uh, uh."

The temptation to rip off his arm and beat him with it was hard to resist. Instead, she graced him with a black look and tried again, with the same result.

"When did you get coffee, and why didn't you bring me one?" she demanded.

The smug bastard lifted the drink higher, forcing her to press closer. His infuriating grin spoke volumes about how much he enjoyed the body contact. To be contrary, she backed off fast.

"I had a friend drop it by," he said with a shrug and another swallow.

Friend. Code for a woman.

"Friend, huh? Well, now I understand why only one drink. Can't have your scores of women thinking you aren't the great lone wolf."

Spinning on her heel, she stalked to the waiting vehicle.

"Hey, where do you think you're going?" he called.

"Not that it's your business, but I'm heading to Erica's surprise party."

"Without your coffee? I mean, you're the woman I'm sleeping with who takes it with two creams, no sugar, right?"

His sin-worthy smile made a comeback, and a second cup appeared, hinting Mason might be a magician or her keen observation skills were sadly lacking. He wiggled it back and forth, dangling the prize.

With narrowed eyes, she considered her options.

One: she could accept the coffee as a very sweet gesture on his part and ignore who had procured it.

Two: get in the hired vehicle, run through a drive-thru, visit Zack and Erica, then finally go car shopping.

Three: knee Mason in the nuts for making her stand in a

parking lot like an idiot while debating her hopeless caffeine dependency.

Four: murder him on the spot, guzzle both cups, and take her chances with the law.

Three moved up the ranks the fastest, with four close behind. For the moment, she'd tuck murder in her back pocket.

Mason, apparently recognizing her internal war, approached, handed her the coffee, and kissed her brow like he had a right. She grudgingly allowed him to lead her back to his car.

The jerk even held her cup while she buckled up.

"Toasty, huh?" he asked, not bothering to hide his smirk.

The feel of buttery leather seats was miles ahead of whatever her hired driver could offer.

"I don't know the etiquette on sending him away," she confessed.

"I'll take care of it," he said. "We'll work it out."

His thoughtfulness ranked near the top of the list of things she appreciated about him. Well, right after those abs and the unfair perfection of his ass.

The second he settled behind the wheel, she cleared her throat. "For the record, we are not sleeping together. Not anymore."

"If you say so," he said flatly, noncommittally, as if the conversation bored him.

Her irritation spiked. "I do!"

"Okay."

"Okay."

"Fine."

"Fine." Her lips curled into a sneer. "Asshole."

"Now you're just *begging* to sniff me. No means no, Shonda."

She turned to the window to hide her smile. But it faded almost instantly.

Getting sucked in by Mason's charm again would be a rookie mistake. And today, he poured it on thick as pancake syrup.

Her mind wandered to where he'd slept last night. Probably at Deirdre's. Her neighbor in 2B had never met a man she didn't want to bang, and more than once, she'd propositioned Shonda's dates. Managed to snag a few of the less scrupulous ones, too.

"Where did you sleep last night?" The question escaped before she could slam the lid on her suspicions.

Filter, Shonda. Filter!

"A nice redheaded woman offered to put me up."

She nearly ground her molars to dust, barely holding back a throat-punch with his name on it. After all, he was driving. Safety first.

"I didn't take her up on it. I stayed awake outside your door like I said I would," he said conversationally. "I'm really rather surprised you'd leave me to freeze after I saved you from a fiery death."

Curious despite herself, she asked, "What did you do to stay warm?"

"At half-hour intervals, I cranked up the heater in my car."

"And this morning's coffee kindness is what? You're suddenly reformed and decided to repent the error of your ways?"

"I considered the possibility." He grinned before sobering. "But what you see is what you get, love."

Yeah, her main problem was wanting exactly what she saw. Badly.

THE LOW HUM of voices faded as Mason stepped onto the patio. Standing over the grill, Zack stared into the flames as if they held answers.

"I thought I smelled something burning."

He jolted and glanced down at the meat before flipping him off. "Nice, asshat."

"Oh, someone has it bad." Mason chuckled, giving his brother a light shake by the back of the neck.

"Shit, man, have a care."

Amused, he opened his mouth to fire back, only to freeze when movement caught his eye.

Shonda was preparing to leave.

Where the hell did she think she was going? If she believed he'd let her leave when someone was out there planting bombs in cars, she was—

"You should apologize," Zack said, cutting him off mid mind-rant.

"The fuck I will." He already had, but there was no need for his brother to know.

Zack scoffed, visibly annoyed. "Don't be an ass. You obviously have chemistry. Why not see where it leads?"

"Piss off. Did I ask you?" Mason's anger wasn't warranted, especially since Zack meant well. But he felt too wound up for reasons he couldn't clearly define.

"The fuck I will. You're being stubborn." Zack reclaimed the plate of burgers he held. "Go ask her to stay for dinner. No one is saying you have to marry the woman. But you can get your feet wet again by dating a nice girl. And she is nice. I knew her in school, and Erica speaks highly of her."

His brother disappeared inside, leaving Mason standing in the heavy quiet. Maybe he had a point. Starting slow didn't sound terrible, did it? Slow was safe. Hell, if he were honest with himself, he'd admit his life was godawful lonely. Shonda chased the loneliness away. Her sass, her smile, those warm, dancing eyes...

He stepped inside, angling toward her, but froze mid stride.

Tension rippled throughout the room. Zack stood rigid, staring at his phone as if fearing it might detonate in his palm.

"Zack? What is it?" Erica's voice barely rose above a whisper, uncertainty trailing every syllable.

He didn't move.

"Hey, man? What's going on?" Mason snatched the phone and read the message for himself.

"Enjoying your party? It will be your whore's last."

"Jesus Christ!"

The stillness fractured, and the room buzzed with movement, whispers, cries, or hands reaching. As one, their collective gaze landed on Erica, who was eerily silent until Zack reached for her.

"Daddy, is Erica going to be all right?" Jacob tentatively asked.

Mason's gaze found Shonda. Pale and stunned, she looked moments from bolting. He had no idea how to calm her, but he wanted to mimic Zack's hold on Erica and pull her close.

He understood the need. It echoed his own after yesterday's explosion. Shonda hadn't mocked how clingy he'd gotten. And her kindness set her apart.

Zack abruptly released Erica and rushed to the trash can, barely making it before he retched. Mason made a move to follow, but their mother waved him off.

"I've got this," she said.

Silence followed. Mainly, no one knew what to say. All of them were locked in their own prison of turmoil.

When Zack returned, fire lit his eyes. The fury shimmering off him could've scorched the walls.

Mason stared in awe, barely recognizing the change. His brother didn't lose control. Ever. He avoided conflict unless absolutely necessary. But the stalker had created a warrior hell-bent on protecting what was his.

"No!" Erica's voice cracked. "Somebody stop him!"

Spinning around, Zack threw up a hand to prevent his brothers from intervening. "Don't you dare touch me. I'm ending this."

"Whoever it is doing this is probably long gone, bro." Dane's was the voice of reason. Always calm. Always logical.

"I don't want you going out there, Zachary." Their mother's tone left no room for argument.

"You don't understand. None of you do!" Zack drove a fist through the wall beside him, cracking the drywall on impact. *"Goddammit!"*

"Zack, look at me." Erica's soft, persuasive voice had the ability to bring his pacing to an end. "Currently, she's fixated on me. But I'm worried if you confront her, going on the assumption I'm right and it is a female, she might snap. In her mind, she thinks you're hers, but if you deny her, that puts a target on *your* back as well as mine."

"What do you propose we do? I'm done with waiting for the police department to find a fucking clue." He resumed pacing again. "What the hell are they even doing? Sitting on their asses, eating donuts? Because they sure as shit aren't working to find out who it is."

"Please."

One utterance. Spoken low, filled with pain, brought him back to himself.

Zack held out his hand. "Who has my cell? Give it to me, please."

Mason slapped it into his palm. "Don't do anything stupid," he warned. Previously, their roles would have been reversed, with his brother the levelheaded one of the two. But whoever the enraged person was in front of him, well, he wasn't anywhere close to reasonable.

"Fuck off," Zack muttered, already dialing a number. He spoke, then listened, finally ending with, "I don't want excuses,

Buck. Find her, or I will. I can promise you, if I do, it won't be pretty."

He disconnected the call with a jab of his thumb and hurled the phone before storming off.

Erica was wrecked, though not a single tear fell. Mason respected the hell out of her self-control.

He glanced at Shonda, whose eyes shimmered with the fury and helplessness she tried to hide. Giving into the irresistible urge, he headed for her. They met in the middle of the room and fell into each other. Not surprisingly, her warmth grounded him. He inhaled deeply of her sweet scent, calming the riot in his mind.

"Did you just sniff me?" she asked under her breath.

His laughter threatened.

God, her timing!

"Come on, love. Let's help clean up. I don't expect anyone is in the partying mood anymore." With a quick, tight squeeze, he reluctantly released her.

CHAPTER

FIFTEEN

"I feel awful shopping for a vehicle when Erica is going through hell," Shonda said as they cruised the car lot.

"Why would she care?" Mason asked.

"She helped me pick my last two cars. It's our BFF thing. She chooses what she loves, and I pay for it."

He halted mid-step, unable to process.

She walked ahead a few paces before registering his absence. Glancing back, she raised her brows. "What?"

"You let Erica choose your cars?" he echoed, incredulous. Who the hell handed over such an important decision? Automobiles were personal. Sacred. Selection was based on comfort, texture, engine…

"Well, yeah. I hate negotiating, but with only one unreliable car service in this godforsaken town, I need a vehicle."

Moving past his shock, he peered in the window of the closest sedan. "What about a rental until she's back on her feet?" he suggested.

"No, I have to seal the deal before Eva gets back. She'll push me into something flashy like a Porsche, Corvette, or maybe that all-electric Audi everyone's talking about. Really, I don't need the headache. When she doesn't get her way, she makes my life a living hell."

He blinked. "The Audi etron GT?"

She lifted her arms in a meh-who-knows-or-cares shrug.

Again, he stared. Their conversation was the weirdest to date, and he couldn't believe what he was hearing.

"Shonda."

She didn't bother to look up from the price sticker she'd been studying.

"Not to sound indelicate or anything, but do you have the finances for any of those?"

The amused sparkle in her eye and lip bite assured him she did. And why did he find her careless humor crazy attractive?

He shook his head. "If you're serious, why the hell aren't you going for one of those?"

"They aren't practical for everyday life," she said simply, pausing by a deep blue pearl model Nissan.

"How is a top-tier, hybrid hypercar not practical for everyday life? It's not like you have kids or carpools."

A quicksilver scowl came and went, and she firmed her lips.

Ten seconds ago, they were enjoying themselves. Which was odd, because he really hated vehicle shopping, too. But the speed with which her attitude cooled made his head spin.

"What did I say?"

"Nothing. This one is fine. I'll take it."

No, he'd definitely put his foot in his mouth. Her dullness didn't lie.

Christ, why couldn't they go twenty-four hours without an argument? He dropped his chin to his chest and exhaled a sigh.

"I'm sorry."

He had no clue what he was sorry for, but if they could go back to her happily kicking tires, he'd repeat it fifty times.

"Mason, you have nothing to be sorry for."

No hint of guile could be found when he stepped closer and tipped her chin up. Those beautiful moss-green eyes were clear and honest, but somehow not okay.

"Then what upset you? And before you tell me you weren't, I'll remind you I don't like liars."

A wry smile curled her lips. "I haven't lied to you… yet."

He crowded her against the car she'd chosen and traced the line of her jaw with his fingertips. "Yeah, I'm going to have to call bullshit."

Her sharp gasp labeled her offended.

"When did I lie?" she demanded, indignant and adorable.

His hands slipped beneath her coat, burrowing under her sweater. Her stomach contracted from his freezing touch. "This morning, when you said we weren't sleeping together anymore," he murmured next to her ear, capturing the lobe lightly between his teeth.

Her choked laughter made him feel ten feet tall. The sound brought lightness to his soul and could anchor a man if he let it. Another sobering thought, but one he shoved away as fast as humanly possible, not wanting to mar a future memory for himself.

"Do you actually like blue?" he asked, trailing lovebites along her graceful neck.

"Hmm?"

"Blue. Do you even like the color?" She never wore it, and there were only spotted traces in her home decor.

"Depends on the shade," she replied, ending on a moan as his hands flirted with second base.

"What's your favorite color, love?" God, her skin. He spared a fleeting worry for any nearby cameras, but concluded he didn't give a damn. They were fully clothed, single adults.

"I find I'm partial to ice blue."

"What a coincidence," Mason murmured against her lips. "I've been told my peepers match that description."

Pretending to check, she pulled back and widened her eyes in mock surprise. "Why, so they are!"

He dipped his head to steal a kiss. The spark hadn't fully ignited when the loud, awkward clearing of a throat nearby doused the flame. With a heavy sigh, he eased away, stuffing his hands into his jeans to shield the erection forming with zero regard for timing or location.

"Mason? I thought that was you!"

The woman was too cheerful and overfamiliar.

He shifted to find a perky blonde beaming at him.

"Frank was next on rotation, but when I saw it was you, I traded leads," she said.

He nodded politely and reached for Shonda's hand, preventing her from edging away.

His radar sensed the incoming storm, but they'd weather it together.

"Good to see you again, uh..." His mind blanked. Not ideal with two expectant females staring at him.

Christ. He was fairly certain they'd hooked up at least once.

Carly? Mandy? Brandy?

"Uh, Brandy," he said, not confident at all.

"Candy," the saleswoman bit out through clenched teeth.

"Right. My bad."

She gasped. He winced.

Fucking A. Why did these things keep happening? He needed to be faster on his feet. Shonda's muffled snort tried to drag a laugh out of him. He didn't dare meet her eyes, or he'd lose what little control he possessed.

Shonda took pity on his awkwardness.

"Candy, I'm interested in the blue Maxima." She stepped forward, effectively inserting herself between them and motioning toward the car behind her. "And while seeing Mason is always an experience—"

"Hey," he cut in.

"—I'd like to make my purchase as fast and painless as possible. Can you help me, or should we see if Frank is available?"

He had to give her credit. She was poised and direct, one hundred percent in charge when she chose to be. Another check mark on a list of skills he probably shouldn't find sexy but did.

"Can you give us a second, Candy?" When she didn't budge, he sighed and tugged Shonda a few feet away. "Are you sold on the blue?"

"What do you have against blue?" Her brow furrowed.

"It's bland. I think the red or black would suit you better."

"Oh, how *cute*. Next, you'll be picking out china patterns together." Candy's syrupy tone didn't quite mask her bite.

Shonda stiffened. "You know what? I think I'll take my business elsewhere. And you can be sure I'll let Stuart know how catty his employee was today."

Her threat landed, and Candy's arms uncrossed instantly. "You know Stuart?"

"Yes, the owner of the dealership. You know him, right? We go way back," Shonda replied breezily. "I had dinner with him and April a couple of weeks ago. Lovely couple."

Candy blanched, but Mason didn't feel bad for her. Instead of with cruelty, Shonda had handled the situation with finesse, making her point without going nuclear. With a few well-phrased sentences, she'd guaranteed the other woman would put professionalism above personal feelings.

Candy forced a smile. "There's no excuse for my behavior. If you'd prefer, I can find another associate."

The embarrassment staining her cheeks bothered him. The longer he stood on the lot, the more he recalled from their lone date. She was a single mom with two kids to support. How many cars could she possibly sell in their tiny town with a competing lot across the road?

"I don't think that's necessary," Mason cut in. "You're a highly trained staff member, or Stuart wouldn't have hired you, Candy."

Shonda's gaze pinned him, and a blend of awareness and admiration shone from her eyes.

She knew. Of course she did. Small-town gossip reached everyone eventually. Her smile was full and warm, making him uncomfortable. He hated that she believed him to be a better person than he was.

"I've changed my mind," she said, glancing back at the line of cars. "I'll take the red one."

IT DIDN'T COME as a total surprise to Shonda when Mason disappeared a few hours later, and Dane showed up in his place.

"I brought Chinese," he stated with bags raised high, as if tempting her.

"Shopping for a family-sized sedan freaked your brother out, huh?" she asked as she swung the door wide for him to enter.

"Pretty much."

"Pfft. If it wasn't pathetic, it would be funny."

"True," he agreed. "I ordered crab rangoon. Erica said it was your favorite."

Shit! If Dane had told Erica he was coming here, she'd know something was up. "How much does she know?"

Dane froze in place, confusion written all over him.

"Was she not to know I was bringing you dinner because you're lonely?"

"Wait, what? Who said I was lonely?"

"My brother."

"In case you've forgotten, you have two," she replied dryly.

"In case *you've* forgotten, only *one* has been hanging out with you," Dane countered with a laugh. "But if he's so forgettable, maybe he's doing it all wrong."

She laughed, charmed by his easygoing manner. "I'm pretty sure I adore you."

"Don't tell me you told Mason that. He'll be on the next plane to anywhere."

"Pfft. Do you take me for an idiot?"

"Nah." He grinned as he unpacked the food cartons. "I can already tell you have a higher IQ than his last three conquests combined."

Shonda laughed again, surprised she could, and removed two plates from the cabinet. "Does he know you talk about him like you do?"

He shrugged. "If he doesn't, he should get *his* IQ tested."

They bonded over orange chicken and verbal digs at Mason's expense.

"Do you mind if I use your phone to text your brother?" she asked some time later.

"Please don't tell me he never gave you his number."

In addition to her high color, she imagined her compressed mouth, wide eyes, and raised brows gave away her embarrassment.

"He did, but he rarely responds to texts."

"Do you suppose my brother knows he's an asshole?" Dane asked, handing over his phone.

"Yes, I tell him constantly, and you don't strike me as shy."

His hearty laughter warmed her cold, tired soul.

"I tell you what, if you really want to get back at him, let's run away and get married," he suggested with a flare of his eyes and an engaging grin.

"I ask you to keep her company for dinner, and before the

plates are cleared, you're planning an elopement?" Mason's deep, not-so-amused voice interrupted their teasing.

Hand on her pounding heart, Shonda waited until it resumed some semblance of normalcy before responding.

"How did you get in here?" she asked.

"You were too wrapped up in each other and forgot to lock the door. Think that's the wisest course of action?" Mason dropped a duffel bag beside the sofa, and damned if it didn't produce an angry thud.

"If we're picking courses of action, I vote she marries me," Dane volunteered, hand raised as if he actually had a choice.

Mason and Shonda ignored him.

"No," she said. "I should have double-checked and locked it behind him."

Astonishment unhinged his jaw. "Are you agreeing with me, for a change? Should I mark the date down?"

"Hardy-har-har." She crossed her arms.

Mason's laughter boomed.

Grinning, he closed the distance between them, hauled her from the chair, and kissed her.

"Say goodbye, Dane," he commanded.

"Goodbye, Dane."

Hands on her waist, he lifted as she jumped and wrapped her legs around him like a monkey.

His second kiss was deeper and mind-altering. If she had any sense of self, she'd recognize she was a damned pushover when it came to him. But Mason was a bad habit she couldn't shake.

"Seriously? You're tossing me over for tall, dark, and brooding?" Dane asked as Mason carried her away. "Sure, I'll clean up here and put the food away. Don't mind me."

"Oh, we won't," Mason said.

"Way to play hard to get, Shonda," Dane called after them.

CHAPTER
SIXTEEN

A parade of days marched by. Shonda kept things between them playful and light, as if suppressing her emotions would miraculously shield her from the eventual fallout. Their non-relationship was "Casual" by Mason's definition. The terms of their arrangement remained clear, and she never mentioned the word *love*.

While she understood they couldn't continue indefinitely, she was content to enjoy whatever stolen time he allowed. Being with him felt better than being without. Regardless of the hardass line in the sand, he was honest about intentions and, as far as she knew, they were mutually exclusive.

He hadn't invited her to his place, and she told herself it didn't matter.

But it did.

A lot.

If she had any foresight, she'd never have let him cross the threshold of her apartment. His stamp was everywhere, and one day, probably soon, she'd pay for letting him stake a claim.

Their minor arguments had faded as they found a working

rhythm. He'd begun texting and calling, which felt monumental in their own right. Yet she never initiated contact. Pushing would send him running.

On the nights he didn't come by, Shonda flatly refused to sit in a quiet void and absorb the sting. She made plans. Friends. Dinner. Erica. Anyone who could serve as a distraction from the hollow ache in her chest. And she damned well never let herself fall apart. Because what she wouldn't do was chase him. She wasn't that woman, and never would be.

Her happy bomber had gone silent. No fresh threats lurking under the hood of her new car, painstakingly parked in a gated garage under lights and cameras. Sure, she wasn't naive enough to believe it was over. Neither was Mason. But every now and again, she was able to clear her head of the nagging worry.

One of the sweetest things he'd done was arrange for patrol cars to swing by her place when he was absent. And he'd gone to the extent of securing routine patrols for her mom's and dad's places, too.

If leaving her place, Mason used back roads, checking mirrors so frequently it boggled her brain.

Simple trips to the grocery store turned into a cloak-and-dagger event. They always used his car, rigged with a sensitive alarm able to detect the brush of a leaf on its way to the ground.

Tonight, he circled the block twice before pulling into the parking lot.

"I feel like we're in a spy movie," she quipped, bracing as he executed another evasive maneuver.

He didn't crack a smile. "Better safe than sorry."

His terse response set her nerves on edge. He didn't appear angry per se, but tension coiled around him like a taut wire ready to snap. Every inquiry about work, his day, or anything hinting at a personal share was met with a blank stare or a grunt.

When he reached for the door handle, she caught his arm.

"Mason, what's wrong? Are you mad at me for some reason?"

"No."

He tried to pull away, but she held firm.

Leaning forward to meet his eyes, she asked, "Is it impossible for you to have a real conversation with me? Anything more meaningful than what we plan to eat for dinner or what movie we want to watch would do."

"Oh, for God's sake. Here we go." He slumped back with an exasperated huff. "This is where you encourage me to share my feelings, right? To commit to calling you my girlfriend?" His cold gaze locked on her face. "It's not happening, Shonda. Give it rest."

The disdainful attitude stung harder than any slap. He'd twisted a vulnerable moment into a needy demand she didn't make. For a split second, she wished he *had* hit her. At least then she could label it for what it was. Abuse. A perfect reason to walk away.

Her therapist would say her inability to quit him went back to childhood and her feelings of being unlovable. Perhaps it did, but she wanted more from life and the people in her world.

She sat motionless, staring at his gloved hands clenched around the steering wheel. Her shell cracked open, revealing the sobbing inner child, the one deserving of attention and caring.

"I'm done."

Her statement was toneless and final, but once out, the oppressive weight lifted from her shoulders. Before he could react, she flung her door open and stepped out, hustling in the opposite direction from the store.

"Shonda, get back here," he snapped, voice fury-laced.

She didn't break stride. Each step cemented her decision to be done with the self-torment. Done with longing for things she couldn't have. Done with the best sex of her existence.

Her last thought almost paused her flight, but she was nothing if not dogged.

"I'm not fooling around," he called after her. "Get back here. It's not safe for you to walk home in the dark."

No, it wasn't. But it was safer than being near him, where she might fold and pretend she didn't crave or need more.

His muttered "goddammit" echoed in the quiet night. The snow made everything sound sharper but less personal.

A minute into her hike home, and she was cursing her stupidity. She should've worn a heavier jacket. The full thirty-minute walk wouldn't kill her, but by the time she arrived, she'd be a fucking Popsicle.

A car door slammed behind her.

Mason would either chase her down or leave her there to stew in it. When no footsteps followed, her stomach sank and her romantic fantasies fled. Stewing it was.

No matter how many times she told herself she wouldn't cry, her body refused to behave. Scalding tears spilled over her chilled cheeks, and she angrily swiped them away. No way was the bastard going to be the reason she turned into a red-nosed, puffy-eyed mess. Not if anyone was around to see.

But of course, someone was.

From nowhere, a rock-solid body collided with hers, knocking her to the ground. Her purse vanished from her shoulder, ripped away as her body hit the pavement. Her right arm took the brunt of the fall, and pain shot through it as she scrambled to her feet. With a battle cry, she gave chase, but her boots skidded across the icy sidewalk, sending her sprawling again.

Tires squealed.

An instant later, Mason's car screeched to a hard stop beside her.

He jumped out, wild-eyed. "Are you all right?"

She nodded, ignoring the burn in her shoulder, and waved him off.

"Go get that rat bastard and run him over, will ya?" she ordered.

His grin was sharp and deadly. Diving back into the car, he peeled off in pursuit.

As soon as he was gone, she berated herself for sending him after the thief. Her hip throbbed like hell, and a single step toward the store was a reminder of how hard the fucking ground had been. She was brutally cold, bruised, and emotionally wrecked. The perfect trifecta of miserable.

Ten more steps reminded her she didn't have a wallet to cover the cost of a ride. The five after brought frustrated tears to her eyes again. Six additional steps, and she was thoroughly pissed, prepared to murder whoever was making her life a living hell.

At last, the store came into view.

She was roughly twelve feet from the doors when Mason pulled up beside her, a lingering fury in his gaze.

"The guy must've had a car waiting," he said with an annoyed shake of his head. "I've called the police, and they should be here soon. Come get warm."

The thought of those heated leather seats wrapped around her was tempting and caused her to waver.

But if she got in his car, she'd be unable to sever the tie.

"Thanks, but I'll wait inside."

He scoffed and held the door open. "Don't be ridiculous, Shonda. Get in the car."

His assumed compliance triggered her.

"Ridiculous? *Ridiculous?*"

So what if her screeching portrayed her as mentally unstable? She had every right to be angry.

"You know what's *ridiculous*, Mason? You, treating women like they have cooties if you spend more than twenty-four consecutive hours together. Another *ridiculous* thing might be your gamophobia."

"What the hell is gamophobia?" he snapped as if she'd accused him of murder.

"Look it up, asshole."

She stormed inside and made a beeline for the service desk.

"Shonda Grant, right?" the man behind the counter asked, circling around to her side.

Recognition hit as she registered the sandy-brown hair, azure eyes, and a ready smile.

"Tommy McAdams?" What were the chances of seeing her childhood friend when she needed a kind face the most? "Wow! It's been forever! How are you?"

She lurched forward and hugged him, the years falling away. He was her first unrequited love at age eight. But of course, young love never stood a chance.

"Look at you," she said. "All grown up and a heartbreaker."

His laugh was pure sunshine, and it tugged a smile from her.

"You look…" He paused, frowning as he took in her tear-streaked face, ripped jeans, and wild hair.

"Like a hot mess?" she offered with a watery grin, recalling her predicament.

"I was going to say beautiful, but I doubt you'd believe it, seeing as how you're a little worse for wear at the moment."

The kindness went a long way in soothing her emotional hurts.

"Thank you."

"What happened?" he asked.

"Would you believe I was mugged?"

"In Stonebrooke?" The disbelief in his voice was understand-able. Nothing ever happened in their sleepy little town.

"I know, right?"

"God, are you okay? Do I need to call the police? What can I do?"

"I've got it covered, cuz. They're on their way," Mason's voice answered from directly behind her, smooth and deep. He startled a squeak from her.

She had to be in bad shape if he failed to trigger her body's early warning system.

"Mason. Hey, man. Were you outside when it happened?" Tommy asked, eyes wide.

"You could say that." His tone was dry, and the silence afterward was weighted and strange.

Shonda jumped into the verbal gap. "The phone, Tommy?"

"Oh, yeah, come on back."

"No need," Mason forestalled them. His voice was clipped but fully loaded when he added, "I brought you here. I'll damn well take you home."

"I'll call Eva, but thanks." Pride kept her spine stiff, even as her bones ached to curl into his warmth. Accepting his help meant surrendering and pretending what had happened in the car didn't make her bleed. She couldn't go back to their unsuitable arrangement.

"You're being a stubborn fool," he ground out, closing the distance between them.

She backed until her shoulders hit solid muscle. Tommy's arm caught her, supportive and keeping her upright. The gesture drew Mason's cold stare straight to the contact point. He lifted his withering glare to his cousin's face, as if sizing up a threat.

Tommy's chest vibrated with his low chuckle. "That's not going to work with me, cuz. The McAdams clan is made of sterner stuff."

"How about if I threaten to break your fucking arm off?" Mason growled, dead serious.

"Ah, it's like that, is it?"

Tommy couldn't have come up with anything better to get Mason to back off. The hostility dissipated, leaving indifference in its wake.

"Not at all. Knock yourself out." Mason spun on his heel, calling over his shoulder, "I'll be outside, giving my statement to the police. Text me if you want to have a beer sometime, Tommy."

Ice settled around Shonda's heart, numbing the ache. It allowed her to remain unaffected and casual when she faced her new champion.

"Let me know if you need a ride," he said gently, full of the easy kindness he'd always possessed.

"I'd take you up on it, but Eva has the spare set of keys to my place." She offered a small smile. "Thanks, though."

"So, you and Mason, huh? It's hard to believe."

Her brows drew tight. "Why?"

"You've always been a nice girl, and they're not really his thing."

His innocent comment was like a dagger dipped in acid, then plunged straight into her fucking chest. She managed a sickly smile and reached for the phone receiver on the wall.

CHAPTER
SEVENTEEN

Valentine's Day sucked, pure and simple. The holiday was created for saps and die-hard romantics. Commercialism at its finest. A day to spend an ungodly amount of Benjamins in an effort to impress. Who really believed expressing one's emotions with a too-expensive gift or over a dinner would get and hold the girl? It made love between couples transactional.

No, thanks!

The business line rang, jarring Mason from his righteous disdain and reminding him to focus.

"Fuck Cupid," he muttered. Raising his voice, he called out to Todd. "Hey, how about you do your job instead of flipping through a magazine, and answer the phone?"

The meathead paled in the face of his irritation. "Sure, dude. Sorry."

Technically, Mason should be the one apologizing, but if he gave an inch, Todd took an entire fucking football field's worth of yards.

Since Erica's stabbing, Mason had been doing double duty. But he didn't blame Zack for refusing to leave her side. His brother was in love, and the threat to Erica still existed. With Dane and him taking up the slack for the business, Mason didn't have time to take a piss, much less pretend he was the romantic sort and shower anyone with paper hearts.

It was his primary excuse for not seeking out Shonda to apologize. The gentlemanly thing to do would've been to make sure she wasn't suffering ill effects from last week's mugging, but she had others, like her family… and Tommy.

The real truth lived in his ire at her relief when his cousin had hugged her protectively, as if she required saving from *him*.

Mason swore under his breath at the bullshittiness of it all.

As if he would ever hurt her!

Granted, he'd probably looked exactly as he felt, as if he wanted to rip Tommy's arm from its socket and stuff it down his throat. Taking umbrage at another man touching her was to be expected, right? Shonda had been sleeping with him and should be loyal.

"Loyalty doesn't exist outside immediate family," Mason reminded himself for the millionth time.

Unable to remain seated, he shoved back his chair and strode to the wall of windows overlooking the parking lot. It was pretty empty for this late in the day. Apparently, all the saps and diehards were still smarter than he was, at least when it came to playing the romance game, anyway. They had someone to go home to at the end of the day.

And wasn't being alone the root of his problem?

Shonda had made him care. Made him remember how fun it was to be in love—when it was good, before the ugly end.

He didn't love her, and maybe he wouldn't ever catch feelings, but he *did* care.

Envisioning her home alone, without someone to make her day special, bothered him. The only visual more troubling was the possibility she wasn't alone. She might've taken Tommy up on the ready invitation he'd been silently offering that day. Perhaps a guy like his cousin was simpler, less complicated, and easier to love.

Mason scoffed at the drivel clouding his brain. If he kept it up, he might as well tattoo her name on his arm.

Having made up his mind to return to work, he pivoted on his heel.

And hesitated.

He should definitely check on her. Perhaps scavenge whatever the local florist had left, and bring her flowers. Gourmet chocolates, too. Both would go a long way toward making up for his craptastic behavior.

The sheer irony of his situation? The night of her mugging, he'd been moody with Valentine's Day fast approaching, and although he wanted to spend it with her, he didn't want her to get the wrong impression.

He needed a decent night's sleep, and those only seemed to happen when he cuddled her close. He shouldn't be opposed to using classic romantic tools to grovel, right?

Fuuuccckkkkk!

At least Zack and Dane weren't bearing witness to his vacillating back and forth. He'd never hear the end of it.

Resolved to see Shonda, Mason hurried to his office, shut off his computer, and stepped into the reception area.

Dane was reclined with his feet up on the desk, a magazine in hand.

"What the hell are you doing here?" Mason asked irritably.

"Waiting for you to come to your senses and take your smokin'-hot girlfriend to dinner," Dane replied, not bothering to look up from whatever held his attention.

"She's not my girlfriend," he snapped.

For the longest minute, his brother stared, his expression indecipherable, before shrugging and perusing his magazine.

"She's not!" Mason insisted, feeling weighed and wanting.

"Then you won't be bothered by her going to dinner with Tommy tonight."

Mason ground his teeth against the stinging sense of betrayal. Theirs was a goddamned fling. So what if she moved on first?

"Over my dead body," he ground out.

Yes, he'd struggled to hold his response back, failing spectacularly. But fuck it.

Dane's laughter followed him to the door.

Mason stormed back. *"What?"*

"You're in denial, bro. Besides, Tommy's over by the free weights."

Mason's gaze shot to the mirrored wall behind Dane to ascertain the truth.

Sure enough, Tommy was at the start of a workout. One Mason had designed for him.

The tension eased from his shoulders, but his desire to strike Dane was overpowering.

"You're a *dickhead.*"

"And you're an asshat," Dane countered with the bird and a mocking grin. "We all have our cross to bear."

Since the urgency to stop Shonda from dating Tommy was gone, Mason rested his elbows against the counter and relaxed. "Why'd you lie?"

"It was only a half lie. Shonda *is* at home getting ready to go out." Dane's smile was pure evil.

Straightening, Mason glared. "With who?"

"Me."

The desire to rearrange his brother's features was a visceral reaction to his taunt. Rage was eating him up and stealing his ability to reason or be civil.

Dane's eyes were crinkled with amusement as they watched

him. "I played the woe-is-me card. She decided to have pity and keep me from wallowing over my lost love."

"What lost love?"

Dane's wicked grin widened.

"Wait, why are you still here if she's expecting you?" Mason demanded, his fury fog clearing. "Are you standing her up?"

With his head half-cocked, Dane shot him a "you're the dumbest fucker on the planet" look.

Mason's brain caught up, painfully slow. Its ability to think logically kicked back into gear, and he removed his self-disgust from the shelf, dusted it off, and replaced it in a position of honor.

"Thank you, dickhead."

"Anytime, asshat."

SHONDA CHECKED herself out in the full-length mirror and ran her hands down her hips, smoothing invisible creases. The dress was a scandal waiting to happen, and she loved it. A blood-red knockout designed to hug her curves and put a man's imagination to shame.

Eva had swept in earlier, a Cat-5 hurricane in heels, pretending the months-long silence was just a blip in their otherwise glittery mother-daughter fairytale. She'd insisted on a shopping spree, dragging Shonda to her favorite high-end boutique to make amends with someone she couldn't quite bring herself to understand. With laser precision, she'd plucked the stunning red number from the rack and handed it over.

The material was the answer to every unspoken desire. And the moment the sleek, silky fabric slid over Shonda's skin, it was game over. Eva might be a master at emotional evasion, but damn if she didn't have an eye for fashion. One win in a sea of epic maternal failures.

A knock sounded at the front door, pulling her from the mirror. She glanced at the clock.

Dane was twenty minutes early.

Luckily, she was habitually early, and she only had to slide on the matching ruby stilettos to complete her ensemble.

"A few extra seconds won't kill him," she said aloud.

Besides, if she had to endure the awkwardness of a sympathy date, she might as well look incredible doing it. It was doubtful he'd notice or benefit from it since he was heartsick over his breakup.

But Eva's rule lived rent-free in her head: always dress your best, no matter what life throws at you.

Shonda fastened the tiny buckles at her ankles, took a final breath to steel her jittery nerves, and crossed to the peephole.

Broad shoulders, tailored jacket, angular jawline.

Yep, definitely Dane.

But her body didn't quite buy it. An electric charge danced beneath her skin, making her buzz before she was halfway across the room. Shaking off the sensation, she flung the door open with a ready smile.

Shit.

Wrong man.

Her heart kicked against her ribs, half in fury, half in surrender.

"What are you doing here?" Her tone was sharper than intended.

Mason didn't speak as those dangerous eyes swept the length of her body, lingering on every place they shouldn't. The passion in his gaze wrapped around her, sucking the air right from her lungs. When his attention dropped to her heels, he smiled. Every single one of her traitorous nerve endings lit up.

"Those are *great* fucking shoes," he said roughly, as if the compliment had scraped its way out of his throat.

Her body, the traitor, reacted instantly. Warmth rushed up her neck, her thighs tightened, and a flutter began low in her belly. Either he was a goddamn wizard, or her standards were somewhere beneath a cat's belly in a crawlspace.

"Th-thanks."

And now she was stammering. Fantastic.

She fought to reclaim a shred of composure. "Where's Dane?"

Mason braced his hands on the doorframe and leaned in, acting as if the space was his and she was his woman.

She sure as fuck wasn't.

"Would you be upset if I said he wasn't coming?"Mason asked curiously.

"A little. I went to the trouble of getting ready. The least he could've done was call."

Without waiting for a response, she stalked to the kitchen. Mason could leave or not. Either way, she was parched and needed a drink. She poured a glass of water and downed half in one go.

Behind her, the door clicked shut.

She finished the rest and waited, heart pounding.

Then came the muttered curse.

The door opened. Closed again.

Her body, along with her ego, deflated.

Typical Mason. He'd probably bolted after he realized what day it was, unable to stomach the implications.

With a disgusted sigh, she refilled her water and walked toward the living room.

And promptly dropped the glass.

In the center of her space, Mason was holding two dozen long-stemmed roses in one hand and a shiny Mylar *Be My Valentine* balloon in the other.

Knees trembling, she lowered herself onto the couch, too dazed for words.

Her brain scrambled to make sense of the image, but it refused to compute. What was he doing? And more importantly, what the hell did it mean?

The expectant light in his eyes dimmed. With a tired sigh, he set the flowers on the coffee table and tied the balloon string to a protruding rose stem. His movements were stilted, face unreadable.

"Happy Valentine's Day, Shonda." His tone held no arrogance, no seduction. Only the awkwardness of a man in unfamiliar territory.

As he stepped around her to go, Shonda's heart lurched. It occurred to her that he might interpret her silence as a rejection.

"Mason."

He paused in the foyer.

"Don't go." Her voice came out broken. She repeated herself, louder this time.

Wordlessly, he turned the lock.

Pulse spiking, she ran to him and jumped into his arms.

Their mouths met in a clash of hunger and regret, with noses bumping in their haste. This week had been too damn long, and only with him did she feel this alive.

Her fingers worked at his tie, tugged at buttons, pushed aside fabric. One arm curled around his neck, her hand fisting in his thick dark hair; the other slipped inside his shirt and pinched the sensitive nub of his nipple. He groaned and slid his hands beneath her dress, exploring until they found the lace barrier that barely qualified as underwear. She moaned against his mouth, and her body melted into his touch.

No one made her feel as desired as Mason. Not before. Not since. Perhaps no one could. Mason's special brand of magic was the exact reason she had difficulty letting go.

"I intended to take you to dinner," he murmured against her jaw.

She barely registered the words. "Huh?"

"Dinner," he repeated, tongue flicking the shell of her ear.

"I'm not particularly hungry. Are you?"

"Ravenous."

Shonda arched back, meeting his eyes.

Pure molten lava.

Her thighs tightened around him. "But not for food, right?"

He gave a low laugh, then winced. "You might want to ease up, love. My internal organs would like to survive this evening."

A surprised giggle escaped her. She loosened her grip.

"Take me to bed, Mason."

"Ah, those are the sweetest words I've ever heard."

CHAPTER

EIGHTEEN

fter two rounds of toe-curling, stress-busting sex and a quick shower, Mason offered to take her out for a late dinner.

"If it's all the same to you, I'd rather order a pizza and stay in," she said. Her energy was depleted from a long day of work and their bedroom calisthenics. "Unless you had your heart set on going out."

"Nope, pizza works for me. But I'm definitely taking you out soon. I'm going to insist on that dress, minus the underwear."

"I've never gone commando," she admitted, lifting the wineglass he'd poured for her.

THE ACTION of his reaching for his phone was arrested mid-stretch. He glanced back over his shoulder, expression caught somewhere between disbelief and delight.

"Never?"

She shook her head and bit her lip. "Never."

"Dear lord! First you didn't know what the Mile-High Club

was, and now this? Your sex education is lacking in all the best ways, love. We're going to rectify that. Soon."

"If you haven't rectified it by now…" She shrugged, guzzling her wine and stretching to refill it.

He grinned, climbing from their nest to cross to her bookshelf. When he settled back in, he had their old school yearbook. Flipping through, he paused now and again to study a photo.

"What are you doing? Seeking to relive your glory days?" she asked curiously.

"Pfft. Not hardly."

"Really?" She rested her head on his shoulder. "I'd lay odds there's a Sharp on every other page, with you beating out your brothers in a two-to-one landslide."

"Funny," he replied dryly.

Pinching his side, she added, "I'll go further and say you don't let anyone come to your place because you don't want them to know you have your high school and college jerseys in shadow boxes hanging around the bedroom."

He snorted. "You have me all figured out, don't you?"

"Yep." She laughed, snuggling down into the covers with a jaw-cracking yawn. "Seriously, what are you searching for?"

"The last time I was here, I noticed this on the shelf. I thought I'd see what younger Shonda looked like."

She groaned. "And you had to start with my freshman year? You couldn't pick my senior year, when I'd lost the braces and developed breasts?"

He stared at her as if the concept of her being ugly was foreign to him. "You're lying."

With a resigned sigh, she leaned in and flipped a few pages, then tapped her picture.

Though his face was expressionless, he missed nothing as he studied the photograph.

Admittedly, not one of her finer days.

"Yeah, who wants a flat-chested teenager when they could feel up your glorious tits in person?" he said as he tossed the book and dove for her.

They wrestled for control of the covers, and when he pulled her on top of him, their laughing gazes locked.

God, she loved him. The feeling was bittersweet, all things considered.

Suddenly, kidding didn't feel appropriate anymore. They'd been over less than twenty-four hours ago. But the second he showed up with the Guy's Guarantee for Valentine's Day Sex package, her good sense abandoned her and her body assumed command, locking her brain out of its control center. None of their issues were resolved.

"Mason, before you order dinner, can we talk?"

His brow arched with concern. "Why does your tone worry me?"

"Because I'm a fearsome woman warrior?"

"That might be it." He grinned. "Okay, lay it on me. What's running through that beautiful head of yours?"

She ran her finger along the edge of the sheet, buying time. If she blurted what she was thinking, it would come out all wrong, probably triggering him into running.

"Come out with it, love. Rip the bandage off. I'm a big boy. I can take it if you don't want to see me again."

His dark expression claimed differently, but she wouldn't go there.

"That's not it." Her resolve began to stall out, but she pushed through. "I *do* want to see you again. But you have to know I'm falling for you. Our time together isn't a fling for me anymore." She blew out a shaky breath. "I was willing to play by your rules —at first—but you keep changing them. It's impossible to interpret your continual return. And the sweet gestures... from anyone else, it screams caring."

He didn't reply, and the silence was weighted.

Summoning the last of her courage, she charged on. "The flowers, the balloon… please tell me what I'm supposed to take from those?"

"Why does it have to mean anything more than what it is?" His vibe shifted, becoming harder and guarded. "I brought you flowers and chocolates because every woman deserves them. The balloon was a throw-in from the florist."

Cold permeated her bones. "You didn't pick the *Be My Valentine* balloon?"

He thunked his head back against the headboard and closed his eyes.

"No."

"You really don't want a future together, do you?" she asked, dreading his response.

The flicker of hesitation in his eyes and the set of his jaw spoke volumes. She steeled herself against the coming truth.

"I told you at the airport. I want you on a level I've never wanted another woman. For longer than I've ever wanted another woman." He rolled his head to meet her gaze. "Why can't that be enough?"

Everything around her blurred, and the ache pressing behind her eyes became so intense it bordered on physical pain.

He'd been honest, and she needed to be, too.

"Because I'm too old for 'casual fucks,' Mason," she said calmly. Though where she found the Zen was anyone's guess. "I want more. I want to build something lasting with someone who loves me. I want a home with the two-point-five kids, maybe a dog, and my two fat, old cats." Scrunching the covers to her chest, she shifted to kneel in front of him. "If I wait much longer, my age starts to work against me. I'll be middle-aged, with no prospects and a uterus that might be entering hostile territory. Can you understand where I'm coming from?"

His reply was soft, nearly reverent. "I can."

"And?"

"I can't give you what you want."

Her lungs locked, and she had to force herself to nod.

"Fair enough. Then I'm going to ask you not to come back, okay? I n-need to…" She pinched the bridge of her nose and tried again, steadier this time. "I need to manage the process of getting over you, and your hanging around won't facilitate a healthy break."

His lashes brushed against his cheeks as he shut his eyes. Unerringly, he clasped her hand and brought it to his mouth, pressing a kiss to her knuckles, firm and lingering. Exhaling heavily, he nodded.

"Okay," he agreed.

It was a solid minute before he released her, rose, and dressed, never pausing to check for her devastation or the arduous struggle to hide it.

"Walk me out?" he finally asked.

Plunge a knife in my chest?!

"Sure."

She slid into a robe and followed him to the foyer.

At the door, he cupped her face, leaning in to press his forehead to hers.

"Don't ever think you're not good enough, love. My leaving has nothing to do with you."

She grimaced, remaining silent.

Mason gave her a little shake. "I mean it. It's all on me. I'm the one who's broken. I'm the one who can't be fixed. You're perfect."

Her composure shattered, and the sobs she'd been holding back tore loose. He caught her as she collapsed against him, burying her face in his chest.

"I'm sorry, Shonda," he whispered raggedly, sounding as distraught as she felt. "I'm so goddamned sorry."

SHONDA COULDN'T SLEEP.

Oddly enough, the final breakup with Mason wasn't the reason she'd kept tossing and turning. Her decision, as painful as it had been, was the right call. While it hurt to make the course correction, having released her grief, she could strive to forget and move forward.

The act of quitting their toxic back-and-forth gave her clarity.

And in that stillness, her thoughts shifted to Erica.

There had been no call, text, or juicy play-by-play detailing Erica's night with Zack. Yeah, she could have written it off—had they gotten intimate, ghosting a bestie would be natural—but the silence felt wrong. Off in a way she couldn't explain, and unease slithered through Shonda, creating a persistent chill she couldn't shake. The urgency to speak with Erica was suffocating her.

She tossed beneath the covers, willing herself to sleep, but the longer she waited, the more the tension grew, coiling tight inside her stomach. Eventually, she sat up, flung back the sheet, and reached for her phone. Her thumbs barely typed out "How did" when the device rang in her hands.

The number wasn't one she recognized, but her compulsion to answer was strong.

"Hello?"

"Shonda? Hey, it's Zack." His voice was sharp-edged, bordering on frantic.

Instantly alert, she pressed a palm over her racing heart. "What's wrong?"

"Erica and I had a fight. A knockdown, drag-out. She…" His gulp was loud and unfiltered. "Look, Shonda, I'm not asking you to betray any confidences or anything, but have you heard from her? She left the hotel, and I can't find her. I've driven around town, trying to think of all the places she might've gone. I've even checked the hospitals." His hysteria was escalating. "If she isn't with you…"

The following silence was telling. Erica was in danger.

Knowing a psychopath was on the loose, she wouldn't have vanished without checking in. Under standard girlfriend circumstances, she would've shown up on Shonda's doorstep with her mascara streaked, muttering about men, demanding wine, and ready for revenge plotting.

"I'm on my way. Are you at home?" she asked, as she dragged on her jeans.

He was, and ten minutes later, she arrived at a scene straight out of a police procedural. The house was swarming with uniforms, Zack's brothers flanked him in a defensive line, and the tension was thick enough to choke her.

She walked in on him mid-meltdown.

"Why are any of you still here?" Zack shouted, hands flailing. "Go out and do your fucking jobs!"

Although Shonda wasn't surprised by his rage, Bucky Whitmore was, and he blinked at the vitriol directed at him. As a department supervisor, he usually played things by the book. But clearly, even good-natured Bucky had reached his limit. He shoved Zack hard enough to make him stumble.

"Zack, you need to calm the fuck down."

The harshness of the move and the steel tone prompted Zack to comply.

"I'm sorry," he replied after a long minute. He made a point to shake each officer's hand. "I really do appreciate what you are doing. I'm…" Raw desperation flickered behind his attempted composure as he shook his head.

If Erica hadn't been missing, Shonda might've found the

whole incident tragically romantic. The man was beside himself, unhinged with worry, and still trying to keep it together for the people around him.

"We'll find her," Bucky promised, clapping his shoulder.

Zack nodded, throat working as he tried to hold back the panic. "If you'll excuse me."

Recognizing the signs of unraveling, Shonda followed him. If she wasn't mistaken, he was about to become completely unglued.

"Breathe," she urged, sitting beside him and rubbing his upper back.

"I-I…c-can't…"

"You can, or you wouldn't be speaking right now."

With a jerky nod, he worked to regulate his breathing. Mindlessly looking for an anchor, he grounded himself by gripping her thigh.

Mason chose that precise moment to enter, and his gaze immediately zeroed in on Zack's hand. The black expression on his face could've curdled blood.

"The only reason I'm not ripping it off is because you're hurting," Mason said, deceptively calm. "After this, all bets are off."

Oddly, his possessiveness had a calming effect on Zack. In what had to be an instinctive move meant to irritate, he slid his hand slightly higher. Not quite offensive, but it drew a warning growl from Mason.

"Just making sure that's the way the wind blew," Zack said.

"Dickhead."

"Asshat."

The exchange might've passed for banter if their eyes hadn't been lit with equal parts grief and rage. When Zack stood to pace, Mason sat down beside her.

A small, quivering voice pierced the room. "Dad?"

They all shifted to find Jacob in the hallway, pale and wide-eyed.

Zack was at his side in seconds. "Hey, lil man."

"Is it true? Is Erica missing? Was it my mom who hurt her?"

Zack hugged his son fiercely, gaze landing on Dane, who stepped into view behind Jacob with an unreadable expression. He shook his head.

"Who told you that?" Zack asked.

"I heard Grandpa yelling at Grandma," Jacob said. "He said it was all Grandma's fault. That she cud-cod…"

"Coddled?" Zack supplied.

"Yeah, coddled her too much. That maybe if she hadn't hidden the fact that Mom hadn't died in the fire, this would never have happened."

Shonda managed to suppress a gasp, and beside her, Mason's face turned to stone.

Judith had known the entire time!

"Jacob," Zack said, "I need you to stay here with Shonda while I go talk to your grandparents. Can you do that for me?"

The boy gave a quiet nod.

"I've got him," Shonda said, wrapping an arm around his thin shoulders. "Come on, buddy."

Mason followed Zack out, and Shonda did her best to distract Jacob, but the raised voices from the other room made that impossible.

"Is my mom going to kill Erica?" he asked, eyes brimming.

She wished she could lie and tell him there was no chance, but the truth hung heavily between them.

"It's okay. You don't have to answer," he whispered. Clever kid he was, he'd already guessed the truth.

Her heart broke for him.

After an epic shouting match, the police cuffed Judith and

walked her out. Charlie retreated to his home to wait, and Dane assumed the task of comforting Jacob.

"Come on, Fry Guy," Dane said, scooping him up and slinging him over one shoulder. "Let's go."

Hours crawled by with no updates or new leads. Fatigue crept thicker than fog, settling behind Shonda's eyes and dulling her mind.

"Come here, love," Mason said, offering his arms as a lifeline.

For the count of five heartbeats, she hesitated, wishing she had more fortitude to stay detached. But she was stretched thin, and she craved the comfort of the man she loved, regardless of whether he returned her affection or not. Shonda curled into Mason's side, appreciating the feel of his embrace.

He cradled her head against his chest and stroked her hair with slow, soothing motions. The strong, rhythmic beat of his heart beneath her cheek became her lullaby. Eventually, sleep claimed her.

CHAPTER

NINETEEN

Mason replayed the night's events in his head, rehashing his argument with Shonda on a never-ending, torturous loop. Regret, acidic and bitter-tasting, rode him hard, but there was no going back and erasing the suffering from her eyes.

The ping from an incoming text shattered the silence. Color drained from Zack's face, signaling another dramatic twist. Dane and Bucky crowded around him. Shifting Shonda with care, Mason eased from beneath her and joined them. The photo on the screen knocked the breath from him.

Blindfolded, bound, and deathly pale, with blood streaked down her face, Erica lay on the ground.

"Jesus!" he and Dane exclaimed in unison, both thoroughly rattled.

But Bucky remained contemplative, dissecting the image with surgical precision. After a few beats, he said, "Send that to me."

The instant Zack complied, Bucky forwarded it on.

"I've sent it to the lead detective on the case," he said. With a reverse pinch, he expanded the image. "If I had to guess, I'd say

Erica's being held in a garage. See here? That's some type of floor coating."

Zack leaned in. "You're right! Look at the back wall. I can't be positive, but doesn't it look like it might be pretty dark? Like maybe the wall was burned?"

Before anyone could respond, Zack bolted for the dining room and snatched up a laptop. He entered his passcode with shaky hands and flipped through a series of photos until one stopped him.

"Here! Right here. Same coating on the floor. That's Erica's garage!"

He thrust the laptop into Bucky's hands and went for his keys and coat.

"Zack, wait," Bucky barked. "You can't rush in there. She might have a weapon and could hurt Erica if she feels threatened."

Mason could have kissed Bucky for his cool head. In this chaos, it helped to have someone keep Zack from acting on pure emotion.

"Right. What's our next step?" Zack asked impatiently. His fury was a living, breathing thing, vibrating off him. "And don't say we wait, because I can't."

With a simple tap of the phone, Dane redirected the conversation. "Why would she send this? She had to know you might recognize the place."

"Maybe she didn't think that far ahead. Maybe she just wanted to torment me so badly, she didn't consider it," he suggested.

Damn it all if Dane didn't have a valid point. The entire setup felt off.

"I'm not buying that," Mason said. "She's been extremely careful not to get caught until now."

"Fuck! You're right." Zack dragged his hands down his face and steepled his palms in front of his mouth.

His obvious torment shredded Mason's soul.

"What do we do?" Zack's question was hoarse and hurting.

"*You* do nothing. Let us handle it." To stop his protest, Bucky held up a hand. "I'm serious about this, man. We're trained for situations of this nature. You're not. I'll call it in that Christie might be holed up there. But if you go charging over, half-cocked, you could get Erica killed."

"Dammit, Buck! I'm dying over here," Zack protested.

Mason understood in a way no one could. If he were in Zack's predicament, he'd react exactly the same way. To be unable to protect the person you loved the most had to be devastating. His gaze zeroed in on Shonda, who was wide awake and watchful. One arm was wrapped across her stomach as if she were hugging herself, and with her opposite hand, she covered her mouth as if preventing an involuntary scream.

"I could always arrest you for obstruction and throw you in a cell to cool off, I suppose," Bucky said.

"Are you trying to get me back for suspecting you earlier?" Zack asked, half serious.

"Partly." His half smile flashed before his expression turned solemn again.

Zack pivoted toward the hallway. "I'm going to check on Jacob."

The next moments were pure madness as he tore through the house, screaming Jacob's name. Mason and Dane rushed to follow suit while Bucky checked the exterior of the house.

"*What the fuck?*" Zack shouted. "How the hell does an eight-year-old boy just disappear from a house with a half-dozen cops surrounding the outside and five adults on the inside?"

"Stay calm," Dane ordered.

With ice-cold blood running through his veins, Mason had to force himself to stop and think. Where the hell would Jacob go? To see his grandfather? Props to the kid for stealth, but when he found him, hopefully unharmed, Jacob would soon learn his life was too fucking precious to be risking his neck on boneheaded moves. To say nothing of aging his dad as he had.

"Do you think he might have gone to Charlie's?" he suggested.

Wasting no time, Zack grabbed his cell and pulled up Charlie's number. After a long series of rings, he shook his head. "No answer."

Dane and Zack ran for the door, and Mason stopped Shonda with an arm around her waist as she moved to follow.

"They've got it." At her understanding nod, he sat down beside her and gathered her close. How bizarre that he was the one needing comfort.

"I have a sinking feeling," she told him.

He did, too, but overcome by the rising tide of anger, worry, and pure fear, he couldn't speak. It went against his nature to do nothing, but Bucky was correct. Their interference could get Erica killed.

Approaching footsteps echoed through the house, and Mason rose to greet his brothers. Their expressions were identical: two individuals who had been sucker-punched by fate.

Mason hugged him, and sobs wracked Zack's body as the adrenaline caught up to him.

"We think she has Jacob, too. We found Charlie in a pool of blood, unconscious," Zack rasped.

"Apparently, Christie hit him over the head and texted Jacob, pretending to be Charlie," Dane clarified.

From somewhere behind him, Mason heard Shonda gasp. "Oh my god."

Yeah, his morbid thoughts exactly.

"Since our hands are tied, I feel like we should be there for Charlie," Dane suggested flatly, eyes haunted.

They all agreed.

Charlie had been a surrogate dad to them. As the local police chief, it had been well within his rights to arrest and send the young Sharp hoodlums to juvie when they erred on the wrong side of the law. Instead, he'd proved to be a positive influence and dedicated his off-time to guiding them down the right path.

"Is it possible Jacob got away? Maybe he's lost in the dark?"

Shonda's question was fragile optimism wrapped in worry, and Mason adored her for providing a flicker of light in a dark moment.

"Anything is possible." Dane's eyes softened, figuring out what she was trying to do, too.

"I can wait here, in case…" she offered.

She didn't finish, but they all heard the "in case Jacob miraculously returns" anyway.

CHAPTER

TWENTY

The message came through that Jacob wouldn't be coming back.

Zack discovered his son was in the grip of the same lunatic who had Erica. With nothing left to do, Shonda drove to the hospital.

Everyone crowded into that sterile waiting room was worried sick, and she was no exception. Not only for Erica and Jacob, but for Charlie, too.

The man had been a fixture in town since her childhood. He was also the same person who had caught her and Erica smoking a joint behind the movie theater as freshmen. Instead of hauling their butts to their parents for punishment, he'd issued a single warning, giving them a fatherly hug and making them feel they'd personally let him down. His censure had been worse than any grounding.

While she was present for news on Charlie, being near Zack meant real-time updates on Erica as well. What she hadn't accounted for, though she probably should've, was Mason's emotional retreat. Apparently, he'd met his comfort quota and slipped back into his Fortress of Solitude.

Fine. She was long past the shock of Erica's kidnapping and didn't need his attention to stay upright. It was important to remember who had ended things, she reminded herself. Wasn't she the one who'd said she was done riding the merry-go-round of mixed signals?

As if she'd reached out to him with her thoughts, Mason appeared before her. All six foot four inches of rugged, maddening male.

"It appears Zack isn't returning with our coffee. I'm going to pick it up. Do you want any?"

"Sure." She cast a glance around and counted heads. "Do you want me to go with you to help carry anything back?"

"I think I can handle four drinks." His tone was clipped, making her feel foolish for offering.

"Okay. Two cre—"

"I know how you take it." Abruptly, he stalked away.

So she wouldn't chase him and beat him over the head with her bag, Shonda pressed her fingers to the bridge of her nose and counted to ten. Adding another twenty to be safe. Everyone was fraying at the seams, and strangling him wasn't considered a valid coping mechanism.

Twenty minutes passed.

Which was about ten minutes longer than it should have taken to wrangle a few cups of caffeine. Maybe someone should've gone after Mr. High and Mighty to help him manage the Herculean task of juggling a tray after all.

Not that she cared.

Other than a headache from the lack of caffeine, why should she care whether Mason needed help? He'd made himself abundantly clear. He didn't want ties.

She wasn't built to be a fuck buddy. Sure, another woman

would jump at the bait, convinced she could convert him. But Shonda had learned the hard way. Believing anyone would change their ways always ended the same, with one person brokenhearted and the other long gone.

Her faith in happily ever after was thin these days.

Her wayward thoughts chased each other around her brain on one giant hamster wheel, wearing her down. What-if. Should-she. Could-she. The loop was endless. And in the background was the bigger fear of, *God, please let Erica be okay!*

"Shonda, dear, would you mind checking to see what's keeping Mason?" Connie Sharp asked with a warm smile on her face.

Dane popped up. "I'll go. I need to make sure Zack's all right, anyway."

"I didn't ask you, dear. I asked Shonda," Connie replied. Her sweetness didn't mask the steel underneath. "You'll stay to keep me company."

Shonda liked Connie. She really did. But the woman had been all too eager to nudge her and Mason into each other's arms since they met earlier. And if Shonda found it annoying, she could only imagine what commitmentphobe Mason was experiencing. Did Connie not know her son at all? Did she believe the king of emotional detachment would willingly wade into a relationship? The poor woman was deluded if she did. The continual push would send him backpedaling in the opposite direction.

"I'll be happy to check," Shonda said, hiding a wry smile. "Be right back."

Amusement flickered in Connie's knowing eyes. It caught Shonda off guard. What had she been like in her youth? Wild? Reckless? Softhearted? Had Connie been a carefree heartbreaker, like Mason? Or staid and family-oriented, like Dane? Probably a mix of the two, similar to Zack, who seemed to laugh easily and love with every fiber of his being.

"Thank you, dear," Connie said.

"Think nothing of it," Shonda replied, dry as desert.

She found Mason leaning against the kiosk counter, fully engaged in a flirty conversation with a female employee. The woman's V-neck did little to hide the sexy lace bra or the nipples it was supposed to shield. Subtlety was not part of the barista's wardrobe.

Shonda remained torn about interrupting. Her stomach knotted as the woman laughed suggestively and bent closer to whisper in his ear. Mason's smirk didn't falter as she pressed a piece of paper into his hand. As a matter of fact, he appeared utterly relaxed.

The green-eyed monster Shonda had buried under logic and self-respect tore free and leapt straight for her throat.

"Excuse me," she called, the rudeness ringing through the quiet lull of the coffee line. "Your mother is waiting on her order, and the line's backing up. Think you could let this poor girl get back to work?"

Mason's glance swept the growing line of patrons before landing on her with a wintry weight. Her stomach pitched. Although he didn't reply, the annoyed glint in his eyes said plenty.

Shonda had overplayed her hand. It didn't matter that she'd called it quits last night. By creating a scene, she'd driven the final nail in the coffin of their relationship.

And the knowledge stung far more than expected.

He tucked the phone number into his back pocket, stepped around her without a word, and sauntered away. The effort it took to keep her expression neutral was monumental. Her only consolation was a moving line.

"Can I get a slice of lemon pound cake?" she asked politely.

If Erica could find solace in sugar, maybe she could, too.

Shonda passed a ten to the smirking barista and accepted change with a clipped smile.

Mason had vanished, for which she was grateful. Her emotional meltdown wouldn't have an audience.

Okay, maybe one witness.

Dane leaned against the wall outside the women's restroom, arms folded.

Of all the rotten luck.

"Shonda." His warm understanding made it harder to pretend.

And he had to have known. Having gotten them coffee earlier, he was sure to have seen the pin-up-worthy barista and known she was Mason's type. He'd tried to save her by offering to fetch Mason and their missing order.

"It's fine," she croaked. "Really. Do you mind?"

She gestured to the bathroom door behind him.

"Not at all," he said, flashing a roguish grin as if her world wasn't imploding.

She stepped forward, but before she could pass, his arms came around her, and his mouth covered hers.

Holy hell.

The bag with her cake hit the floor as her hands gripped his shoulders. His kiss was firm and unapologetic, coming close to helping her forget.

"What the actual fuck?" Mason's furious snarl brought a threatening energy.

In Mason's need to separate them, Dane was shoved aside and Shonda was jerked backward in a rough grip.

"If you don't want her, there are plenty of hot-blooded males who do," Dane taunted.

It was the absolute wrong thing to say to a feral person.

Mason's fist landed, breaking Dane's nose with an echoing crack.

"Oh my God!" Shonda gaped at the blood gushing down his face. "What the hell is wrong with you?"

"Me?" Mason was incredulous. "I'm not the one kissing my brother."

A round of snickers rippled through the onlookers, and his brows clashed as he registered what he'd said. Even Dane, slumped against the wall with his head angled to stem the flow, snorted.

"You know what I mean," Mason snapped.

"The last I checked, you were accepting phone numbers from coffee girls," she retorted. "You don't get to weigh in on who I do or don't kiss." She shoved him to get to Dane. "Feel free to go to hell, asshole."

"Gladly."

His angry strides helped him disappear around the corner, leaving Shonda staring after him, mind blank and heart thudding from the adrenaline rush.

"Uh, sweetheart? Any chance you could get me paper towels or napkins to stop the bleeding?"

She crashed back to earth.

"Oh God! I'm so sorry!" Scooping up the forgotten bag, she pulled out the stack of napkins and handed them over.

"I'm going to smell lemons for the rest of the day," he joked.

"I doubt you'll be smelling anything any time soon." She examined the angle of his nose. "What were you thinking with your moronic move?"

"Did you enjoy it?"

Dane's sparkling humor was misplaced, and she stared in disbelief.

His brows shot up in question.

"That's beside the point," she mumbled, warmth creeping into her cheeks.

"No, I'd say it's exactly the point. We both enjoyed it and pissed off my brother in the process. Win-win, wouldn't you say?"

"There's something seriously wrong with the men in your family." She grabbed his hand and tugged. "Let's go. We need to find a doctor. I don't like the angle of that nose."

"Yeah, it hurts like a bitch."

"Well, if it's any consolation, you took that shot like a fucking champ. Anyone else would be out cold."

"Is it any wonder why I adore you?" he teased.

"Come on, Romeo."

He slung an arm over her shoulders. "For support."

"Uh-huh." She jerked to a halt as she recalled why she'd sought Mason in the first place. "Oh shit."

"What?"

"Your mother is going to murder me."

"Not hardly. Who do you think gave me the idea to kiss you?"

Shonda's mouth dropped open. "No!"

Dane's answer was a shit-eating grin.

"She's the devil." Ten paces later, she stopped and scowled. "Wait. You didn't want to kiss me?"

"Are you serious right now?" he scoffed. "Hell yes, I wanted to kiss you. More, if truth be told, but you're Mason's girl."

"Now we're adding delusional to your family's flaws," she said sourly.

"The two of you can keep pretending, but the rest of us have eyes."

While they waited for the doctor to set his nose, Dane clasped her hand and said the one thing that stopped her inner spiral.

"My sophomore year, you walked down the hall in your cheerleader uniform, ponytail bouncing in time to the hemline of your sexy skirt. I had to carry my backpack in front of me for a full fifteen minutes to hide what it did to me."

Shonda ducked her head and bit her lip to hide a grin.

"Shonda?" His deep, serious tone brought her gaze up. "It was worth the broken nose."

She smiled. "You say that now."

"I'll say it forever."

"Why couldn't you have been the brother I fell in love with?" she asked with a heartfelt sigh.

The second it left her mouth, she wished she could snatch it back.

But Dane didn't flinch or appear surprised by her slip. "Timing. If I'd been your flight mate, you wouldn't have looked twice at him."

"Probably." She squeezed his hand. "Thanks for not making it weird. And I'd appreciate it if you didn't say anything to him about…" She gave a vague wave, unable to mention love a second time.

"Mum's the word." He smiled, then winced. "You owe me TLC. Caring for me should piss him off more."

Shonda barked a laugh, and thanks to Dane, she had the feeling she would be okay. Eventually.

CHAPTER

TWENTY-ONE

Connie came in search of Dane, replacing Shonda in the procedure room. She assured her any blame was on Mason for his poor behavior.

With no further duties to occupy her, Shonda drifted back to the waiting area outside Charles's ICU. Mason was parked on the far side of the room, arms folded, scowl firmly in place, as he projected icy disapproval.

Curbing her desire to tell him off, she sank down and closed her eyes.

Thankfully, Zack returned, taking a seat beside her, effectively breaking the oppressive spell of Mason's silent fury. But as the hours rolled on, the oddness of his behavior set her on edge. Zack wasn't his usual engaging self, and his silence, added with the covert glances at his phone, was a dead giveaway.

"You're awfully quiet," she murmured.

He shot her a guilty look, and she leaned in, keeping her voice low. "What are you planning?"

He darted a quick glance around before returning his gaze to hers.

"Nothing."

As if. Did he think she'd fallen off the turnip truck yesterday?

"You are, and I want in on it," she insisted in a harsh whisper, slashing a quick look at Mason before refocusing on him. She nearly laughed when Zack shot him a grin.

Mason averted his face.

"Nicely done," she murmured with an appreciative smile.

"Years of practice."

"Your brother is an easy mark. Now spill."

"You aren't going to let this go, are you?" he asked with a weary sigh.

"Not on your life."

As he studied her, Shonda forced herself not to squirm. Did he see a pathetic excuse for a woman who had outstayed her welcome to steal longing looks at his clueless older brother? She hoped he considered her as nothing more than Erica's concerned best friend. Anything else would be humiliating.

Another check revealed Mason glowering at them.

"What's he so angry about?" Zack asked.

"He probably thinks I am going to seduce you to the dark side like I did to Dane," she quipped, making no effort to keep her voice down.

Zack sputtered. "You and Dane? What did I miss?"

"While you were outside, your mother sent Mason for coffee. When he didn't promptly return, she sent me to find him," she explained. "Connie had the bright idea to convince Dane to steal a kiss. Mason broke his nose."

Zack laughed for the first time in hours.

"It's not funny!" she exclaimed.

He laughed harder as Mason surged to his feet, flipped them off, and stormed out the door.

Shonda giggled. "Okay, so maybe it's a little funny."

"I wondered where they were. Thought maybe they were making a dinner run."

"No, your mom drove Dane home. She said she wanted to take a nap, but would return with food for everyone."

"So you've been stuck in here, subject to the silent treatment for the better part of the day with my idiot brother and me. Poor girl."

Waving impatiently, she said, "Okay, enough stalling. Now we're alone, tell me what's going on? And don't you dare say 'nothing.' I want to help."

"I can't involve you in this, Shonda." He popped up to pace. "Christie is clinically insane. It's impossible to know what's going on in that messed-up head of hers."

"I'm involving myself. Erica's the only family I have left. We're sisters of a sort," she insisted.

As a kid, Shonda had spent many holidays alone. Eva was always gallivanting to places unknown, and Luigi rarely showed, claiming the restaurant couldn't survive without him. As she got older, Shonda would drive to Erica's house to hang out.

Erica was her person. The closest thing to a sister she had.

Wordlessly, Zack unlocked his phone, pulled up his messages, and gave her the device. The photos were horrifying, and Shonda cried out.

"Ohmygod!" Erica's battered and bloodied face triggered her vomit reflex, and Shonda swallowed hard. "Have you shown these to the police?" she asked.

"Not the recent ones. Christie wants me to meet her. Alone. You can see where she intends to call me."

As she studied the background of the pictures, a half-baked plan formed.

"Zack? You know I'm an ex-Realtor, right?"

His brows dipped in confusion until the realization hit, and hope flared in his eyes.

"Tell me you recognize those rooms."

She nodded. "I believe I do. I remember taking people on a tour of the place. It's abandoned now. I think this house is part of a subdivision in Stapleton. The city condemned it a few years back."

Zack jerked her to her feet and gripped her shoulders.

"Where is it?" he demanded.

"Get your fucking hands off her!" Mason's low growl echoed from the doorway.

Shonda felt a thrill at his possessiveness, followed by self-disgust. Someone should smack her and say, "Snap out of it, you idiot!"

"Jesus, Mason. I'm not hurting her."

"But you are," Mason said, menace still lacing his silky tone.

Zack studied her, and whatever he saw convinced him Mason wasn't overreacting. Finger by finger, he loosened his grip.

"Jesus! I'm sorry. I…" He reached out and eased aside the neckline of her shirt, revealing her bruised shoulder. "What the fuck? Who did this?"

She winced and avoided looking in Mason's direction. If Zack found out they'd kept the explosion and mugging from him, he'd lose his mind.

Too late.

He lost it anyway.

Livid, he swung in his brother's direction. "You did this?"

"No, give me some fucking credit. She was mugged last week. Earlier, I forgot and grabbed her arm a little too hard."

Oddly, she thought Mason had missed her wince, down in the lobby.

"I'm sorry, Shonda." Full of contrition, Zack added, "I didn't know, and I definitely shouldn't have touched you without permission."

"Yeah, so how about you step away from her so she can fix her shirt, Mr. Grabby," Mason groused.

Infuriated by his sense of ownership, her temper erupted.

"Why should it matter to you?" Shonda snapped.

Fuck him and his high-handedness. She could damn well fight her own battles.

As she spun to leave, Zack caught her hand.

"Shonda, where's the location of that house?"

His desperation checked her flight. For him and Erica, she'd make nice a little longer.

"I'll need to check my old files for the exact address," she said. "Can you follow me back to my apartment?"

"No!" Mason bellowed, stepping between them and cutting off Zack's ready retort. "No one is going anywhere until you tell me what the hell is going on."

"Dammit, I don't have fucking time for your jealousy, Mason. Get a clue already," Zack shoved him hard, sending him back into the wall.

For a moment, Shonda feared she was about to witness the clash of titans. Two virile, pissed-off men toe-to-toe, ready to battle. But Mason surprised her by backing down first.

"I wasn't jealous. I'm not a complete idiot." He shot her an undecipherable glance. "I recognized that the two of you are planning something. Did you find where Christie's holding Jacob and Erica?"

"We think so."

"Let's go then. I'll drive."

"No. Someone has to stay for Charlie," Zack said. "We can't leave him alone."

"The doctor said he wasn't waking anytime soon. I already spoke to Mom, and she'll be back shortly," Mason informed him. He placed a large hand behind Zack's neck and guided him toward the exit. "No more arguments. Let's go."

MASON PALED upon seeing Erica's condition, and his gut churned. He'd never been able to tolerate the suffering of women, children, or animals. Perhaps his gut reaction was why he'd lashed out at his brother earlier. He refused to believe another man's hand on Shonda sent him over the insane-with-jealousy cliff. Casual lovers rarely cared to such a degree, and he sure as hell didn't. Loving a woman wasn't on his list of things he intended to do. Ever. For him, it led to lies, betrayal, and eventual heartbreak. Women didn't stick.

Perhaps he was an asshole. Maybe women sensed he was lacking in a fundamental emotion and sought it elsewhere.

"Mason, we can do this," Zack said, aware of his kryptonite but not of his tumultuous inner dialogue.

"No, it's okay. I'm okay," he stated, grim but determined.

They each selected a set of files to browse and compare against the pictures Christie had sent. As they'd finished searching the last of Shonda's files, the phone rang.

Unknown number.

Giving a gesture of "stay silent" to the others, Zack put the call on speaker.

"Hello, lover," Christie purred.

Fury clouded Zack's features, but he remained deceptively calm when he answered.

"Christie."

"Are you ready to play a game?"

"I thought we were already playing one. Haven't you drawn us into this farce against our will for the past six weeks?" he retorted.

Mason mouthed, "Don't piss her off."

Her laughter came across the line. "Yeah, it's been pretty fun."

He nodded his approval when Zack said, "I want to speak to Jacob."

"Not your little whore? You surprise me, Zack. I mean, I know you sent the kid to live with my parents when your slut moved in," she said nastily. "I thought maybe she meant more to you."

A muffled cry of pain came through the speaker, likely Christie torturing Erica.

Beside him, Zack struggled for control. "Please. Just to see if he's all right."

"Sure thing, lover."

The clip of her footsteps on hardwood indicated that she'd entered a different room. It revealed another clue: her hostages weren't together.

"Jacob, talk to your father," she ordered.

"Dad? Dad?"

"Hey, lil man. You doing all right?" Though he kept firm control of his voice, tears streamed down Zack's face.

His obvious pain brought a lump to Mason's throat, and Shonda appeared similarly affected.

"Yeah, but I think Erica's hurt. She—" Jacob was cut off by his mother.

"Enough. You've heard him. He's fine. I'll call you in an hour and tell you where to go."

"Christie! Christie, wait!" Zack shouted.

She disconnected, leaving dead air and a frantic father.

"Don't let him go. I may have something," Shonda told Mason as his brother stalked away.

He got up to trail him. "Zack."

"I need a minute, Mason," Zack snapped.

"Shonda thinks she found the house."

CHAPTER

TWENTY-TWO

"When I couldn't find it in the files, I did a reverse-image lookup on my phone. It's located at 116 Eastside Lane, in the center of Wisteria Estates over in Stapleton. I was right. That's about thirty minutes from our location," Shonda said as she adjusted her laptop screen for them.

"You're shitting me! The same address as Zack's? What are the chances of that?" Mason asked, stunned there were two listings.

"Pretty good. You'd be surprised how many duplicates there are and in fairly close vicinity, too. It made showing houses a nightmare some days."

"I'm not surprised. To Christie, it would be the ultimate joke. Any way we can get a blueprint or floor plan?" Zack asked her.

She didn't look optimistic. "This time of day, all the courthouse offices for permits and planning are closed. But let me call a friend."

Twenty minutes and an email later, they had memorized the online layout of the house.

"Pull up maps on your laptop. Let's see if we can get an aerial view of the landscape and neighboring houses," Zack directed Shonda.

"Smart," Mason muttered. His brother's clarity during this crisis revealed a whole new side to him. Who knew he had a tactical mind?

"I have my moments." Zack shot him a wry grin, but his eyes lacked any matching humor.

"No house directly behind," Shonda pointed out. "But on either side, the neighbors appear to have tall, wooden fences."

"Could we plan a backyard approach? Think she'll be on the lookout for us?" Mason asked.

Zack paused to consider, finally nodding his head. "If I had to guess, she will have stuck Erica in the front room and Jacob in the back of the house."

"What makes you say that?"

"Erica is the bigger threat if she got loose. She'd want to have her within sight at all times. It stands to reason if Christie is watching out the front for any attack, then she would have Erica tied up there, where she could keep an eye on her." Zack ran a hand through his hair in agitation. "I don't think she would view Jacob as a potential problem. She'd be more inclined to leave him alone for longer periods. In a rear room, he's far enough from the road that if he yelled, he probably wouldn't be heard." He shared a look with Shonda. "Erica wouldn't call out and risk Christie hurting Jacob in retaliation. She cares about him too much."

"I agree," Shonda said.

"Makes sense." Mason considered the angles. "Zack, I think we should call the police. A SWAT team might get in there with no casualties."

"They won't show up without fanfare. I don't trust that she won't set the house ablaze the second she sees anyone close," he said raggedly. "I can't take the risk."

They shared a worried look. Shonda was first to break the

silence. "Okay, here's what we do. I have a handgun in the safe. If you know how to use it, one of you can take it. I'll grab the first-aid kit and be waiting out by the fence line. We get Jacob out first. Have him run to where I am, if he's capable. If not, shoot me a text, and I'll come get him. That leaves you two to split up and search for Erica."

The plan was a good one, and Mason couldn't find any holes.

"Once I have Jacob, he and I will run for the car and phone the police. So you'll only have about seven or eight minutes to get to Erica from the time you release Jacob. Mason should have the gun."

"You think *he* is the clearer-headed one of the two of us?" Zack asked, apparently shocked she would believe it.

"In this case, he is. Otherwise, I would say you most definitely are."

"Thanks for the show of support," Mason replied caustically. One would think he walked around beating his fists on his chest, the way everyone spoke about him.

"Hey, you're the firm believer in people telling it like it is." Her sourness wasn't unwarranted. There was a lot he could unpack, but he didn't dare. Not only would the timing be shit, but it wouldn't make a difference in the end.

The two of them were done. They had to be for both parties' emotional and mental well-being. If he allowed himself to truly care, when she finally left him—as she doubtless would—he'd be incapable of putting all the pieces of his heart back together as easily as he had in the past. The other times weren't necessarily a walk in the park, but Shonda, yeah, if he ever allowed himself to love her, there would be no recovery. Alone was better. Safer.

"Where did you learn tactical planning?" Zack cut in. Probably afraid Mason would fall back on his baser impulses and behave poorly.

"I've helped Erica plot a few novels."

Her cheeky grin dragged a laugh out of Zack, and he hugged her.

"Hey!" Mason didn't appreciate how quick his brothers were to touch his girlfriend.

Girlfriend?

Shit. He was in deep trouble if he was thinking in those terms. First breaking Dane's nose, then getting his feathers ruffled because Zack gave her a friendly hug, and now silently staking a claim? What the hell was wrong with him? Hadn't he literally just decided they were best apart?

"Snooze, you lose, pal," Zack quipped.

"Whatever. Let's get going. We only have half an hour before Christie's next call. It might take us that long to get there. If she leaves in the meantime, we're screwed."

Mason led the way to the SUV, trying to regroup and shrug off his revelation.

BY THE TIME they arrived on the road behind the house in Wisteria Estates, Zack still had ten minutes before Christie was due to ring him.

Mason and Zack carefully walked the wooded lot as they'd discussed earlier. The backyard was wider than it was deep, which they decided could work in their favor.

Mason returned to give Shonda the all clear.

As they were heading back, he heard Zack yell, "No!" in the distance, and they took off at a run.

He gestured for them to stop, then pointed to his phone. "What I mean to say is, I don't want anyone to die, Christie."

Beside him, Shonda tensed, but other than stiffening, she didn't react. And damn if Mason didn't appreciate a levelheaded woman.

Zack's frustration was high as he improvised, saying, "She'd planned to go to Florida today. She was leaving me. Wasn't that what you wanted? Can't you just let her go? What do I have to do to get you to let them both go unharmed?"

Whatever Christie replied triggered Zack's terrified response. Never, in his entire life, had he been so shaken or pale.

Mason's gnawing worry escalated to a very real fear. But following his initial reaction was fury. That crazy bitch had thrown his family into the fiery pits of hell, and he fully intended to end her reign of terror. End *her* if he had to.

"What do you mean?" Zack asked. The tremor in his voice gave him away.

Incapable of hearing the conversation playing out in real time, Mason remained laser-focused on him. Feeling beside him, he gripped Shonda's hand and wove his fingers with hers in a show of unity. He preferred to believe they drew comfort from one another, and it wasn't him being dependent on her calm presence beside him.

In his mind, the "what if" of how he would feel in Zack's position played on repeat. What would he do if Shonda were in Erica's place? Go insane. And he'd tear hell apart to get her back.

After another minute of conversation, Christie ended the call.

"She knows we're here," Zack stated flatly.

"How the fuck…?" Mason trailed off to examine their surroundings.

Despite being heavily wooded, the lot was sparse of vegetation. Winter in North Carolina created a barren landscape and didn't allow the best concealment if one was viewing the empty area. But it was highly doubtful Christie could spot them at this distance. Which meant they'd missed something.

He released Shonda and retraced his steps, searching each tree trunk for a camouflaged cam.

And sonofabitch if he didn't find one.

"There."

"What is it?" Zack asked.

"A camera," he replied in disgust. "Why the hell didn't we consider that she'd have security measures in place?"

"She wants us to step into the backyard. And there's no guarantee she won't pull something or shoot us where we stand," Zack said, expression grave."I can't ask you to take that risk."

Before he uttered the last syllable, an explosion rocked the ground, and burning debris dropped mere feet in front of them.

"No!" Zack shouted, running for the house.

Mason tackled him right when he would have flung himself into the inferno. Years as a protective big brother had him instinctively covering Zack's head and locking him within his embrace. If let free, he'd charge into the blaze and self-harm on a lost cause.

Zack was rabid in his grief, clawing and fighting to be free. Regardless of how fucking much the fist to Mason's face hurt, he wasn't letting him go.

"Jacob!" Zack screamed. "I've got to get to Jacob!"

Wrecked, Mason rocked Zack, praying his unrelenting embrace held.

Their devastation was complete.

Hours later, while Mason answered the lead detective's questions for what felt like the hundredth time, he monitored Zack from the corner of his eye. Perched on the step at the back of the rescue vehicle, his brother was a shell-shocked zombie, allowing the paramedics to treat his minor cuts and burns. The police attempted to question him, but his dazed mind was reflected in his dead-eyed expression.

As if a power switch flipped him back to life, Zack dropped

his blanket, climbed from the back of the rig, and stalked toward the pair of body bags. His hand was on the zipper of the closet when Bucky reached him. Though he tried to dissuade Zack, he was met with resistance.

"Excuse me." Mason had stepped away from the detective, but stopped as Dane approached Zack.

He blew out a breath, confident their younger brother could reason with him.

Although he took persuading, Zack eventually climbed into Dane's black SUV.

Mason stalked over and set the full force of his rage on Bucky.

"You find her, Buck," he snarled. "I don't care what you have to do, or who you have to rough up to do it, but you fucking find that black-hearted bitch."

"Don't you think we've been trying?" Bucky fired back.

"Not hard enough!" Mason snapped, pointing at the bodies. "Not fucking hard enough! My n-nephew..." His voice broke. "My nephew lies there. Proof of your department's incompetence. And don't think for one second Christie's done. She'll come after Zack next. If anything happens to him, I swear to God..."

The threat was an implied promise, though Mason wasn't dumb enough to verbalize how badly he wanted to tear the fucking world apart. But if Psycho Christie hurt his brother, all bets were off the table.

TWENTY-THREE

Another thirty minutes passed before Mason was given the okay to drive Shonda home. He was highly impressed with how she'd stood beside him, uncomplaining, as she provided detailed information and unthought-of insight to the officers. But she'd been swaying on her feet, and he had called it quits. Odds were, if law enforcement didn't have enough with the first three rounds of questioning, a fourth wouldn't suddenly solve the crime and direct them to Christie's whereabouts.

He pulled into her complex's parking lot and cut the engine.

Mutually drained, they stared at her building in silence. Minutes ticked by before either found the energy to move.

"Come on," he said, his voice raspy to his own ears. His damn throat ached like a bitch from the rush of smoke. "I'll see you inside."

"You don't have to."

"I do," he argued, shifting to meet her devastated eyes. "For my own peace of mind, Shonda, I really do."

Once they were out of the vehicle, Mason reached for her

hand, gripping it tightly as they made their way up three flights of stairs.

"I'll go in and check everything out. You wait here, and please, keep your phone in hand," he said.

"Do you really think Christie will be in my apartment?" she asked with a furrowed brow.

She was right to be skeptical, but Mason wasn't fucking around with anyone else's safety. Especially not hers.

"I don't know what to think," he admitted. "In addition to the mugging, your car being blown up, and your mother's house fire, we're dealing with a fucking mad cow."

"Good point." She tucked her hands in her coat pockets. "I'll wait."

After satisfying himself that no one was hiding in the apartment, he announced the all clear.

"Be sure to reset your alarm," he reminded her.

"I'm not a child, Mason," she snapped. Fatigue and grief drew her mouth down, but her eyes snapped with annoyance.

If he had the energy, he'd have grinned at her fire. She was beautiful despite the soot and filthy hair.

"I know you aren't." He hauled her close. "And I'm sorry about Erica, love. I know she was a sister to you."

"I can't believe she's gone," she choked out. "We rarely went a day without talking. To think that she…" The catch in her voice slayed him, and his heart ached for her. "And poor Jacob," she whispered. "I don't know how you're upright."

The dam burst, and sobs wracked her body.

Barely inside the doorway, Mason slid to the floor with Shonda cradled in his arms. Between hiccuping sobs and sniffles, she relayed another favorite story of her and Erica's girlhood exploits. She recapped their lives, recounting humorous and poignant moments. Each telling of a poor rich girl's loneliness.

Mason swiped at the dampness on his cheeks.

Two people near and dear to him had lost the people they loved most in the world. Fuck if he didn't remember what the devastation felt like. He was only eighteen and hadn't yet graduated from high school when he got the call about Melanie's accident and resulting death. He'd been wrecked.

Looking back, it felt like another lifetime—as if the tragedy had happened to someone else.

Yet he continued to allow the past to dictate his future, didn't he? And the reason why escaped him. The idea of gambling with his heart a second time made him queasy. Look how it had turned out for Zack. The Sharps had always been unlucky in love, and based on today's events, they always would be.

Mason glanced down. Shonda's head was cradled in the crook of his elbow, with her cheek pressed against his chest. The ghostly lines of her despair had left tracks in the ashy residue lingering on her cheeks. Pressure built in his chest, and his pulse hammered uncontrollably, giving him the shakes.

Leftover adrenaline or terror of the drowsy female in his arms?

Panic boiled up, cooking him inside out.

Because of his cursed inability to love, changes had to be made. Shonda was right when she said they needed a clean break. It crushed him to acknowledge it, but there would be no more coming back for another hot, steamy weekend. It didn't matter that sex with her was the best he'd ever experienced or that cuddling her made him feel more complete than he'd ever felt with anyone. If he waited any longer to walk away, his ability to end things would be compromised. And he'd be sure to drive home the point that any problem lay entirely at his door, not hers. Never hers.

Having determined the best course of action, Mason rose, hefted her up, and carried her into the bedroom. One last time, he allowed himself to experience the guilty pleasure of undressing her, running a warm washcloth over her petal-soft skin, and tucking her into bed. And because she was sleeping, no one called him out on his sentimentality. He certainly wasn't going to tell on himself. Hell, he could barely own it.

Dropping a quick kiss on her forehead, he shifted to leave. Her murmured protest created an unending ache.

"Mason?"

"Yeah?"

"Will you stay the night?" Her hopeful question unmanned him, and he closed his eyes against the sting of tears.

"No. I need to see how Zack is holding up." Only a half lie, he told himself.

"Oh, okay."

The instant understanding was another lash on his black soul. How was one woman so damn forgiving? Regardless of her humiliation at the coffee kiosk today—God, was it only today?— she sought his comfort.

"Shonda—"

"Don't say it." Her sigh was soul-weary. "Not tonight. Please."

"How do you know what I was going to say?" he asked.

"It doesn't take a genius. There's goodbye in your voice." A hiccup in her last word indicated her struggle to remain strong.

And coward that he was, he didn't turn, too afraid to witness her pain.

"Goodbye, Mason."

The finality had him spinning around.

Too late.

She'd already rolled over, presenting her back and shutting him out.

"Shonda—"

"If you'll lock the door on your way out, I'd appreciate it."

"I can stay," he found himself offering.

"No, thank you. I'm not a fan of pity. And I'm sure it's past time you left. You've got to be crawling out of your skin to be free right about now."

"Sho—"

She hissed her rage as she sat up. "Have some goddamned decency and *get the fuck out already!*"

He reeled in shock.

GOD! Why was he lingering?

If he didn't leave, Shonda would lose it—worse than she already had.

Her breakdown over Erica and Jacob was justified. Who wouldn't cry for a dead friend? But soon she would be a bigger mess. And all because she loved him. Mason, the King of Casual. A man who didn't return her feelings.

Unrequited love was a kick in the teeth in the best circumstances, but the added embarrassment of crying in front of him, for him, was oh-so worse.

Breath suspended, she counted the seconds until he headed out of the bedroom. Her broken exhale was a mix of disappointment and heartache.

She'd survive this.

There was really no other choice, was there?

Her pain was too great, and she let the tide sweep her out to sea. The bulk of her sobs were for Erica, with quite a few self-pitying ones thrown in for herself. Her best friend in the world, the woman who knew her better than anyone and the only person who truly loved her, was gone. How was she expected to cope?

Abruptly, she sat up.

Erica's parents!

She had yet to deliver the horrific news. And dear God, she didn't know how to break it to them. The Suttons had doted on

Erica. Detailing their daughter's grisly murder by some psychotic bitch would kill all three of them.

Shonda crossed to the bathroom to splash water on her face. She refused to meet her ravaged gaze in the mirror.

Wasn't it a damn good thing Mason had left?

Her resemblance to a misshapen gargoyle was revolting, resulting from her crying jag. Swollen eyes, red-tinged eyebrows, a nose to rival Rudolph's… And currently, she was a full-blown mouth breather, thanks to her stuffy nose.

She winced when she finally caught sight of her reflection. Tossing down the hand towel, she grimaced. What the hell did any of it matter? Eva wasn't here to scold her for not crying prettily enough.

Misery required a pint of sea salt caramel gelato, and she was certain she had one in the freezer. Junk food was the only way to truly drown her sorrows without taking a long walk off a short pier.

Of course, at some future date after gaining fifty pounds, she'd need to buy a gym membership, but maybe by then she'd be unrecognizable to Mason. For sure, he'd do his damndest to forget her existence.

Yeah, no gelato. She couldn't risk the calories. Comfort could be found in booze instead. As far as she knew, vodka was low-cal.

Erica could have told her. She'd been the Research Queen.

A second round of grief blurred her vision as she blindly stumbled her way to the kitchen.

A dark figure by the island blocked her path.

With a bloodcurdling scream, she transformed into a ninja warrior, kicking and swinging, fully intending to gouge her intruder's eyes out.

"Jesus, Shonda! It's me!" Mason backed away, hands up in surrender.

"What the hell, dude? I thought you'd left," she screeched.

Grabbing her side, she bent to catch her breath. "Christ alive and his holy grail! What were you thinking?"

"I couldn't leave you. Not like that."

Fucking great. He felt sorry for her. Exactly what every girl wanted. *Not.*

"I absolve you of all guilt. I'm fine, and I want to be left alone."

Uncomfortable under his watchful gaze, she averted her eyes and stormed to her liquor stash.

A minimum of two shots was imperative before making the dreaded phone call to the Suttons.

"Shonda—"

She rounded on him like the wounded, angry animal she was. "What do I have to say to get you to go? Leave! Get. The. Hell. Out!"

"No."

He'd stated it so matter-of-factly, she wasn't sure she heard properly.

"Excuse me?"

"I said, no," he replied succinctly. "I'm not leaving."

"The fuck you aren't!" she raged.

"You can be as mad as you want. It won't change the fact I'm not leaving you at a time like this."

"You are the most contrary sonofabitch I've ever met. Do you know that?" With jerky movements, she yanked open the cabinet, grabbed the vodka, and drank straight from the bottle. "Fucking arrogant asshole."

CHAPTER
TWENTY-FOUR

Over Mason's propped-up feet, he watched the Shonda Show. He nursed a single beer, because at some point after about four or five mouthfuls of vodka, she'd decided she didn't want to drink alone. But getting drunk with her wouldn't be smart. Before morning, she'd need assistance—most likely holding her hair as she emptied her stomach's contents, and then to make it to bed.

She was so enraged at him earlier that she'd failed to realize she was clad only in her lacy bra and ass-hugging boy shorts. He'd figured it was kinder not to point it out and embarrass her.

With a grin, he took another sip.

First, she'd toasted to Erica. Next was Jacob, Zack, the imminent death of Christie if Shonda got a hold of her, and anything else she could think to drink to. Even sloppy drunk, she was a sight.

"Oh! I froggot to crawl the Shuttonsh!" she shouted, weaving and bobbing toward the counter.

Mason was up and heading her off before she got halfway.

"Uh, love, it can wait until morning." Also, he had absolutely no idea what she'd said.

"They're gonna be sho shad," she cried pitifully.

Ah, Erica's parents.

"I'll tell you what. Why don't you give me their number, and I'll call them?"

"Shrood be me."

"I get that, but it might be hard for you to explain right now, love." He steered her back to the sofa, mentally chanting, "I will practice constraint," as she shifted and wrapped her arms around his neck. Yeah, he might wish to bury his grief in sex, but it didn't mean others coped the same way.

And there was always the issue of consent. He wasn't that guy. Ever.

Easing her arms down, he settled her on the couch and tucked a blanket around her.

"Shrur. Now you wanna be all nice and shrit," she grumbled, reaching for the bottle and frowning when she noticed it was empty.

"What's the code to unlock your phone?" he asked.

Palms in the air, she gave a double-shouldered shrug. If she weren't so fucking adorable, he'd strangle her.

"Okay, plan B."

Facial recognition. By the time he'd convinced her that he didn't secretly work for the FBI or CIA and unlocking her phone wasn't part of a conspiracy, he was annoyed. Anyone who'd dealt with his wasted ass in the past was owed a heartfelt apology.

As he waited for Erica's parents to answer, he worked out what he would say. They were kind when they had no cause to be, accepting his condolences and promising to contact him when they booked a return flight to Stonebrooke.

They didn't blame Zack for the terrible tragedy Christie had wrought, and Mason was grateful for their generosity toward his brother. He provided his number in the event Shonda was unavailable. With a last promise to take care of her and any future details regarding Erica, he hung up.

Next, he texted Dane to check on Zack a second time and also to fill him in on the Suttons' plans.

SCRAPING noises woke Mason from a fitful sleep.

Since wasted Shonda had a serious inability to keep her hands to herself, he'd taken the couch. It allowed him to keep an ear out in case she needed him. His plan had been to stay awake, but he dozed off. As the scraping continued, he struggled to get his bearings and determine the sound's origin.

He tilted his head.

The front door.

If he didn't know any better, he'd swear someone was picking the lock.

Soundlessly, he rose and padded to the foyer.

The door eased open an inch, making it no further than Shonda's ridiculous security stick.

Last night, she'd insisted it would keep out unwanted bombers and pyromaniacs alike. To put her mind at ease and stop the ensuing argument, he'd shoved the damn thing under the handle.

And fuck all if the valiant little stick didn't do its job.

Heart rate kicking up, he considered his option. There was only one.

In a bold move he'd probably question for months to come, he yanked the bar free and dove for the intruder. Surprise was on his side, and he managed to spin the guy around and shove him face-first into the wall, trapping his arm behind his back.

"What the hell, dude?" the intruder cried.

"Shut up!" Mason snapped, giving the man another slam

against the drywall. "Who the fuck are you, and what are you doing, breaking into Shonda's apartment?"

"She's my cousin! I have a key for when I'm in town."

He didn't slacken his hold. "Cousin? What's your name?"

"Billy. Can you chill, man? You're ripping my arm from the socket."

Mason took stock of Billy. Golden hair to his chin, roughly five-ten, and surfer speak. He scoured his memory, attempting to recall if Shonda had mentioned him. He drew a blank.

A rough frisk came up empty except for a wallet. The guy's driver's license identified him as Billy Grant from Miami Beach, Florida.

Mason shoved him in a side chair and ordered him to stay put. "Don't move. If I have to chase you down, I'll beat the hell out of you. Got it?"

"Yeah, man. I got it," the younger man said sullenly.

Keeping an eye on Billy, Mason poked his head in Shonda's bedroom and called her name. When she didn't answer, he shouted again.

A bleary green eye popped open, struggling to focus.

"Do you have a cousin Billy?" he asked, exasperated from the hassle and lack of sleep.

"Billy?"

"Yes. Surfer type from Florida."

"Um…"

"It's a yes-or-no answer, love," he said dryly.

"Then I'd have to shay… maybe?"

It was too much to hope she had sobered up with a few hours of sleep. Mason wanted to bang his head against the wall in frustration. Right now, a guy was sitting in her living room, trying to look so damn innocent, and he could very well be the same one who had mugged her. His timing was seriously suspect.

"Shonda, I need you to come out here for a minute."

She staggered up, underwear askew. One breast was on full display, along with an ass cheek.

"Love, you might want to grab a robe."

Her owl-eyed blink was laughable, but Mason held himself in check. With a shake of his head, he rubbed the spot between his brows. He was never going to let her consume more than two drinks in the future. He didn't possess the patience for this aspect of her over-imbibing.

"Dude, I could come back," Billy offered, standing and inching toward the door.

"Park it!" Mason barked.

Of course, Bullheaded Billy Boy had to push it with another step.

"One more inch before she confirms your identity, and I'll break both your legs," Mason growled.

His last threat rang true, and Billy Boy dropped into the chair, fear in the wild eyes he cast around as he looked for an escape.

When Shonda was safely clad in a robe, albeit a slinky one, she ambled toward him. About two feet away, still out of sight of Billy, Mason stopped her. "Please fix your bra and belt your robe, love," he suggested in a low voice.

After straightening her clothing as much as she was able, she joined him for a bleary-eyed peek at her intruder.

"Billy!" she cried, throwing her arms wide as if for a hug.

Mason, having anticipated her move, stepped in front of her and secured her robe tighter.

"So you know him?" he asked.

She squinted over his shoulder. "I think sho."

And because she didn't sound positive, he gently drew her back to his chest and wrapped his arms around her. "Shonda. I need you to focus. Is this guy your cousin or not?"

"Yessh. Itsh Billy."

"I told you, man," the guy said, suddenly smug.

Mason's dislike was instantaneous. "Whatever, I need a beer."

"Could you get me one if y—"

The death glare he cut Billy stopped the bastard mid-sentence.

"Yeah, on s-second thought, I'm n-not all that thirsty," Billy stuttered.

Keeping him pinned in place with a lethal look felt like pulling wings off a butterfly, but young Billy Boy wasn't going to take advantage of Shonda in her fragile state.

In any state.

Mason recognized the type. The kid was probably running from trouble and had brought it to her door. Well, whatever was brewing would end now.

After grabbing a beer for himself and a water for Shonda, Mason returned to the living room to find her sprawled out on the couch. Discomfort radiated off Billy like UV rays from the sun.

Good.

Maybe if the little shit realized no one was putting up with his weaselly ways, he'd be quick to hightail it out of town.

Mason placed his beer on the coffee table and repositioned Shonda with her head resting on his thigh. No reason for her to be in pain in the morning. Well, other than the massive hangover she would suffer. As he smoothed the hair away from her cheek, he marveled again at the softness of her skin. God, he loved touching her.

Abruptly, he shut down that line of thinking. Not the place, nor the time.

"Okay, kid, spill. Why are you here? And why now?"

"What do you mean? I'm just here to visit."

"Yes, and I was born last Friday," Mason scoffed. "What kind of trouble are you in?"

"No, really. I—"

"Enough!" he snapped. After the trauma of the last twenty-four hours, he was on an extremely short, frayed leash. If it broke,

Billy Boy was in for a world of hurt. "Do you really think the wide-eyed, innocent routine actually works? You can't possibly be that stupid."

The guy remained quiet.

Smart move.

At the moment, Mason was tired to his very soul. With his fatigue came a cranky-ass attitude and a heightened intolerance for games.

"I'll ask one more time. If I don't get a straight answer, you're out on your fucking ass. What kind of trouble are you in?"

A snaky emotion filtered through Billy's moss-green eyes as he cast a glance at his cousin, followed by one akin to fear mingled with regret. An instant later, he pasted on a who-gives-a-shit grin.

"Okay. Let me put this another way," Mason said silkily. "What have you gotten her mixed up in?"

"Could be classified as corporate espionage, I guess."

Mason choked on a sip of beer. Yeah, definitely not what he'd expected. He would've been less surprised had the answer been drug cartel-related.

"Excuse me?"

Please, God, let him have heard wrong, for Shonda's sake.

"Corporate espionage," Billy reiterated, seemingly blasé. The surfer persona disappeared as if it had never existed. "I work for an international marketing firm based in Miami, and our advertisements contain hidden codes. It allows competitors to get insider information. What exactly they contain, I don't know. But the idea is ingenious and keeps those involved from having to meet in person. Lessens the risk of getting caught."

"Let me guess, you've used Shonda's design talent to create these ads."

"No. There are many of us skilled in ad-set creation. And if I couldn't do it, I'd sweet-talk another co-worker. Unfortunately, she was killed last week in a hit-and-run."

"Jesusfuckingchrist!" Mason breathed. "It had to do with this, didn't it?"

Billy refused to answer.

Deciding to circle back around later, he asked instead, "Does Shonda know what you're into?"

"No. Are you kidding? She'd kill me!" Her cousin seemed genuinely appalled and fearful.

"And I won't?"

The threat wasn't subtle, nor was it meant to be. Mason had no idea how much jail time Shonda would serve if she were caught and convicted of a crime she had no knowledge of. He replaced his thigh with a pillow and inched forward in his seat.

"Did you know she was mugged last week, and did you have anything to do with that?"

Though he hesitated, Billy answered. "Yes."

"Yes, you knew? And yes, you were behind it?"

"Yes to both counts."

"Why?" Mason barked.

"I was looking for a hard drive or a notebook with the new codes to her division," Billy confessed.

"So this is the same company Shonda currently works for? She mentioned they were headquartered in Miami."

"Yes, she got me my job," he confirmed. "Early last week, after Phoebe was killed, the company revamped security measures again. She was VP of Marketing and Sales in Miami, and Shonda is the only other person who has access to the database I needed."

Why the guy was so forthcoming, Mason couldn't begin to guess, but he didn't trust the fucker as far as he could throw a boulder.

"I thought her company only dealt in television and radio stations."

"Dude, they're owned by GenCon Industries. GenCon owns half the fucking world, and they're heavy into the development of cyber technologies."

Mason swore enough to make a hardened criminal blush. Yeah, he'd heard of GenCon Industries. They dominated all areas of the global tech market. If Billy, who Shonda had apparently secured a job for, was caught, it would reflect poorly on her. They might even think she was in league with him.

Wasting no time, he whipped out his cell and called John Moore, the corporate attorney for Workout World.

"John, I'm sorry to wake you"—Mason checked his watch—"so early in the morning. I need some legal advice, STAT."

"Shoot."

He laid out all the information he had on hand, peppering Billy with questions where he needed things filled in. John's advice was for Shonda to hire a damned good attorney, turn her cousin in, and throw herself at the mercy of the company heads. Having no prior knowledge of the criminal activity going on around her helped. They had the police reports from the break-ins, the car explosion, and the mugging to back up her story.

"Consider yourself hired on her behalf, John."

"That's all well and good, Mason, but she needs a criminal attorney. I'd be happy to take a back seat to whoever she hires and help where I can with corporate law. There's someone I can recommend. I'll give him a call to see what we can do to make sure she isn't affected by this mess."

"Thanks, John."

After he hung up the phone, Mason stalked to where Billy sat, smug, leaning toward gloating. He hauled the smaller man from the chair.

"Now. Let's talk about that car explosion, motherfucker," he said, planting his fist squarely in the center of Billy's face. The crunch of bone was satisfying as hell.

CHAPTER
TWENTY-FIVE

Stabbing pain shot through Shonda's throbbing skull when she opened her eyes. She slammed her lids shut and sucked in a breath. Why the hell was it so bright in her bedroom? She never went to bed without closing the blinds. Squinting in the direction of her window, she groaned.

They *were* closed.

A swipe of her tongue across her teeth indicated her cotton mouth wasn't the sole reason for the horrid taste in her mouth. At some point, she'd vomited. There was no mistaking the rancid flavor of bile. She moaned and rolled on her side.

"Too fast, too fast," her brain screamed.

The life-affirming scent of coffee permeated the air, and she'd give her left arm if she didn't need to move to get some. She whimpered at the thought of walking to the kitchen, much less standing up.

Why the fuck did her body hurt so badly?

She only recalled a few swigs of vodka. Granted, she wasn't much of a drinker, but booze had never affected her to this degree before.

Pushing up from the bed was a mistake, and she froze until the world stopped spinning.

"Death, take me now," she whispered, wincing as her voiced plea reverberated inside her head.

She sensed a presence in front of her and jumped.

DEATH WORKED FAST!

"How about we keep dying at bay for a little longer, love? Have some coffee."

Mason.

Yeah, so almost the same thing. He'd brought death to her heart in the nonliteral sense of the word.

"Not so loud," she begged.

He chuckled. She contemplated murder and would probably have carried through if she weren't in agony. In her current state, she would doubtless leave clues behind.

"Why are you here? I thought you'd left," she croaked.

He tugged at his slacks and squatted in front of her. His appearance, so fresh and utterly gorgeous, pissed her off. She could almost guarantee she looked like a crack whore after a wild night of partying. Hair in all directions, little to no makeup to hide her pale face, and mascara smeared.

She followed the line of his gaze to her skewed bra. Hastily, she straightened it and closed her robe. Had he undressed her? She eyed him with suspicion.

"I didn't take advantage—much." His wolfish grin flashed. As soon as his dimples appeared, she had to do a double-take to make sure the last of her wardrobe hadn't dissolved into thin air. In the interest of preserving her modesty, she tightened the robe's sash and knotted it. Not quite a chastity belt, but the sex ship had sailed a long time ago.

"I thought we agreed you were supposed to dial back all your sexiness," she muttered.

When he sobered, continuing to stare, yesterday's events rolled in.

Erica and Jacob were gone.

Sadness, swift and fierce, punched her in the chest, making it difficult to catch her breath. Nausea hit, not only from the alcohol consumption but from the image of her friend's charred body, along with Zack's sweet little boy.

"Oh, God!"

She shoved Mason on his ass and leapt over him in her rush for the toilet. As she crashed to her knees, he moved in behind her to hold her hair.

This is taking it above and beyond casual friendship, a little voice whispered.

Shut the fuck up, little voice! You don't know what the hell you're talking about, Shonda scolded.

When the contents of her stomach were fully purged, she shifted to rest against the vanity. Mason pressed a cup of water into her hand. As she sipped it, he ran a cool cloth around her neck and across her forehead.

"Better?"

His concern enveloped her, providing comfort on a basic level. The fingers stroking her hair, the arm holding her back against his chest, and the legs sprawled on either side of her made her want to weep. How could one person with a gazillion gallons of love to offer refuse to give it, other than pouring it out in minuscule increments? Did he not realize it reeled a woman in and made her long for permanence?

Maybe for the time it took to get through the funeral services, she could accept his scraps and lean on his unrelenting strength. And once the horror was over and the dirt had been shoveled onto the coffins, she'd send him on his way. For good.

Having reached a plan on how to move forward, Shonda nodded. "Thank you."

"I'll assume you need a shower. Do you want your coffee first, or do you prefer me to wait and reheat it?"

"First, please."

He left and returned with a mug and pain reliever.

"When you're done here, we need to address a problem," he said. His regretful tone suggested he'd spare her if he could.

Giving him a single nod, she allowed him to pull her to her feet. Catching her reflection, she winced.

"I was right. Crack whore," she mumbled.

Mason was delightfully confused as she ushered him out. The fact he hadn't made a suggestive remark or offer to scrub her back confirmed her dreadful appearance.

Twenty minutes later, feeling a step removed from the walking dead, she ambled into the kitchen. Mason, spatula in hand and apron tied around his lean hips, stood over her range, scrambling eggs.

"I wasn't sure what you could tolerate, but sometimes greasy food helps."

She dry heaved and slapped her palm over her mouth.

Turning off the burner, he picked up a plate and offered option two. "Dry toast?"

She accepted a slice and parked her butt at the counter. A muffled sound from the other room startled her. Inching back, she peeked around the wall and gasped.

Tied to a chair, with a gag in his mouth, was a very bruised and bloody Billy. His moss-green eyes, so like hers, pleaded for help.

Shonda straightened up, catching sight of Mason's grim face.

"That's what we need to discuss," he stated gravely.

Laughter exploded from her.

Sure, she probably seemed like a lunatic, but who cared? Her life couldn't be any more insane, and she should just go with the flow. With any luck, she'd be committed and given the good drugs.

"Let me guess. You suspect Billy has been trying to off me?" she said when she'd regained a semblance of sanity.

The shock on Mason's face almost set her off again. She used her mug to hide her smile.

"Well, yes. But it's a helluva lot more serious, love."

"Of course, it is." She sighed. "Because my life isn't shitty enough."

All trace of humor vanished, and she ate her dry toast in silence, chasing it with coffee.

As Mason explained their encounter, he also admitted to roughing Billy up as a warning against future attempts to harm her and helping him rethink the error of his ways when he was eventually released from prison. And sonofabitch if she didn't fall in love with him all over. Not that any good would come from falling deeper into feelings.

Her new lawyer, John, had spoken to another attorney, and together, they devised a solution for Shonda's legal woes. Luckily, there was documentation for the island incidents and the car explosion. John told them the outcome was fairly straightforward and had his paralegal type up a statement for her to turn in to the department heads as well as the human resources department.

Shonda spent the morning placing calls and hosting video chats.

Unbeknownst to Billy, Mason had caught his smug confession on his phone's recorder. The audio file helped when Shonda played it back, but not much.

"You're to report Billy's involvement to the police for his nefarious behavior and turn him over. We also expect your resignation by the end of the day, Ms. Grant."

"Understood. Thank you, Mr. Bascombe." She owed no

loyalty to her pissant cousin for what he'd done to her. "And again, I'm grateful for your lenience."

"We're sorry to lose you."

And she was sorry to be lost. None of it really mattered. Unemployment afforded her the opportunity to mourn the sister of her heart.

By the call's end, her headache had grown exponentially, and she feared her head would explode with the slightest provocation.

"So how do we do this?" she asked with a tired sigh, after closing her laptop.

Mason cut a sharp, lethal glance at Billy. "Say the word, and they'll never find the body," he promised. The threat was wrong on every level, but she enjoyed her cousin's terror.

"I'm honored you'd do that for me," she replied cheekily.

"Perhaps we should put him in your new car, blow it up, and say he was setting a second bomb."

Billy's already fear-filled eyes grew wider.

"Nah. I'm partial to my new baby. Jail is good enough. It's going to take him a while to get out for attempted murder. GenCon has a whole team of lawyers willing to send him away for the theft alone."

She approached Billy and untied his gag.

"Care to explain? I thought..." She clamped her jaw closed against the hurt. Yes, she'd believed he loved her, but he was one more in a long line who'd let her down on that front.

Betrayal was a bitter pill. She seriously had to lower her expectations of people.

Billy, sensing weakness, went for the Oscar. "I'm sorry, Shonda. I love you. You're my cousin. The only real family I have. But I needed the money," he whined, continuing until he registered she was unmoved.

She untied his legs and pointed to the hall bathroom. "Get cleaned up."

Triumph shone on his smarmy face, and he had the nerve to bend in an attempt to kiss her cheek.

"Don't," she snarled. "Don't you dare touch me." Tamping down her murderous rage, she added, "You should get cleaned up for your mugshot. Can't have anyone believing you were beaten to coerce a confession."

Ugliness replaced his elation, and his eyes darkened with hatred.

And there it was. The truth of his feelings. It shouldn't taste like ashes in her mouth, but it did.

Billy paused to sum up the new, take-no-shit Shonda, then cast Mason a calculating glance before storming down the hall.

She collapsed in the seat he'd vacated. Her palms cradled her forehead as she stared at the floor, half wishing she could cry. Yet the tears wouldn't come. She was all sobbed out.

The scrape of a sliding chair brought her head up.

Mason joined her, and for the longest minute, neither spoke. As he opened his mouth, a thud came from the bathroom. Shoving open the door, they found the window was open, the screen missing, and Billy gone.

"Motherfucker!"

Mason rushed for the front door as she peeked over the window ledge.

Billy was up and loping away.

"So much for turning him over to the police."

As the blue Maxima sped by, Mason calculated the odds of it being the one from the car lot. By the time he reached the top landing, he was in a full-blown rage. Because one, he and Shonda would probably never make out against another vehicle. Two, he was exhausted due to a lack of sleep. And three—this one pissed him off the most—Billy had outsmarted him.

He hadn't realized there was a window in the guest bathroom, but he should've checked. And really, did the kid have a death wish, jumping from three stories up? How did he not break his fool neck?

Mason entered to find Shonda was fluffing pillows and generally straightening the place. She appeared to be on autopilot.

"Shonda."

"What?"

"Why don't you take it easy today?" he suggested.

"I can't. I have to keep moving. The place needs to be nice for Erica's parents."

Her eyes were bone dry, which concerned him. She was being too stoic, too matter-of-fact when she should have been a basket case.

"If you shoot me a text with the flight number and time, I'll pick them up," he offered.

"I can get them."

"It's not a problem—"

"You have enough to do, Mason, and I'm not a fucking invalid," she snapped, savagely flinging a freshly plumped pillow down. "I can drive thirty minutes to the airport, retrieve a grieving couple, and bring them back here, all without your help."

"Look, I'm trying to be supportive here, Shonda. But I'm not taking your shit."

"My shit?" She visibly trembled with fury. "My shit? You have some goddamn nerve. This"—she waved her index finger between them—"has been your way from minute one."

She punched another pillow, and he was thankful it wasn't his face.

"'I don't do long-term. If you want this, know that it's only for the duration of our stay,'" she mimicked in a piss-poor imitation of him. But the speech sounded right. Hands on hips, she rounded on him. "Well, you know what? We've played it your fucking way. And now I'm asking you to respect *my* wishes. You don't get to pop in and out of my life on a whim, all under the guise of checking up on me. Not anymore."

Shonda's fury died out, leaving her hollow-eyed and spent.

He hated how badly it made him feel.

"I love you, Mason. And I can see by your horrified expression you don't feel the same. The thing is, after everything that's happened, I couldn't go another day without telling you." She deflated and sat. "But there are no expectations, okay?"

His heart hammered as his vocal chords shriveled up.

With a sad, decisive nod, she said, "I also know you'll run for the hills. It's all good. I swear." She closed her eyes. "But could you please go? You don't have to smooth things over or make life better for me. You can't. And I need alone time to process everything."

Part of him urged him to stay and make it work, but the strongest part of him wanted to escape, as she'd predicted he would.

"I'll text Zack as soon as I pick up Pete and Mary," she promised. "They can meet up to discuss arrangements after."

With a nod, he left, cursing himself for hurting her and adding to her grief.

CHAPTER

TWENTY-SIX

The drive to Dane's house the following day took Mason ten minutes, and thankfully, it wasn't a lot of time to relive Shonda's goodbye. Hell, even if it had been longer, he lacked the mental and emotional capacity to relive it. Sleeping the previous night had been an exercise in futility. The entire evening, he stressed about Billy returning to murder Shonda. On five separate occasions, he grabbed his keys, prepared to sit outside her building. But he wanted to honor her request. With Billy's crimes in the open, the danger had likely passed.

Mason arrived as Zack rejoined the living, and he'd barely made it inside when the slamming of a car door caught everyone's attention.

Dane admitted Bucky and another plainclothes cop, who introduced himself as Detective Fields.

"Bucky. Detective. What's up?" Zack asked tiredly.

"Zack, we're sorry to disturb you at a time like this, but may we speak with you?"

He led them to the living room.

"The coroner pulled DNA samples from the bodies found on

the scene. We'd like to test yours against the boy they found," Fields informed them.

Unease danced along his nerves, but Mason remained silent and waited for them to get to the point.

"Is that all? A phone call wouldn't have sufficed?" Dane asked.

Zack sat forward. "What aren't you telling me?"

The two officials exchanged a speaking glance.

"Buck," Zack growled.

"The DNA came back to a woman who was reported missing four months ago. We're still waiting on that of the boy."

The silence was heavy as the implication sank in.

The bodies were likely a plant, meaning Erica and Jacob weren't dead. Or not yet, anyway.

"I can go to the hospital or to the station right now," Zack said, hopping up.

"Actually, that's the reason why Byron is here. He's head of our forensic team. He brought the swab kit."

"Let me get this straight. You're saying the woman found in the ruins after the explosion was *not* Erica?" Connie asked, seeking the clarification they needed.

"That is correct, Mrs. Sharp," Bucky confirmed.

"So it is probable she is still alive." When he nodded, she asked, "If that is the case, maybe my grandson is, too?"

"Yes."

She started to cry, and Zack jumped up to hold her close. "It's a good thing, Mom."

"I know. I just… I have to tell Charlie," she said.

"No," Byron said, standing. "We want to keep this under wraps for the moment."

"But Charlie is Jacob's grandfather. He has the right to know," she protested.

"Mrs. Sharp, no one but those in this room can know we

suspect the bodies belong to anyone other than Ms. Sutton and your grandson. It could hamper our investigation and alert Christie Bauer we're on to her deception. Do you understand?" he asked, not unkindly.

"Yes, but we can swear Charlie to secrecy," she said, patting Zack's chest and seeking his support.

"He's right, Mom," he said slowly. "We need to keep this under wraps until we locate them. If Christie finds out, she might hurt them for real."

"What about Erica's parents and Shonda? They'll be here any second."

Zack cast a worried glance toward Bucky and the detective.

The smaller the circle, the more likely they were to keep the secret.

"I don't think we should tell them, Mom," Mason said.

"Mason! You can't keep something like this from Erica's parents or your girlfriend," his mother said, appearing appalled he'd actually consider such a thing.

"Shonda's not my girlfriend," he snapped. "For Christ's sake, Ma. Stop with that shit already!"

His rage came from nowhere he could discern, but he was sure as shit over the constant assumption about their relationship, or lack thereof. The entire situation was tired.

As his rotten luck would have it, Shonda and the Suttons walked in during his rant. She wasn't quick enough to mask her hurt, but she did have a ready excuse to leave.

Agitated, he rubbed the spot between his brows, wishing he were anywhere but there.

"Shonda, hold up," he ordered, trailing her outside.

"I'm fine. We discussed it all yesterday. It's not like I haven't known the score from the start. Nothing's changed," she said as she circled her vehicle to get to the driver's side. "Go take care of your family, Mason."

"Goddammit!" he swore. "I said, *wait!*"

"Good grief. Please, don't let's rehash this." Her weariness tugged his last remaining heartstring. Her eyes were dull, practically lifeless, as she said, "I'm truly fine, but it's annoying to hear you protest so loudly whenever everyone's around." She jerked open the car door. "It's humiliating because you make it sound as if I'm throwing myself at you at every opportunity. And I'm not. You know that."

"Shonda—"

"The situation is shitty, and unfortunately, our worlds are overlapping because of Erica. Otherwise, you'd get out clean. I swear."

"Shon—" He surged forward.

"Keep your platitudes, Mason. We both know there's nothing more to say, don't we?" She cast him a sad smile of goodbye. "Please tell Erica's parents I'll give them a call tonight to find out what they've planned for services."

Anxiety and guilt converged in his chest, suffocating him.

She really intended to walk away!

Her finality cut him in ways he could never express aloud.

"Erica's not dead," he blurted. "They haven't found her, but the DNA of the body in the morgue wasn't hers."

He was in deep shit for revealing the news, but his mother was right. Leaving her in the dark, regardless of police logic and his agreement two minutes ago, was wrong.

"And Jacob?" she asked.

"They've come to gather Zack's DNA sample to compare with the child's body. We're hopeful it's not him either."

She nodded and offered a tight smile. "Thanks for telling me. Have Zack or Dane text me when they hear anything more."

"Shonda," he called as she was about to duck into the driver's seat. "You're welcome to stay."

A long beat passed. "No, Mason, I don't think I am."

"You're exhausted and upset. Let me drive you home."

What the hell was wrong with him? Good Christ, could he be any more wishy-washy? No wonder she was confused. He didn't know what he truly wanted either.

Not sparing him another glance, she drove away.

It stung.

As Mason stalked back to the house, Dane stepped into view. His censure and disappointment were stamped heavily on his visage.

"Not a fucking word," Mason snarled as he shoved by him.

"Asshole."

He heard, but pretended he didn't.

He *was* an asshole. Worse.

Shonda wasn't shy about calling him out. Yet, coming from her, it almost always seemed like an endearment. And wasn't that the crux of the matter? Whenever she busted him on his bullshit, he adored her all the more for it.

Inside, his mother had whipped up a spread to feed an army. On any given day, Mason would be the first to do it justice. But not today. He couldn't force a single bite past his lips, not when his stomach churned.

And it was all because Shonda had called it quits. She'd given in and accepted what they'd had was casual.

But it wasn't. Not by a long shot.

As much as he tried to tell himself he could walk away, he always ended up back at her door. She was right. His constant return was always under the guise of making sure she was okay. But because of him, she was a hot mess.

Shonda loved him, and it was hard to wrap his feelings around the fact. Under no delusions, he realized he was opinionated, domineering, and demanding. A few nicer qualities could be sprinkled in here and there, but overall, he was no prize.

Yet she loved him.

And he couldn't let her.

For her own sake, he had to find a way to kill whatever she felt for him.

Reaching a decision, he tossed his plate on the counter, grabbed his keys, and drove to her apartment. The lights were out, and he had a moment of panic. What if she'd never made it home? Or what if Billy had come back to finish what he started?

He charged up the stairs and banged on the door, alternating fists and yelling her name when she didn't answer right away.

"Can I help you?" her neighbor asked.

"I'm looking for Shonda."

"Yeah, the whole complex got that," she said, not sparing the sarcasm.

Ignoring her snark, he asked. "Have you seen her?"

"Afraid not." With a careless shrug, she slammed her door.

"Thanks for nothing!" he hollered.

"You should make a point to read *How to Win Friends and Influence People*," Shonda commented from behind him.

He yelped his surprise.

Christ, he was on edge!

"We need to talk, and then you can tell me when the fuck you trained as a ninja."

"Why rehash the conversation? Have you not met your insult quota for today?" she asked, chockful of anger.

The new jaded attitude pissed him off.

"Knock it off, Shonda. I've never insulted you. Not intentionally, at any rate."

"Shall I count the ways?"

Banking his temper, he shifted closer. "No. I don't really care to be reminded how you think I'm a jerk. I'd like to explain."

"Even if I didn't already know, I don't care what your excuse is." She ran a hand through her hair, a sure sign of her frustration. "You're an adult, Mason, with the ability to reason.

You know relationships, if you choose to have them, take work."

"I don't want the work," he exploded. "I want it easy."

"Says every guy on the fucking planet."

"Don't lump me with other losers."

"Then don't be one," she snapped. "I've made it too easy for you for far too long. You come here, screw my brains out, remind me it's nothing more than a *casual fuck,* and then go on your merry way." She leaned forward, gaze furious as she drove a finger into his chest. "That no longer works for me. I'm not your cum-dumpster. Find another idiot to *casually fuck.*"

Her tantrum drew a crowd. While she apparently didn't care, he did. "Stop saying that. Can we take this inside? Your neighbors shouldn't be privy to our business."

"No. If you don't like it, leave."

"Woman, you are getting on my last nerve. I—"

What he would have said was cut off by a text on his phone.

"Must be someone from your hordes of women calling," Shonda sneered, stepping into the darkened apartment.

Guessing her intention to slam the door, he stuck his foot on the threshold. "Look, I have to go, but I intend to finish this."

She jerked the door wider and snatched his phone.

"Jesus!" She gaped. "Zack thinks Christie is at his house? Why doesn't he just call the police?"

"Because he's not sure."

"Your brothers intend to confront Christie to end this thing, don't they?" She didn't wait for his answer. "Come inside while I change my shoes."

He grabbed his device back.

"Oh, fuck no! You are *not* going," his tone was flat, final.

"I am. You and I can drive together and back each other up, or I can go by myself."

"You forgot there's a third option," he said silkily.

As expected, she challenged him, "Oh, and what's that?"

"I can tie you up."

She gulped in the face of his menacing grin and uncrossed her arms.

"Y-you wouldn't dare." False bravado inched her chin higher.

"Oh, love, I would dare a great many things," he whispered, inches from a kiss. "You might enjoy being tied up."

Before their mouths could meet, she shoved him. "No. Next time you come to me, it better be because you want more than a casu—"

He pressed a finger against her lips. "Don't say it. You've made your point." God, he fucking hated that phrase. Why had he ever uttered it?

"I've got to go," he said. "As it is, I'm going to be late."

"I told you, I'm going, too," she replied stubbornly.

Based on past experience, she would follow him on her own, and her insistence was more than simple contrariness. With the lost job, the near-death, and her friend's abduction, it appeared Shonda had reached a critical point and needed to take her life back. On many levels, he understood, but he couldn't live with himself if she got hurt or, god forbid, killed.

"Mason. Erica is my sister in every way that matters. What if the situation were reversed? Would you sit it out?"

Without a doubt, he'd hate himself later, but he caved nevertheless. "Fine. But you do *exactly* as I say."

"Fine," she agreed, eyes expressionless.

"You're lying," he said. "Have I ever told you how much I hate liars?"

"Have I ever told you how much I hate players?" she retorted.

"Go. Dress in all black and make sure they're clothes you can move freely in."

Suspicious, she asked, "You won't leave me?"

"No. Now get dressed. We're out of time. Zack is determined to end this tonight."

TWENTY-SEVEN

Mason drew up about a hundred yards from Zack's house. They had inched their way around the block and checked the area for the best approach, careful to avoid driving by his place. Turning around, they backtracked wherever they could. More than once, they stopped and studied the nearest neighbors' yards to be certain Christie hadn't implemented her camera trick.

Dane messaged them with Zack's suspicions and detailed their plan. Mason was to go in through the patio door. Once inside, he could sneak up and disarm Christie while Zack distracted her. Dane was the secondary backup and would stay hidden until the last possible moment.

Shonda was to lie in wait and call for help if things went sideways.

"You good on the plan? You'll listen from outside the window, and if it turns south, you call Bucky," he reiterated because she was bullheaded.

"Why aren't we trusting the police with this? Our last foray into rescuing Erica still gives me nightmares," she said.

"Zack's woman, Zack's call," he replied.

Their eyes locked.

"Stay safe, love."

"Don't do anything stupid," she whispered back.

With a grin, Mason slipped into position. Taking care to be quiet, he inched his way toward the dining room sliders. As he was passing the kitchen, he chanced a peek.

Zack's hands were half-raised, and he was visibly struggling to stay calm.

A step to Mason's right revealed Christie, who was continually opening and closing her lighter. Jacob was tied to a chair, sitting inside a kiddie pool, lost and terrified. The sight of Erica's unconscious form slumped in her seat shot his heart rate up.

Not good.

Blowing out a breath, he disabled the alarm chimes, using the app, and waited impatiently for the required two minutes for it to take effect. He was reaching for the handle when a gun cocked behind him. The barrel was pressed to the back of his head, aborting any action on his behalf.

Fuck!

Zack had been correct in assuming Christie had an accomplice.

Dane was their only hope.

"Get moving," Judith snapped.

"Neither you nor Christie will get away with this. There will be a massive manhunt. You have to know that, right?" he tried to reason.

"Do you think we care? Zack convinced Charlie to commit my daughter to an institution," she said, pressing harder. "Do you really think she'll be taken alive to be drugged and locked up until the end of time? She'll burn this whole place to the ground first."

Mason's heart stuttered to a stop.

Minus his mother, his whole world was in that house. Shonda would also be injured in a blast. His heart restarted, beating double time. Why the fuck didn't he tie her to a chair and leave her behind?

Judith ordered him to stop outside of view as she awaited her daughter's cue.

"Mason, you might as well come out now," Christie tauntingly called a minute later. Directing her next statement to Zack, she said, "I know you'd never come here alone. You don't have the balls."

"Actually, I did come here by myself." Zack was a fraction louder than he normally was, relaying the bluff to Dane and him.

She tsked. "Hmm. Well then, let's see about that. Mother?"

Mason entered, followed closely by Judith, who had a Glock jammed against his lower back. His fury at being caught was a living entity. Palpable to those around him. But unless he wanted a bullet in his spine, there was nothing he could do until they provided an opening.

His brother's dry humor in the middle of the chaos surprised him.

"Dude, you let an old woman get the jump on you?" Zack scoffed. Apparently, his inner child couldn't resist.

"Fuck off, dickhead."

Zack grinned, showing he had no hard feelings.

"Come out, Dane, or my mother shoots Mason where he stands," Christie threatened.

"He's not here," Mason deadpanned, buying him time and hoping she believed the bluff. "That pussy's at home, nursing a broken nose."

"Is that right?" she asked with diamond-hard eyes. Three beats passed. Her mouth curled the slightest bit as she whipped her gun around and shot him in the thigh.

"Jesusfuckingchrist!"

The pain was liquid fire, dropping him where he stood. Applying pressure to his wound, he prayed to whatever god would listen that she hadn't struck an artery.

Zack managed a few steps before she aimed at him.

"I told you not to move," she snarled.

Although action heroes could take a bullet with a grunt and a quip, it was a helluva lot more painful in real life. Blood seeped through Mason's fingers, and his mind grew fuzzy.

Shonda had to have heard the shot and called the police, right?

"Christie, call this off. Please. I'm begging you. Surely the neighbors heard the gunshot. The police still routinely patrol this block looking for you. They'll be here any minute," Zack cajoled.

Behind Christie and Judith, Dane shifted into position, posed with a shovel high above his head, and prepared to strike.

"Christie, for fuck's sake! Light the damned match already. I need to sleep," Erica growled.

Instantaneous fury flared on Christie's visage, driving her forward.

Dane struck.

The shovel connected with her wrist, sending the gun skittering across the floor toward Zack.

And right as Judith aimed at Dane, Shonda stepped into the view, squeezing off two rounds.

Judith fell, and Mason scrambled for her discarded weapon.

With only a single-minded concern for Jacob, Zack jerked him out of harm's way and urged him toward the back door. He spun back for Erica, but Christie beat him.

Standing over her, positioned with her thumb to flip open her lighter, she sneered.

"No!" Zack scrambled like hell for purchase on the slick, gas-drenched floor, slipping and sliding his way back to them.

And it was now or never. Mason squeezed off a round, echoing Shonda's next shot.

Stunned disbelief crossed Christie's face as she looked down at the hole in her chest, and a whoosh of air extinguished the lighter's flame as she crumpled to the ground.

With a groan, Erica eased into a sitting position, and the second she was free of the chair, she shuffled her way to Christie. There was no hesitation in her action as she promptly kicked her in the ribs.

"I hope you're dead, you fucking piece of shit!" Whack.

"Rot in hell!" Whack.

Erica got off two additional well-placed kicks before Zack pulled her to him.

"I think my ribs are broken," she said between shallow pants. "I forgot for a minute."

In the distance, sirens wailed, coming ever closer. They couldn't arrive too soon!

Woozy from loss of blood and action, Mason closed his eyes, snapping them open as he sensed movement beside him.

Judith inched closer to Christie's discarded gun.

"Don't you even think about it," Shonda snarled. With the weapon clasped in her hands, she was a goddamned Viking princess—tall, stance wide, blonde hair escaping her braid. Her fierce expression assured them she'd willingly kill without remorse.

Christ alive, he'd never seen a more beautiful woman!

Dane left to admit the police, as Shonda whipped off her shirt and tied off Mason's wound.

Later, he might blame it on the dizziness, claim he was out of his gourd, but he couldn't hold back his sudden anger.

"What the hell were you thinking?" he shouted. "You could have gotten us all killed. Yourself included."

Dane returned in time to hear. "Shut the fuck up! She saved your ungrateful ass along with everyone else in this room. Her shot was true. *Twice!*"

But Shonda didn't defend herself. She remained silent as she applied pressure to his wound until the paramedics assumed control.

And when Bucky questioned her, she relayed her version of the story with admirable calm. After, she was handcuffed, with the officer apologizing for needing to take her into custody.

"What the fuck?" Mason scowled. "She stopped a human barbecue."

"Procedure. We're taking her for further questioning." Bucky replied, grimacing.

"I don't gi—"

"It's fine," Shonda said, not sparing Mason a glance. "Let's go."

"No! *No!*" It required two paramedics and an officer to restrain him. "You aren't going to treat her like a fucking criminal for being a hero."

"Mason, if you don't knock it the fuck off, we're going to sedate you."

He whipped his head around and groaned when he saw Phillip.

His cousin served as a paramedic and was voted least likely to take shit from a patient.

"Lip, she did nothing wrong. She shouldn't be treated like a damn criminal."

"Tommy told me you had it bad. I didn't believe him." Lip glanced at his partner. "We lift him on three."

"Lip—"

"She'll be treated like a princess, Mason. No worries, okay?"

"And I don't have it bad. We—"

Again, his cousin cut him off. "You can deny it all you want, man. We all have eyes and ears."

They rolled Mason out to the waiting transport.

When he opened his mouth to argue, Lip slapped an oxygen mask over his face.

"Hey Mike, you have any elephant tranqs in your bag?"

Mason glowered.

"Ah, the man doth protest too much."

He ripped the mask back long enough to snarl. "Bite me."

CHAPTER

TWENTY-EIGHT

The detectives and milling police were courteous, providing Shonda with the opportunity to call a lawyer and an unlimited supply of police station coffee. Bucky claimed the inquisition was informal, and they only needed to line up all the events with the crime scene. In a separate room at the station, Dane detailed his own account. Detectives were also sent to question Mason, Zack, Jacob, and Erica at the hospital about whether or when they would be able to provide details for a statement.

It seemed like a lot for two psychos, but who was she to judge?

But it was over, and Shonda was exhausted. She wanted to go home, take the hottest shower known to man, crawl into bed, and sleep for a month. The last weeks had been a whirlwind of nonstop chaos.

When all was said and done, four separate officers asked to take her out for coffee or a drink sometime. Clearly, her Dirty Harriet routine was an aphrodisiac. She politely declined. Dating anyone while she felt the way she did about another man left a bad taste in her mouth.

She was headed through the lobby when it occurred to her that she had no car. Her apartment complex was a good five miles away, and she'd freeze to death before she ever made it home. The empty plastic chairs were tempting.

Deflated, she sat down.

Her phone was in her purse, which was in Mason's car, and she had no numbers memorized.

"Need a ride, babe?"

Dane lounged against the exit, as if he owned the place. Her savior.

"God, yes. I'd sell my soul for a way home," she said, joining him.

With a laugh, he flung an arm around her shoulders. "No pact with the devil needed for a warm car ride."

"Have you heard any news on how everyone is faring?" she asked.

"Erica was in imaging for X-rays and a CT scan, and Jacob is on an IV for dehydration. The plan is to watch him overnight."

A few heartbeats passed before she could summon the nerve to ask after Mason.

"He's in surgery to remove the bullet and repair the damage to his leg." Dane must've read her conflict, and he paused in opening the vehicle door. "We have time for you to shower and change if you want to head over."

"No point. I can see Erica in the morning. I'm sure with Zack, Mary, and Pete, it will be crowded enough."

"And my brother?" Dane asked gently. "He has no one there for him."

"His own fault, wouldn't you say?" The question was rhetorical. She didn't expect an answer. "Besides, he has you and Connie to care for him."

"Not me. I'm not looking after his cranky ass. My face still hurts."

She laughed because it was impossible not to.

Dane was a joy to be around. She imagined long before Mason had become embittered, he'd probably been as flirty and lighthearted as his brothers. There had been glimpses during their time together and had been part of his draw.

"Okay."

"Okay, what?"

"Okay, I'll get a quick shower and meet you at the hospital in about an hour."

FOR THE NEXT THREE DAYS, Shonda took a turn caring for Mason.

Each day, his mood grew darker, and his tone a little grimmer. And she understood why. The poor man was trapped and subject to unending drama regarding their non-existent relationship. His mother was downright relentless, droning on about wanting to see him settle down with a nice girl. How did Connie not realize she was doing more harm than good?

Dane, on the other hand, simply enjoyed busting his brother's balls. At every opportunity, he'd throw an arm over Shonda's shoulders or touch her waist. It didn't matter if she shrugged him off or told him to knock it off. Mason would still fall into a black mood.

His retaliation was as childish as Dane's behavior, which included flirting with the nurses as if he couldn't care less.

And Shonda was over their stupid games. At one point, banishing Dane.

"You need to go, too," Mason told her coldly, directly after she sent his brother packing.

"This again?" she quipped.

The immediate backlash caught her off guard.

"Jesus, Shonda! When will you take the hint? *I don't want you here.*" His eyes were darker and uncaring, as if he truly meant what he said. And perhaps he did. Mason had never asked her to visit.

Her chest ached. Literally hurt to breathe.

She'd take his "hint" and run with it, though. The truth was, they were over before they'd started, because he'd never allow more. Never let someone else close enough to alter any aspect of his well-organized, lonely life. His true feelings on the matter penetrated her thick skull. Mason, like her boyfriends before him, and her parents before them, didn't want her around. How long did it take a normal person to recognize the truth? After all, he'd been hammering it home from day one.

Stupidly, she'd allowed herself to live in a pipe dream, pretending he cared. The small, seemingly loving gestures had contradicted his claim to be a free agent, allowing her optimistic nature to feel a small measure of hope.

With a jerky nod, she spun away, avoiding eye contact with Mason's mother, who stood gaping in the doorway. Doubtless, she was equally shocked by his behavior. No mother liked to believe her son was a complete asshole in addition to being a moron.

Connie would be wrong—*her* son was.

"Excuse me, please," Shonda said with a tight smile.

Of course, Connie blocked the door, and unless Shonda intended to shove her to the ground, getting around her was impossible.

"Hold it together! Hold it together," she mentally chanted. Focusing on the refrain enabled her to hold back the tears burning behind her lids.

"Shonda, honey," Connie Sharp tried to do what she did best: manage the situation.

"Mrs. Sharp, would you please let me by?" she asked, low and desperate.

Wasn't it bad enough she'd been humiliated by her own

actions and Mason's words? Did she have to be trapped by a meddlesome mother, too?

"He didn't mean—"

"Yes, he damned well did," she snapped, anger bubbling to the surface. "Now, please, let me pass."

Perhaps the desperation cut through Connie's stubborn desire to see her eldest son settled and happy. Unfortunately for her, being settled was at direct odds with what Mason wanted. Regardless, Connie silently stepped aside, allowing Shonda a glimpse of freedom.

But as she was ready to make good her escape, Mason's rough voice reached her.

"Shonda."

Her treacherous heart slammed on the brakes, halting her retreat. But pride, bless it, refused to let her turn around.

"I'm sorry. If there was anyone worth changing my mind for, it would've been you."

The sincerity was a baseball bat to the knees. He probably meant what he said, but it was zero consolation. Without offering a response, she walked away. But a few spasmodic steps later, the tight rein on her temper snapped. She charged back to within inches of his arrogant face.

"You know what? *Fuck you!* Fuck your platitudes and condescending bullshit. I don't want or need it," she said. The sharp tip of her nail pounded his pec with every point she made. "I feel sorry for you. One day, after you've shoved away everyone who might've tolerated your grumpy, narcissistic ass, you'll be alone. Life will have passed you by. And you'll think of all we could've had. You're going to know true loneliness."

She breathed deeply before saying, "But me? I'm going to meet a great guy who cherishes me. We'll marry, maybe have a few babies. And when old age rolls around, we'll be surrounded by our extended family. I'll never spare you another thought after today. This"—she wagged a finger between them—"will have been long forgotten. So don't sweat it, Mason."

As grand monologues went, hers was excellent. And had she not been crying, perhaps he would've believed her.

"If it helps you sleep at night, sweetheart, then that's what you should tell yourself." He wasn't cold or mean when he said it, which was worse than a brutal retort.

"I should've saved the bullet and let Christie finish you," she said coldly.

His shocked silence felt way too good.

When Shonda swept out, Connie made no move to stop her. Maybe she recognized Shonda would mow her right the fuck down. Perhaps she realized, like everyone who knew him, Mason really *was* a lost cause.

As she stalked down the hallway, Shonda had never felt so alone. There was no running to Erica with her troubles. The last thing she needed was someone else's stupid drama.

Shonda considered seeking out Dane, but it would only cause additional strife in his family. His bruises were uncomfortable to stomach.

She stumbled.

Verity's offer!

Just last week, an old college friend from Colorado emailed her, feeling her out about a position at her new start-up.

Why not? A scenery change might be the best solution. Besides Erica, nothing was holding her in Stonebrooke anymore. And as much as she'd love to remain part of her world, she couldn't. Her friend's future lay with Zack, and if Shonda were in their orbit, eventually, she'd circle back around Mason's sun.

She slid behind the wheel of her car and pulled out her tablet. Next, she found Verity's inquiry and sent an informal acceptance. The excited response eased some of her anxiety about the spur-of-the-moment decision, and for the next few minutes, they hammered out the details.

Shonda signed off and rested her head on the steering wheel.

Wow! She was really doing this! A fresh start.

A sense of rightness filled her, giving her peace. The jaded part of her didn't trust the feeling. After all, she'd experienced the same with Mason, and look where they went—nowhere.

Her passenger door opened.

Her shrill scream filled the small space, echoing back to her.

"Damn, woman! It's me."

"Dane!" She needed a few precious seconds to recover. "What the fuck, dude? You couldn't knock on my window?"

"You were inside your head and would've screamed anyway," he said with a chuckle. Sobering, he added, "Seriously, though, if you're going to sit in a parking garage, you should lock your doors."

"Trust me, I won't make the same mistake again." She punched his shoulder. "You took ten years off my life."

He chuckled, dimple flashing. She wondered for the millionth time why her heart couldn't have selected him.

"Why so blue, babe? I suspect I know, but humor me."

"I'm not blue. I'm happy."

"Uh-huh."

"I am!" she said, forcing a grin. "I've taken a job in Denver."

"And you're already regretting it."

"No, I'm not."

He raised a brow.

"I'm *not*," she insisted.

Dane remained silent and skeptical.

"Okay, maybe I'm a little shocked at the speed of it all," she said. "But I'm happy I'm still employable after the Billy fiasco."

"Good," he said, nodding his approval.

She stared, feeling slightly betrayed by his enthusiasm. "You think I should go?"

"Yes. And although I'm going to miss your beautiful face, I think a change of scenery is exactly what you need."

Deflated, she asked, "You do?"

"Yep."

His seriousness twisted her heart in knots. She bit the inside of her cheek to stem the building sobs.

"Come here."

With a sniff, she dove into his waiting arms, giving in to her pathetic need to be held.

"My brother has made you a hot mess, hasn't he?" he murmured.

"Can we act like you are an only child for a while?"

His chuckle warmed her. "Sure thing, babe. So does that mean we can make out?"

Shonda punched his chest lightly, laughing as he'd meant for her to do.

CHAPTER

TWENTY-NINE

"For years, I convinced myself that once you found the right girl, you'd settle down. You'd get over what Melanie had done and wise up. But I was wrong," Connie said. Disappointment weighed heavily on her face as she stepped closer to Mason's bed. "Maybe it's the combination of being left by your father and thrown over by Melanie, causing you to be heartless. But it kills me to see you throw away the best thing that's ever happened to you. And Shonda was the very best thing in a long while."

"She's a cheater like everyone else. It took her all of a minute before she was kissing Dane," he retorted. "And Bucky told me she was collecting phone numbers at the police station like candy on Halloween."

"Watch your tone, young man. I didn't raise you to be disrespectful," Connie scolded. "And Dane kissed *her*. Not the other way around. I told him to."

"You *what*?"

"I only told him to kiss her if he found you flirting with the coffee-cart woman," she stated matter-of-factly.

"I wasn't flirting."

"No? Hm, that's not what your brother said. Are you intending to lie to me and say you didn't accept the barista's number?"

His face grew warm. "Okay, yes. I got her number."

Connie smacked him on the side of the head. "Hypocrite!"

"Jesus, Ma. I wasn't going to do anything with it."

The phone number had been for show. To dissuade Shonda from any further relationship expectations. Admittedly, anyone but her turned him off these days.

But he'd get over it. He had to.

"Don't try to kid a kidder, Mason. If you took the woman's number, you intended to have sex with her. I don't understand how you could be so cruel."

"I threw it away," he confessed.

"Good," Connie said. After straightening his blanket, she caressed his cheek. "Shonda loves you. We all see it."

"I don't want her to."

"You've made it abundantly clear to everyone, especially her. Well done."

He hated disappointing his mom, but he'd be damned if he would defend himself.

"I'm tired, Ma." He didn't need to fake a yawn. "Do you mind if I get some sleep, please?"

"So that's the way of it, huh?"

"I'm not doing this with you," he said tiredly. "You can't make me want marriage and rugrats. Please let it go."

Alone was better. He knew how to navigate being by himself.

THE NEXT TWO weeks were spent in a flurry of packing for the move. Shonda's goodbye to Erica was the hardest thing she'd ever done. Leaving her old life behind was like cutting off a limb.

And damned if Erica wasn't understanding and supportive of Shonda's decision. Her compassion made everything more difficult.

As expected, Mason didn't call. The delusional half of her longed for him to beg her to stay. The realistic half smacked the deluded part upside the head.

Dane had popped over on her last day in Stonebrooke to help carry her boxes down the three flights of stairs and load them into her vehicle.

"That's the last of it," she said, sighing and shoving her overnight case to the back, then slamming the trunk.

"Thank God. It is downright embarrassing that an owner of a gym should be so winded, lugging boxes up and down stairs."

"Just down," she said dryly.

"Hush. I can change the story to make myself look better if I want."

The teasing turned serious.

"I think I'm going to miss you most of all," she said tearfully.

"Don't do that. Don't cry. You'll make me get all weepy, too. How would that look to your neighbors? I'll have to leave town because of all the razzing."

"Shut up, you ass. I don't know what it is about the men in your family, but every single one of you has to ruin a perfectly good sentimental moment."

"It's a gift."

She rolled her eyes and went in for one last hug.

"Take care of yourself, babe. Shoot me a text whenever you stop for the night and then again when you get going in the morning. I want to know when you arrive safely."

"Yes, Dad." Grinning, she kissed him on the cheek.

"It's all fun and games until you're kidnapped by a highwayman and taken to his lair, where he satisfies your every sexual fantasy."

"On that note, I'd better get going so I don't miss him," she quipped.

"Yeah, maybe I didn't think that one through all the way."

"Nerd."

His teasing did what he intended, shifting her mood back toward an upbeat one.

"The moving van comes tomorrow," she informed him. "Erica said she'd be here for it, but knowing her, she'll try to help haul boxes. If you're available, will you make sure she takes it easy?"

"Of course. Or I may make Zack do it. She might be more inclined to listen to him."

"Don't count on it."

They shared one last hug before Shonda climbed into her car to start her journey to Colorado and her new life.

IN THE DAYS following his release, Mason limped around his home, lashing out at anyone who disturbed his peace or brought up Shonda's name. Not dissimilar to an animal in pain.

And he was.

When he could take no more of his own mood, he grabbed his keys and headed for her apartment.

His fist connected with the door twice before it was jerked open by an exceedingly irritated Erica. Frowning, he pushed past her—careful of her newly pregnant state—and charged into the living room.

The labeled boxes kicked his pulse up.

"Shonda!"

Silence.

"Shonda, come out here. We need to talk."

Erica laid a hand on his arm.

"She's gone, Mason. She left yesterday."

"Gone? What do you mean, gone?"

Disbelieving, he brushed her off and searched each of the rooms. Part of him wanted to believe the stacks of taped boxes were an optical illusion. Surely she hadn't turned tail and run? Not Shonda. She was a fighter through and through. An optimistic one to boot. She would've stayed until he came to his senses.

"She took a job offer out of state," Erica said, shadowing him.

"What are you talking about? Where?"

Her silence made him sweat.

"Where is she, Erica?"

"She doesn't want you to know," she hedged.

"Where. Is. She?"

"I'm sorry." And she honestly seemed to be, but he wasn't accepting of it.

"Are you honestly going to stand there and not tell me?" he asked in disbelief. "You owe me."

Her raised brows forced him to question the wisdom of his claim. But if he had to use the getting-shot-on-her-behalf card, he would.

After an internal debate, she came to a decision. "Fine. She left for Colorado."

"Where in Colorado?"

His patience was thin, and if she didn't tell him, he feared he would wring her neck.

"Yeah, well, it's all you're getting. If you want her bad enough, you'll make an effort to find her."

"This isn't one of your stupid-ass romance novels," he ground out. "Give me the damn address."

"You aren't endearing yourself to me. In fact, you're pissing me off," she said, jabbing him with her nail.

He rubbed his chest. "Why does everyone keep poking me?"

"You put her through hell," Erica charged, ignoring his complaint. "But did I say anything? No! Because I know what you've been through. I understand what it feels like to be betrayed. But I'll be damned if I sit here and have you yell at me because of your own stupidity. Go to hell."

"I swear to God…"

"What? What will you do?" she taunted. "Nothing, that's what. Zack would kill you dead *if* I don't first."

And suddenly, he couldn't take the uncertainty and pain anymore. Yeah, he'd screwed up. More than once. He needed to make things right.

Exhaling a ragged breath, he tried again. "Please."

Her guard slipped.

Thank God for romantic saps.

"I promised her I wouldn't tell you, and I can't break my word."

He dropped onto a plastic-wrapped chair. Defeated, he stared out the slider windows over the dead winter landscape. He'd fucked up. Big time. And there was no coming back. They could've had a good thing if he had gotten out of his own way.

"But…" she hedged.

Hope was a funny thing. It refused to let one wallow in self-pity or let go when they probably should. Mason sucked in his breath, raised his head, and waited.

"I suppose if you happened to overhear me telling the moving men the address, I wouldn't exactly betray her trust," she said slyly.

He jumped up and planted a big smacking kiss on her.

"Hey!" Zack protested, strolling in at the wrong moment.

"Yeah, up yours, dickhead." With a grin and a flip of the bird, Mason settled in to wait for the movers. "By the way, I'm going to need to take time off."

Erica smacked him upside the head. "Smarten up and apologize to her for chasing her away."

He scowled but was thankful she hadn't done worse.

"If you hurt her again, Mason, I swear by all that's holy, I will tear you apart. Piece by piece, starting with your balls. Understand?" she promised.

"Christ, you're scary," he muttered, holding up his hands when she would've smacked him again. "I understand. Swear! And I won't hurt her ever again."

"Good. But know I'll be sharpening my garden shears just in case."

CHAPTER
THIRTY

As the moving van pulled up in front of the driveway to the home she'd leased, Shonda swallowed the impulse to tell them to turn around and head back to Stonebrooke. She'd been gone for less than a week, and she missed her small hometown. Although she'd settled on Thornton, a place thirty minutes from the bigger city of Denver, the population was larger than she was used to.

But it was a new life, right?

She must remember the transition was for the best.

Firming her resolve, she opened the garage door for the movers. When a car pulled up behind the truck and Mason unfolded his tall form from the driver's side, she checked the desire to hit the button to lock him out. She was also reeling in shock.

But then her anger blazed.

What the hell was he doing here? And why now? How had he found her? Two people knew of her location, which meant either Erica or Dane was the rat fink. They'd have words later, when she was unpacked.

Across the distance, he met her furious gaze. He was damn lucky she didn't have power tools, or even a single hammer, in her garage yet. The temptation to inflict bodily harm for disrupting her new life would be too hard to resist.

Breaking his hypnotic hold, she greeted the approaching driver and did her best to ignore Mason, who was stalking her way.

"Why did you leave Stonebrooke?" Mason demanded after the man went about his business of directing his team.

She stared at him, incredulous. "You traveled halfway across the country to ask me an asinine question?"

"Answer me, Shonda."

Of all the fucking nerve!

"No. I don't think I will." She lifted her chin and pivoted to leave.

He caught her arm, his firm grip inescapable.

"Please," he said, softer. His expression changed from autocratic to yielding, the steel in his gaze giving way to warmth.

Butterflies woke in her belly, and she wished they'd go right back to sleep. She had plenty of crap on her plate without fighting her body's responses.

But really, why did he have to make her life difficult? Was his ego so fucking fragile that he needed to hunt her down and assure himself she was pining for him? Was it to completely crush her spirit in some twisted, sick game? She wished him to perdition.

"Mason, this is ridiculous and redundant. I don't know why you're here, and I'm past caring. Take a page from my book and move on."

"No. No, I…" He trailed off, frustration vibrating off him as his protest dried up. "I was wrong."

If she weren't emotionally numb and immune to his bullshit, she might've been swayed into forgiving him. Or at least asking what he was wrong about. She suspected she knew, but she was over it. Something precious was broken beyond repair in his hospital room.

"People don't change," she said, throat aching with regret she refused to show. "I believed you were someone I could love. You weren't."

He swallowed hard. His sudden anguish surprised her. "Give me a second chance, love."

"Second? Don't you mean third? Fourth?" she countered harshly, looking away from his tortured, mesmerizing gaze. She focused all her attention on a frozen mountain peak in the distance, hoping to steal a bit of its icy reserve. Finding the strength to stand firm was an effort.

"I'm not doing this, Mason," she said roughly. Her self-doubt and feelings of inadequacy were too much to bear on a good day. She certainly had no intention of living it on a daily basis. "Not now. Not ever. I owe myself more. I deserve better."

"I need to make this right. What can I do?" The aching sweetness of his plea fell on deaf ears.

"Nothing. But what difference would it make if you could? You were perfectly clear—you don't love me, nor do you want a long-term relationship. I get it. I've always gotten it. But your ugliness hammered it home at the same time it drew blood."

In the face of his silent suffering, she sighed. "Quite honestly, I'm exhausted. I don't have it in me to worry about how bad your family made you feel with their relentless badgering. That's why you're here, right? To once again apologize? Give it a goddamned rest already."

He shook his head, emotions keeping his reply locked up tight.

She easily recognized what was happening to him because she'd gone through the same exact thing at their final parting— blatant disbelief at no longer being wanted. And regardless of how caring he'd seemed, she was never anything other than a plaything to him. The truth had been an iron fist to her solar plexus, the blow damaging in every conceivable way. With careful precision, she'd switched off the caring centers in her brain and heart to survive the last few weeks. If she let him back in, it would be beyond foolish.

"Please, go away. I have a lot to do today. This drama wasn't on the schedule," she said coldly, presenting her back to him.

He remained motionless, not objecting to her leaving.

If her heart spasmed, she ignored it. What girl didn't want to be chased? But in the past, she'd danced too close to the flames and been barbecued. There wasn't a chance in hell that she'd venture near the fire again.

Mason waited until the crew was preparing to leave before he next approached her. During the interim, he went shopping, buying two dozen long-stemmed crimson roses, with the hope she might soften her stance and hear him out.

"You can't avoid me forever, love," he said, dogging her steps up the walkway.

"I can, and I will," she retorted, storming toward the front door.

Right when she would've slammed it in his face, he caught it, narrowly avoiding a smashed nose.

"Get out!" she demanded.

Her fury was justified, but it rattled him. If he could just get her to listen…

In the back of his mind, he recognized pushing was wrong. He'd blown apart what they were building, multiple times, and respecting her boundaries was important. But dammit, he had to try, right? What would life be without her in it? An endless wasteland of minutes grouped together until death knocked.

"Shonda, I'm asking for five minutes, then I'll leave." He held out the flowers. "Please."

Her eyes shifted to his gift, and satisfaction blossomed in his chest, giving him confidence. Hopefully, he scored major brownie points in the romance column.

"These are for you, love," he said tenderly.

A soft smile curved her lips, and he liked to imagine she was recalling their delicious night of lovemaking on Valentine's Day. She accepted the arrangement, careful to avoid his touch.

His confidence ebbed, and a strange uneasiness gripped him.

"Start talking," she said, swinging the door wide. "You have your five minutes." Purposefully avoiding his gaze, she rooted in a box until she pulled out a pair of scissors and a vase. With great precision, she unwrapped the bouquet and separated the roses.

His relief was all-consuming, followed by disbelief that she was actually giving him the opportunity to apologize for his past actions. He opened his mouth, prepared to wax poetic, but snapped it shut as soon her actions registered.

Disconcerted, he stared, mind blank.

There she was, happily decapitating the head of each rose and shoving the naked stems in the vase.

"What the hell are you doing? Do you know how much I paid for those fucking flowers?" He rushed to save the remaining buds, freezing when she waved the scissors in his face.

"They're *my* flowers. I'll damn well do what I want to them. Right now, mutilation makes me happy. And you're down to three minutes."

Her eyes flashed dangerously, and Mason shivered.

"You're crazy, you know that?" Recovering himself, he pointed a finger at the mess, keeping it out of scissor range. "Certifiable," he stressed.

"Then you should be ecstatic to be free of me," she replied, giving a careless shrug.

"I should," he agreed. He inhaled a fortifying breath. "But I'm not."

She hesitated a heartbeat before snipping another bud.

"I love you, Shonda." The rawness in his soul was laid bare. "You might think speaking those words isn't worth much, coming from me, but the last time I said them was the night my girlfriend, Melanie, died."

Her head whipped around, and her gaze bore into him.

Pity flashed in those expressive eyes, and he swallowed the ugly reactive response of wanting to erase it with a cutting remark. The trigger was from childhood, when vulnerability was painful. But opening up to ridicule or pity—two things he hated with a burning passion—would allow him to lay the past to rest and possibly have a better future.

As quickly as her sympathy appeared, it was gone, replaced by doubt.

"You've not told your mother, brothers, or nephew in all these years?" she asked.

Her skepticism was valid, and he didn't fault her for asking.

"No," he confessed. "Not really. Maybe Jacob. But with the others… it's always been understood."

And with his revelation, he saw what he'd been missing. What he'd been denying to those closest to him. How had an uncaring father and a cheating skank emotionally crippled him to this degree?

"I'm glad for your self-discoveries, Mason. Truly. But—"

"Don't," he croaked, unable to bear being sent away. "Don't say it doesn't matter to you. Don't say it's too late."

"Then tell me, what should I say? Should I forgive your treatment of me, as if it's perfectly acceptable behavior? Should I be okay with how you express love? Sparingly, if at all, by the way." She exhaled her exasperation. "Because if what we've shared until now is an example of what I can expect if we start an *actual* relationship, I'll politely decline."

Mason's entire core froze under her arctic stare.

Where had her fire gone? The passion they'd shared? Had he destroyed the last kernel of her affection with his thoughtlessness? Stolen from her the same way Melanie and his father had from him?

In the face of Shonda's rejection, he felt physically ill.

Denial rose up, fierce and overpowering. His involuntary step forward caused her to shift backward.

Her retreat saved her life.

The crack of the gunshot was unmistakable. The vase with the stems shattered into thousands of fragments, cutting where they landed.

"Get down!" Mason lunged at Shonda and covered her body with his. A hail of bullets pinged around the kitchen, splintering cabinets and denting appliances. The final one ricocheted off the granite counter, lodging in his abdomen.

He grunted.

"Fuck me. Not again!"

CHAPTER

THIRTY-ONE

What did he mean by "not again?"

"Mason?" Hysteria crept into Shonda's voice, making her wince at its shrillness.

"Please tell me your purse is close by, with your gun in there," he said.

"No." She pushed against his dead weight to determine the problem.

He swore under his breath and rolled to free her. "Okay, plan B. You get the fuck out of here. I'm assuming you're familiar with the layout of this place?"

"Yeah, familiar enough. Come on." She rose in a half-crouch and attempted to drag him with her. His resistance was unexpected.

"You go," he said. "I'll be right behind you, love."

The strained edge gave him away. His tight, pale features added to the tale.

"You're lying," she said flatly, kneeling to search for his wound. "Where were you hit?"

Mason caught the hands tugging at his clothes. "Shonda, you need to save yourself."

"I'm not leaving you. Not without a weapon to protect yourself."

"God, you're fucking fierce. I was a fucking idiot not to tell you how much I adore you before now." With a trembling hand, he brushed back the hair falling over her eyes. "But your remaining here is not up for debate, love. I don't trust the lull." With a pained grimace, he gently nudged her. "Escape while you can. Please."

"Mason—" She swallowed down the fear and regret. There was nothing like a surprise assault to make you recognize the important things in life.

His soft smile was understanding. "Go."

Shonda delivered a hard kiss, then dashed for the dining room, all the while praying she'd calculated properly. With luck, she'd have time to get to her gun safe before their assailant got to Mason. Yes, he'd intended for her to leave the house and go for help. But there was no fucking chance in hell she'd leave him at the mercy of a crazed shooter.

Tiptoeing, she crept into her bedroom. Every few feet, she listened for the telltale signs of an intruder. Hearing nothing out of the ordinary, she ventured forth into her closet.

The safe was a floor model. Opening it was a simple matter of pulling back the faux rug and punching in the code. With the gun's safety in the off position, she returned to the kitchen.

The conversation stopped her in her tracks, and she ducked into the dining room to listen.

"You aren't such a badass now, huh?"

A crack and a thud followed the taunt.

Mason grunted. "You know, Billy Boy, I'd make haste if I were you. Shonda already called the police. You've got a few minutes tops to make good your escape."

It was difficult to hear over her pounding pulse.

Billy? He was the one shooting at them? Why trail them here? Why not simply disappear and start over elsewhere?

"Shut the fuck up and tell me where she went," Billy snarled. "If you do, I'll make your death as painless as possible."

Terror ripped its way out through her chest, and her adrenaline spiked, making her tremble. She could scarcely draw a proper breath. Sweat dampened her skin, dripping down into her eyes. Shonda swiped it with the back of her wrist and shifted the gun to her opposite hand to rub her clammy palm on her jeans.

Breathe, Shonda. Just breathe.

Slow and steady pace. Too fast and she'd hyperventilate.

Mason scoffed. "You've obviously watched one too many movies."

Damn, but he possessed balls of steel if he was able to taunt Billy in the midst of an attack. His careless attitude drove her to the brink. God, he was begging to be murdered! Not smart.

"Have it your way, asshole."

Billy's intent left no room for doubt, and Shonda didn't hesitate. Acting on pure instinct, she swung into the room, aimed center mass, and pulled the trigger.

Two shots through the back, straight to the heart.

As his body crumpled to the floor, she darted a wild glance around the room, ensuring he was alone. Next, she checked for a pulse, not expecting to find one. Her aim was true.

"Jesus! Tell me you didn't go all Natasha Romanoff on this guy without backup rolling," Mason demanded. His movie reference might've been funny if she were in a laughing mood.

"Well, yours is a mighty fine thank you." She plopped down next to him. "But since you favorably compared me to Scarlett Johansson, I'll forgive you."

"Shonda Grant, when I'm mobile again, I'm going to spank your ass," he growled, reaching for her. Cupping her face, he gazed deep into her eyes and shook his head. "What is wrong with you that you can't follow directions?"

"Seriously? I just saved your ungrateful ass, and your anger is what I get for it?" she asked, ending on a ragged note. Her hysteria had returned.

"Love, I'm going to need you to remain calm." He caressed her nape in long, slow strokes.

"Calm? I'm perfectly calm." Her shrillness would break glass if everything wasn't already shattered.

His lips curled.

Okay, so she wasn't very calm. She began shaking in earnest.

"Ohmygod! Mason, I just killed my cousin." Hiccuping sobs convulsed her body.

They weren't for the backstabbing prick Billy had become, but for the gangly teen she'd treated as a brother.

"Shonda, sweetheart," he panted. "You can't break down. I need your strength one more time."

Alert to the danger, she stilled. Gray tinged his skin, cluing her in.

"Call an ambulance," he ordered. "All this blood isn't his."

"Fuck me!"

"I'd like nothing more once I get my strength back," he murmured, collapsing against her.

Eyes closed, deathly pale, and grip slackening, Mason passed out.

Shonda scrambled up, but the blood on the tile created a slick surface, causing her to slip and slide as she ran for the hallway. Tearing through the house, she frantically tried to recall where she'd last had her purse. Mason's arrival, coupled with the shooting, had her discombobulated.

A minute later, she stumbled across the bag on the living room floor. After dumping the contents, she rifled through until she found her cell.

Dispatch remained on the line as she reported details of Mason's condition. They talked her through finding the wound and applying pressure. Since the process was universal knowledge, she suspected they were attempting to keep her from losing her shit completely.

Within minutes, the paramedics were on scene, loading him into their rig.

Thank Christ!

Shonda shook her head in disbelief. How were they playing out the same scene for a second time in less than a month? Constant craziness had become her life.

And exactly like before, because she was responsible for taking a life, the police refused to let her accompany Mason to the hospital. Instead, they cuffed her, brought her to the station, and demanded she recount the circumstances surrounding the shooting. Multiple times, until she thought she'd go mad.

"Do I need a lawyer?" she asked wearily.

Thornton was a helluva lot different than Stonebrooke. There, Bucky and others had her best interests at heart. Here, where she was unknown, she was viewed with suspicion.

"Did you do anything to warrant one?" the grizzled officer asked with a smirk.

"Not if you view self-defense as warranted," she said, rubbing the spot between her brows. Mason could be dead for all she knew, and she was stuck in an endless cycle of interrogation, all in the hopes of tripping her up.

After another hour, they were satisfied with her story.

A kindly officer drove her to the trauma center.

From the back seat, she dialed Dane to give him a rundown of the situation.

"I don't know anything else yet. I'll call you when I do," she promised with a sniffle.

"Don't cry, babe. My brother's too mean to die," he said gruffly.

"That's what I'm hoping."

"Never doubt it. I'll be there as soon as I can catch a flight."

Shonda was left at the emergency entrance, and she staggered into the after-hours admitting area, where they directed her to the ER waiting room. The overflow area was her own personal hell.

Calls poured in from Erica, Zack, Connie, and even Charlie. From Dane, silence. Hopefully, it meant he'd been able to find a flight.

Somewhere in all the chaos, she reached Verity and canceled their dinner plans.

"It's surreal, Verity," she said. "I'm not family, so I'm not entitled to an update."

"Can his mother appoint you on their behalf?"

"She said she'd try, but I haven't heard back yet."

"Do you want me to come wait with you?" Verity offered. "I can reschedule the dinner for another time."

"You know I'd welcome the company, but you have three kids, and it's meal time. You'll have a riot on your hands in nothing flat."

Verity laughed and offered to sacrifice her husband to her tiny terrors.

"Seriously, I love you for asking, but I'm okay," Shonda assured her. "I reserve the right to call you at another time, though."

After hanging up, she settled in for the long wait.

THIRTY-TWO

Two hours passed before a surgeon sought her out.

"Ms. Grant?"

She popped up. "Yes, I'm Shonda. Are you Mason's doctor?"

The woman was tall, blonde, and exactly Mason's type: physically fit with an ass so firm she could bounce a quarter off it. If he hadn't professed to love her, Shonda would be toast.

"Yes. I'm Dr. Elizabeth Phillips," the doctor said, offering her hand and a warm smile. "Mason did well and is in recovery. Luckily, the bullet didn't hit any vital organs, and we were able to stitch him right up."

"So he's going to be okay?"

"We're hopeful. The biggest threat is a potential infection. The next phase is the old wait-and-see game."

"When can I visit him?" Shonda asked.

"I'll call down as soon as he's awake," Dr. Phillips assured her with a glance at her watch. "Did you manage to eat?"

"A granola bar from the machine."

"If you hurry, you can grab a bite from the cafeteria."

For the first time all day, Shonda smiled. "Mason is going to *love* you. His favorite thing is being mothered."

"Why do I have the feeling you're yanking my chain?"

"Should I apologize in advance for his surly behavior?" she offered.

"Lovely."

Her dryness caused Shonda to laugh.

With a grin and a nod toward the cafeteria sign, Dr. Phillips left.

The ringing phone distracted Shonda from getting a meal.

"Dane is currently en route," Zack informed her. "What's the latest on my bonehead brother?"

"His doctor said he's in recovery. The surgery went well."

"Good. And how are you?" he asked gently.

She glanced down, wincing when she noticed her blood-caked clothes. "Wishing I had stopped for a shower. But I'm not comfortable heading back home yet."

"Understandable. I don't know if she told you, but Erica and I put our place on the market. Mainly for Jacob, but the vibe of the house feels off now."

"Yes. I'll never be able to sleep where Billy…" Her stomach churned as she recalled his dead-eyed stare.

"Shonda, listen to me. You did what you had to," Zack reminded her. "It was yours and Mason's lives or his."

"I know." She cleared her mind of the death along with her throat. "So, did your brothers patch things up, or do I need to referee when Dane gets here?"

"It remains to be seen. Do you have one of those sexy black-and-white-striped s—ouch! I was asking for Mason." His voice sounded far away.

"Ignore him," Erica said, taking his place. "Who knew all the Sharps were such horny bastards?"

"Me. And based on the bun in your oven, you did, too," Shonda replied, laughing.

"Are you okay? And I mean truly okay. Not the appease-people kind."

"Yeah, for now. At some point, I need to call my family and explain what happened."

"I'm sorry," Erica said tearfully.

"Oh, God!" Zack recovered his phone. "It's the pregnancy hormones. We'll call you back after a bakery run."

Surprised she could, Shonda laughed. "Give her my love."

"Will do. Give my brother a hard time."

After she hung up, she wandered toward the promise of food only to find the cafeteria abandoned. Her next stop was the snack bar. She mainlined M&Ms as she considered all the reasons Billy would want her dead. The truth was likely to be buried with him, and she might never uncover why he'd set out to destroy her career or murder her.

The one thing she couldn't seem to grasp was how he could hate her so badly. She'd only ever been kind to him.

Shonda wiped away the tears for the charming little boy, dreading the chore of informing her parents. Would her mother even remember her brother's son? Eva could hardly be bothered to recall her own daughter's existence.

"Ms. Grant? Hi. I'm Angel. Mr. Sharp is out of recovery and has been asking for you."

Glancing up, she met the gaze of a pretty nurse with a bright smile. Weirdly, her heart thudded with dread. Call it PTSD, but she'd lose her stinking mind if he reenacted his poor behavior from his last hospital stay.

"Can you tell me which room?" Shonda smoothed her hair and cast a rueful glance at her blood-splattered clothes.

Angel smiled. "How about we get you a scrub top to replace your shirt?"

Her kindness was appreciated, considering the day's events, and Shonda scrubbed her fists against her eyes, fighting fatigue along with a deeper emotional overload.

An arm encircled her shoulders, startling her. "Come on," Angel urged. "Let's get you cleaned up so you can go greet that hot guy of yours."

"Thank you."

By the time she'd changed and arrived on the third floor, Mason had dozed off.

Although exhausted, she was too wired for comfort and perched on the edge of the recliner to wait. Every few minutes, she studied the monitor, assuring herself his vitals were normal. Granted, she was clueless about what the norm should be, but she needed to convince herself he wasn't falling into a rapid decline.

Throughout the night, the staff roused him, talking to him in a friendly but persistent manner and encouraging him to wake up.

She should've told them he slept like the dead.

On the heels of her thought, she shuddered and jumped to her feet. In the distance, the city lights winked out as residents called it a night. The darkness was isolating, and with no one to ground her, Shonda fell into despair.

She'd killed a man tonight. And not just any man. She shot Billy. Twice.

Had the police contacted his mother yet?

Shonda was torn, feeling she should break the tragic news. But she wasn't prepared for the shitstorm it would cause when it finally came out that she had been the one to put the bullets through Billy's heart. Since her uncle's death, neither she nor her mother had spoken to Allison Grant. The sisters-in-law had a falling out after his funeral, making contact awkward. Perhaps a better person would have elected to break the silence, but communication was two-sided.

"Shonda."

Dane's low voice propelled her out of her miserable solitude and into his arms. He held her during her breakdown, listening as she relayed the story between sobs.

"Always hitting on my girl," Mason said hoarsely.

Amid gasps and grins, they rushed to his side.

"Well, if you didn't always leave her alone..." Dane countered. "My suggestion would be to stop hanging out in hospitals. It never ends well for either of you."

Mason's chuckle turned into a cough, prompting Shonda to feel his head for warmth. Fever was something to watch out for, according to his doctor.

He caught her hand and brought it to his lips, and she struggled against another breakdown.

"Thanks for saving my life," he rasped.

"Let's not make this a habit," she replied, fighting against another onslaught of tears. "My nerves can't take it."

"Promise."

His loving smile was one she wouldn't tire of, but being the recipient felt strange.

"And if you are as cranky as last time, I'm assigning Dane as your errand boy," she warned.

Dane snorted, and Mason offered up a lopsided grin.

"Who does a guy have to kill to get a glass of water around here?" he teased.

His comment brought back Billy's lifeless face.

Body clammy and stomach rebelling, Shonda barely made it to the toilet before she was beset with dry heaves. And though she reminded herself it was Billy or Mason, it didn't help.

A cool cloth was pressed against her neck, and a cup of water materialized beside her on the sink.

With a small smile of thanks for Dane, she rested against the bathroom wall, struggling to get her shit together.

. . .

"Is she okay?" Mason asked upon Dane's return. "I wasn't thinking."

"Don't beat yourself up, bro. She's tough, and she'll be fine." Dane pressed a plastic cup of water into his hand. "How about you? Can I get you anything else?"

"No, I'm good. But don't let her mourn for that sonofabitch. He's stabbed her in the back at every turn and then shot me. He would've killed her had she not taken him out first."

Unsurprisingly, Dane remained silent. Of the three of them, he was the thinker and almost always assembled his thoughts before speaking.

"The police are down in the lobby, Mason. They want your statement."

"Yeah, tell them I'm awake, but give me a few minutes with Shonda first."

"Will do."

Their eyes locked for a long moment of understanding.

Mason narrowed his eyes as he noted the fading bruises on his brother's face.

"I'm not sorry for punching you," he said.

Dane grinned. "And I'm not sorry for kissing your girlfriend."

Mason laughed, immediately regretting it as pain shot through his abdomen.

"Ouch. And, yeah, fair enough," he agreed. "We good?"

"Pfft. Like you had to ask." Dane squeezed his forearm and released him. "I'll call Ma and tell her she can rest easy."

"Appreciate that."

"Is it going to bother you if I crash at Shonda's?"

Mason shook his head. "Nah. I'll actually feel better knowing someone is looking out for her while I'm stuck in here."

"Don't kid yourself; she's not leaving your side. But I gotta say, the way you've treated her up until today leaves a lot to be desired. If it were me, I'd let your sorry ass rot."

His brows shot up in surprise. Dane didn't do mean, yet there was definite anger in his tone.

"I thought we had a truce?"

"Can't recall uttering that word. But a truce doesn't mean I can't tell you when you're being a dick, Mason."

Dane had the balls to ruffle his hair before walking off, whistling a jaunty tune.

"Dickhead," Mason called, receiving the bird in response. Again, he laughed, then groaned. It felt good to mend their rift. The tension between them over the last month had been wearing, knocking him off-kilter.

Shonda emerged from the bathroom, ragged and worn.

"Are you going to be all right, love?" he asked.

"I have to be, don't I?"

"You don't need to be tough with me. Anyone else would've buckled by now."

"Billy intended to kill me." She shook her head and walked to the bank of windows, seemingly blind to the scene in the distance. "I don't understand why."

"Money is a strong motivator, love."

Her nod was mechanical, and the silence stretched as she suffered in her own private hell.

"Shonda." When he had her full attention, he beckoned her closer. "You had no other choice. You get that, right?"

"I do," she said, her smile sad. After a beat, her brows met. "You said money was a strong motivator."

"Yes."

"Why?"

He blinked. The truth danced out of reach, weaving in and out, teasing his brain.

Damned drugs!

"I'm not sure," he admitted. "But it felt important to say."

"I have a trust fund, yes. But it's not enough for someone to off me." Her frown deepened. "Plus, if I were to die, having no husband or children, my estate would revert back to my mother and father."

The puzzle pieces fitted into place, leaving Mason cold.

"Get your parents on the phone immediately."

She scrambled for her purse. "I don't understand."

"I'll explain it all at once. Hand me my cell and call your parents from yours. Three-way, if you have to, but *do it*."

He thanked his lucky stars that, for once, she didn't argue.

"They're not answering." She glanced at the clock on the wall. Her expression turned grim. "It's late there."

Bucky Whitmore picked up on the second ring.

"Bucky? Hey, it's Mason. Will you do me a favor? Will you contact the Springdale PD and have them perform wellness checks on both Shonda's parents?"

"What's going on, Mason? Does this have to do with the car bomb last month?"

"I believe it does." Mason explained everything, starting with the break-ins in St. Thomas and ending with the shooting in Thornton. "At first, I thought good old cousin Billy was a fuckup. Now I'm not so sure."

"Go on," Bucky urged.

"He struck me as desperate for money, for reasons he took to the grave. But I think he was working an angle with Shonda's sister."

She gasped.

"Shonda has a sister?" Bucky sounded as startled as she looked.

Mason met her wide-eyed stare with a grimace. "A twin, to be precise. Call in the wellness checks, and then I'll explain the rest."

"What are the addresses?"

He handed his phone to Shonda for information forwarding.

"Bucky said he'd call you in about twenty minutes." She set

his phone on the tray and sat down. "What's going on, Mason? How is it you believe my twin survived? Are you saying my father lied about putting her up for adoption?"

"No. I believe he was telling the truth as he knew it. Remember, he said he was in Italy when your mother went into labor? It struck me as odd when he worded it the way he did. *'By the time I could catch a flight home, you were already tucked into your crib, your sister was gone, and your mother blamed me for everything.'*"

Because she seemed receptive to the idea, he continued.

"Why wouldn't a grieving mother wait for the father to bury their infant daughter together?" he asked. "Why have a funeral without him? The delay wouldn't have been too long."

She gasped.

"What?" he asked.

"You said I had a twin in St. Thomas. You saw her at the bar the night of the second break-in."

He grasped where she was going. "It may have been your sister."

"I think so, and Billy was there. Or at least, I suspect he was. I remember seeing someone who looked like him from behind and thinking it was odd he wouldn't greet me." She shrugged, but still appeared bothered. "I told myself I must've been mistaken. But it was the same night you saw the woman. Your comment made me forget all about him."

"They had to be working together," he mused.

"On the GenCon ads?"

She didn't want to see the connection regardless of the clues.

"Shonda, you said your mother ran out of money."

"Yes, but Papa still makes sure she has everything she needs. He has the chain of restaurants and an old family fortune."

He waited for her to get it. But when she did, her horror hit him in the stomach, right next to the fucking bullet wound.

"You once told me your mother was never there when you were growing up. And it was also the reason she and Nolan broke up," he reminded her gently.

"Yes, she was gone so much of the time, he thought she was having an affair." Pale and shaken, she met his steady gaze. "Do you think she was spending time with my sister?"

"It's a strong possibility. It could also be why her house was set on fire while she was out of town. Because she needed the insurance payout."

"This is insane," she said, shaking her head.

"Agreed, but it doesn't mean it's not real."

THIRTY-THREE

Shonda's mind immediately rejected her mother's involvement. Until she heard or saw any evidence directly, she may never believe it. Mason's theory couldn't be ignored outright, though, and it did need to be expanded upon. Still, a lot of things made sense now.

"This is insane," she muttered again, jumping up to pace off her rising anxiety.

If her mother had raised them separately, it meant she'd planned to separate them when they were still in the womb. Was Shonda meant to go to her father? Was her mother trying to be fair by offering up one of the children? Perhaps after he'd stated he had no time to raise a baby—a constant complaint of Eva's—her mother was forced to keep her and her sister apart. How could a twin be explained after the fact? How could Eva risk a visit between them? As a child, Shonda wouldn't have been able to help herself, and she'd have blabbed about spending time with her sister.

But the truth was coming clear. As the years passed, her mother had become more distant, taking off for longer periods of time. By middle school, if Shonda saw her for one week a year, it was a lot. She'd essentially been raised by a slew of nannies.

Her father had continually thrown money at the situation, not seeing it as a problem. His business was his love, and he'd poured his heart and soul into building a multi-million-dollar enterprise with the name Luigi's in big bold letters.

Allison Grant must be the missing link.

Had she been in on the scheme from the beginning, too? Her involvement was the only explanation for Billy's attempt on Shonda's life and the reason the sisters-in-law were "estranged" from before Shonda's birth.

"They'd planned for me to disappear in St. Thomas and for my sister to take my place," she concluded woodenly.

The truth was difficult to bear. Not only was she unloved, but she was an inconvenience.

"They *were* looking for something in my room, Mason. My passport."

Sapped of all energy, she feared her legs would no longer hold her upright. She collapsed on the recliner.

"What are you saying, love?"

"It wasn't about the money. My mother could've gotten it from my father at any time. He loves her," she said, warming to her theory. When Mason's brows dipped, indicating his confusion, she said, "They intend for my twin to take my place. If I disappear, she could easily step in. It would give her access to my father's millions, and she'd no longer live in the shadows."

Mason was silent as he processed her theory.

"That's diabolical," he breathed.

"Yes, but brilliant. Since Papa tends to be self-absorbed, and we rarely see each other, they must believe he wouldn't know the difference," she reasoned. "With my passport, they intended to make me disappear and for my sister to transform into the new, improved Shonda Grant."

"But they never found it that night," Mason concluded. "You had it when we returned from St. Thomas."

"Correct. I'd put it in the safe within minutes of checking in."

"And Billy was never looking for a hard drive. He was searching for anything that might have your passport number. At the very least, they could've claimed it was lost or stolen."

They shared an oh-my-god moment, both realizing their chance meeting had saved her.

"They never counted on you," she whispered around the lump in her throat. "You foiled them at every turn."

"Damn straight," he said, holding out his hand.

She joined him, craving his touch. The connection with at least one person who gave a shit about her made a difference. "Thank you for saving my life, Mason."

"I can't say it's been my pleasure because of the bullet to the abdomen." He grinned. "But I'd do it again if it keeps you breathing."

Leaning in, she kissed him. "You may come across as a grumpy ass, but I suspect you have a teddy-bear heart."

"Don't tell anyone."

"Your secret's safe with me."

Their tender moment helped in healing Shonda's past hurts. Therapy would take care of the rest.

"I should let you rest," she said, noticing his focus drift.

"Not yet." He tightened his grip. "So, was the GenCon espionage fake?"

Shonda considered it from all angles.

"No, I don't think so. If I had to guess, they wanted to set me up and discredit me." She nodded as their ploy became clearer. "With the combination of the attacks, my resignation, and Eva's burned-down house, leaving me nowhere to find a safe haven, they'd predicted I would leave. Why not when nothing was holding me in Stonebrooke? What better way to assume someone's life? Other than Verity, who hasn't seen me in a few years, no one knows me in Thornton. The transition would be simple."

"Christ, Shonda. When I think about how close they came…" Mason looked as ill as she felt.

"Yeah, if you hadn't picked today to plead your case…"

Anger blazed in his eyes. "How do we prove it?"

"Billy." Shonda smiled.

"I don't understand."

"He was the light in Allison's sky. That was never in question," she explained. "She'll take his death hard, and with luck, turn against my mother."

"I wouldn't be so sure."

"She will, *if* there's no money left to inherit from my father."

"So we get Luigi to change his will to exclude Eva and any other offspring?"

She nodded. "In the meantime, I'll change mine. When Allison sees it's all tied up and out of reach, her reaction won't be pretty. Especially after losing her son."

"Then we can manipulate her, get her to confess, and turn on your mother and sister," he said, admiration lighting him from within. "You're a helluva brilliant strategist."

"Why do you think Erica comes to me to help plot her stories?" she said with a playfulness she didn't quite feel. Later, when she was alone, she could unpack the fact everyone in her family wanted her dead with the exception of Luigi.

Mason shifted and groaned. "In the meantime, while I'm trapped in a fucking bed, you don't go anywhere alone. I want Dane with you at all times."

His concern thawed the remaining pieces of her frozen heart. But she needed assurances. "You trust me alone with your brother? Aren't you worried I'll seduce him?"

His smile, when it flashed, promised ruin when he was recovered. "No, love. I'm certain jealousy will never be a concern for me again. Now come here, because I've waited too long to hold you."

Careful not to jostle him, she climbed on the bed and nestled into his warmth. She inhaled deeply, breathing him in. How was it possible for one man to always smell divine? Shouldn't he reek of hospital and antiseptic? His unique pheromone blend signaled her body, making it hum in recognition.

"Did you just *sniff* me?" he asked, teasing smile in place.

"Can I help it if—"

He trapped her words with a kiss. Poignant, it expressed everything he'd been unable to put into words.

"I love you, Shonda."

She could hold out for pride's sake, or she could give in to what she'd always longed for. "I love you, too."

"How determined are you to stay here in Colorado?" he asked sleepily, fatigue weighing his lids.

"Not very," she replied with a light kiss on his jaw. "I miss Stonebrooke."

His mouth settled into a pleased smile. "Good. I have a house on the lake you'll love."

"Are you actually going to invite me to your place?" she mocked, drawing back in shock.

"I'm actually asking you to move in with me," he returned.

"I don't know," she teasingly hedged as she cuddled against him. "You're a moody bastard."

"Somehow, I don't see you having a problem with my moods."

Four weeks later…

"THE VERDICT IS IN," Shonda said, after hanging up with her father.

Mason paused in the act of sipping his coffee. "For Allison?"

"Yes. Conspiracy to commit murder and fraud. But her testimony is critical, and they've agreed to two years in a low-security prison, with the option for parole in six months for good behavior."

"How do you feel about it?" he asked, worried about her internalizing the trauma.

"I'm not sure. I'm grateful Allison cooperated, but she was party to a murder plot against me." Shonda shrugged matter-of-factly.

Later, when they had downtime, he'd ensure she unpacked her feelings and dealt with them.

"Eva and Shalya were arrested, according to my father," she added. "And get this! Eva requested to see me."

Mason scoffed. He'd lay odds her mother was figuring all the ways she could get Shonda on her side. Guilt seemed the likely manipulation tool.

"Will you go when we return to Stonebrooke?" he asked, supervising the loading of the last moving boxes.

"I've toyed with the idea for the sake of closure. But no. I'm done with her."

Good. Now, if he could only mitigate her hurt and self-loathing for being fooled by people she should be able to trust.

"What about your sister? Are you curious about her or her motives?" He wrapped his arms around her and rested his chin on her head. Together, they watched as the movers closed up the truck and the taillights disappeared over the crest of the hill.

"We know what her motives were, don't we? Money and my mother's approval," Shonda said cynically. "No, I don't need to see her either. Erica's my true sister. She's the one I choose."

Hand in hand, they wandered back up the driveway and into

the now-empty house. Mason stopped at the spot in the kitchen where they'd both almost lost their lives. He hadn't realized his hand had tightened on hers until she protested.

"Sorry, love. I…" He inhaled a shaky breath, shaking his head. "Six inches to the right…"

He didn't have to elaborate; they'd both discussed it in the weeks since his release from the hospital. Had Shonda not stepped back when she did or had the bullet been right of Billy's mark, she'd be the one in the morgue. Mason would have lost her forever, a love truer than Melanie's ever was, and he wouldn't have recovered.

"I think we need to make a better memory for this kitchen," she suggested, tugging at his hand.

Shaken from his moody musings, he met her smiling moss-green eyes.

"You don't say," he murmured against her lips.

"It's important to exorcise the ghosts, so to speak. I mean, according to the doctor, you're fit to resume normal activities in moderation."

"When has making love been moderate between us?" he asked with a laugh.

"Valid." She drew her hoodie over her head. "But there's a first time for everything."

"Have I ever told you how much I adore your can-do attitude?"

He grinned, and her panties were no more.

EPILOGUE

Mason strolled into their kitchen and, with a flourish, offered Shonda a bouquet of naked rose stems.

She lifted curious eyes from her prize. "Um…"

"For you, my darling Morticia," he purred against her neck.

"Oh, Gomez, you shouldn't have!"

"'Unhappy, darling?'" he asked, parroting the character's line.

"'Yes, completely,'" she replied, fluttering her lashes.

"'*Cara mia.*'" Lifting her arm, he rained kisses and love bites along her skin from wrist to elbow.

"'*Mon cher!*'" She giggled as she swatted at him playfully. "Let go. I need to put these in water."

He laughed.

In retrospect, her furious snipping of the rose heads amused him. Instead of releasing her, he tossed the bundle of decapitated flowers on the counter, dragged her against him, and cupped her ass.

He nuzzled her neck, smiling at her happy sigh. If anyone had told him one year ago, he'd be in a long-term commitment, he'd have called them a fucking liar. But he was, and he didn't want to be anywhere else. Ever.

"I love you, Shonda Grant." The sentiment rolled a little easier off his tongue every time he uttered it.

"And I love you, Mason Sharp."

"Marry me," he said, surprising them both. But the rightness wrapped him in a warm cloak. An image of their future formed in his mind, giving him the assurance he needed.

She pulled away to gaze up at him.

Her gorgeous eyes were wider than he'd ever seen them. The uncertainty in them unmistakable.

"Yes, I'm completely serious," he said, chuckling. "I want you to make an honest man of me. Then you can sniff me any time you want. We'll put it in our vows."

Laughing, she punched his chest. "You're an asshole."

"So it's a yes?"

"Yes. A million times, yes."

He bent, prepared to seal the deal with a kiss, but a squeal behind him nearly shot Mason out of his skin. Eight months after the shooting, and he was still jumpy. He was embraced from behind, and for a brief second, he feared another attack.

"I knew it!" Erica cried her delight against his back. "We were in bed the other night, and I *told* Zack you were going to propose."

Mason whirled to see his brother enter, chagrin mixed with merriment on his stupid face.

"What the fuck, man?"

"Sorry, bro," Zack laughed. "She's on a lemon-donut sugar high."

"I'm more concerned that your wife thinks of me while she's in bed with you. You've got a serious problem."

Zack's expression went from amused to thundercloud, darkening more when Erica not-so-subtly sniffed him.

"Did you just sniff me?" Mason asked, incredulous.

"Uh, no!" Erica denied hotly.

But she had, and not only did they both know it, her husband and Mason's brand new fiancée also knew it.

Embarrassment pinked Erica's cheeks, giving lie to her answer.

"Okay, yes," she admitted. "But can I help it if—"

Zack clamped a hand over her mouth and ushered his very pregnant wife toward the door.

"What did I say about incriminating yourself, sweetheart?" Zack asked, admonishing her with a twinkle in his eye.

"You need my brand of cologne, bro?" Mason called to his retreating back.

"It's pure Eau de Mason," Shonda laughingly added.

He gazed down into her glowing face.

A bottomless pool of love was reflected in her eyes.

"I'm the luckiest sonofabitch in the world," he told her.

"Yes, you are, and I have a surprise for you." Shonda smiled coyly as she unfastened the first button of his shirt. Her knuckles brushed his abs, causing them to contract as she shifted lower and unbuttoned his jeans. Within a minute, they were both divested of clothes, and his mouth was on hers.

Giggling, she drew back. "Don't you want to know what it is?"

"Yes, and no." He dove back for another taste, but she stopped him with a hand on his chest.

"My dad chartered a private jet for us to St. Thomas. He intends for us to enjoy a vacation without any worries this time." Shonda kissed along Mason's jaw, cupping his length with both hands. "You can initiate me into the Mile-High Club."

His brain was slow to process, distracted by her steady strokes.

For the longest minute, he stared, unable to comprehend.

Then he caught up.

"Hell, yes!" He lifted her onto the granite countertop and captured her mouth with unerring accuracy. Mason had never tasted anything as sweet as Shonda, and he never would.

FROM THE AUTHOR

*Thanks for taking the time to read **Hidden Resolution**! I hope you enjoyed reading Mason and Shonda's story.*

*The next book in the Stonebrooke series, Dane's story, **Loving Resolution**, is still in the developmental stage while I refine the plot. Be sure to subscribe to my mailing list to learn more when this book is ready to release: https://www.tmcromer.-com/newsletter*

*For fans who enjoy interacting, my Facebook group offers readers "fan only" contests, as well as an exclusive first look at covers, excerpts, and more. **Cromer's Carousers** is the most fun way to follow yet. I hope to see you there!*

Love & Lemon Drops,
T.M. Cromer
www.tmcromer.com

KEEP TURNING FOR A LIST OF MY STORIES!

BOOKS BY T.M. CROMER

Get your printable list here: www.tmcromer.com/printable-booklist

CONTEMPORARY & ROMANTIC SUSPENSE

The Fiore Vineyard Series:

PICTURE THIS

RETURN HOME

ONE WISH

The Holt Family Series:

GOODBYE TO YOU

THIS TIME YOU

INCLUDING YOU

A LIFE WITH YOU

The Stonebrooke Series:

BURNING RESOLUTION

HIDDEN RESOLUTION

LOVING RESOLUTION

PARANORMAL ROMANCE

The Sentinels of Magic Series:

THE AETHER

THE DEATH DEALER

THE SEER

THE TRAVELER

The Thorne Witches Series:

SUMMER MAGIC

AUTUMN MAGIC

WINTER MAGIC

SPRING MAGIC

REKINDLED MAGIC

LONG LOST MAGIC

FOREVER MAGIC

ESSENTIAL MAGIC

MOONLIT MAGIC

ENCHANTED MAGIC

CELESTIAL MAGIC

EVERLASTING MAGIC

CAPTIVATING MAGIC

DISCOVERED MAGIC

The Thorne Witches: Happily Ever Afters Series:

ENDURING MAGIC

BOUNDLESS MAGIC

FRACTALED MAGIC

The Unlucky Charms Series:

PINTS & POTIONS

WHISKEY & WITCHES

BEER & BROOMSTICKS

COCKTAILS & CAULDRONS

WINE & WARLOCKS

HIGHBALLS & HEXES

BIO & FOLLOW LINKS

T.M. Cromer is a multi-award-winning sorceress of the written word and fearless architect of high-stakes paranormal romance. With a flair for twisty plots, slow burns, and swaggering heroes hot enough to scorch the page, she conjures stories that hook readers and refuse to let go. From her cozy PNW lair, flanked by two Hellhounds and an unholy amount of caffeine ambition, she weaves love, danger, and humor into every page. Whether it's witches, sirens, or magical assassins, her characters never behave, and neither do her stories.

When she's not dreaming up new ways to ruin her characters' lives before crafting their HEA, she's daydreaming about swimming with orcas or cackling over a particularly clever line of dialogue. Come for the magic, stay for the heartbreak, and maybe fall a little too hard for a man who only exists on the page.

Want to stay current on what's happening in T.M. Cromer's world? Subscribe to her newsletter to receive release news and promo alerts.

You can also join her VIP reader group on Facebook to chat with her, participate in polls, and stay up-to-date on what's happening. Become a member today!

FOLLOW T.M. CROMER:

facebook.com/tmcromer

instagram.com/tmcromer

tiktok.com/@tmcromer

pinterest.com/tmcromer

amazon.com/stores/T.M.-Cromer/author/B011QK3WXY